INYO-SIERRA PASSAGE

INYO-SIERRA PASSAGE

a novel by Jack Rowe

McGRAW-HILL BOOK COMPANY
New York   St. Louis   San Francisco
Düsseldorf   Mexico   Toronto

TO LAURA

1 2 3 4 5 6 7 8 9 BPBP 8 7 6 5 4 3 2 1 0

LIBRARY OF CONGRESS CATALOGING IN PUBLICATION DATA

Rowe, Jack.
Inyo-Sierra Passage.
I. Title.
PZ4.R8785In   [PS3568.O926]   813'.5'4   79-24077
ISBN 0-07-054085-3

Book design by Marsha Picker

1

THE YOUNG COUGAR was fully grown
and hungry, as he picked his way lower on the mountain
for warmer hunting territory. Winter hair had thickened
his coat, but the liquid strength of still-developing muscle
rippled with every silent movement as he ranged for food.
He was not familiar with these lower ravines, but some
inner urgency had impelled him at dawn to leave the
mountain he had dominated these first months of solitary
life, an instinct that had prompted smaller wildlife to burrow deeper in the earth.

Suddenly he froze, the hackles rising just behind his
flattened ears. A strange smell, unlike the scent he had
anticipated, stung the danger spot behind his eyes, and he
bared his fangs in a silent snarl. After a moment, because
his eyes could see nothing of the threat upwind of where
he crouched, he flowed along the rocky ledge to a sheer
overlook shaded by a twisted pine. On a flat grassy plot
beside a narrow trail he saw the woman.

Her slow, strange movements, gathering and packing implements and clothing into a small bundle, were a curiosity to the cougar. His fear left him, as did his craving for food. A natural computer in his skull signaled that this animal was appropriate neither as foe nor feast. He allowed the tensed cords in his haunches to relax, and stretched out with his head between forepaws as he watched her with flickering yellow eyes. All prior urgency dispelled by this novel curiosity, he luxuriated in a yawn and settled with the careless sprawl of any parlor cat.

Charity Whiteflower bent to the task of rolling up the down-filled sleeping bag with the deliberate calculation of the aged. She was seventy-two or seventy-three years old depending on which government document one chose to believe. It didn't matter. She certainly felt like someone over seventy this morning. Over eighty even. For two days and nights she had lived at elevations between 10,000 and 12,000 feet. The reduced oxygen at those levels had given her a forty-eight-hour headache and a wildly erratic heartbeat. The least exertion aggravated these symptoms of altitude sickness, and her progress along the southern portion of the John Muir Trail had been measured in labored stretches between breathers.

She was aware of the approach of the cougar from the first, but it caused her no alarm. She knew the beast was large and predatory, but she also knew it would not attack unless provoked. In the spring or summer she might have taken steps to protect herself from the possible rage of a mother protecting her young. Winter was not the season—at least not until the snows cut off their feeding.

She tied the tightly rolled bundle with twine and, leaning on it for support, carefully brought herself erect. She was a spare-framed woman who at her advanced years still stood broomstick straight. Her posture belied the anguish in her back. Four nights on a bed of pine needles in the down bag at temperatures hovering near zero had knotted the muscles and slowed the blood. She walked stiffly three paces to the boulder where she had set her backpack, a bright orange affair that contrasted sharply with the khaki workman's boots, trousers, and zippered jacket she was wearing. As though hefting a concrete block she swung the sleeping bag atop the pack and slowly tied it to the aluminum frame.

That step completed, she leaned against the rock and pondered her next move, feeling the eyes of the cat on her back.

By any prudent measure, Charity Whiteflower, whose tribal name was Flower of the Great White Mountain, a name that she alone among all living persons remembered, should not be where she was. A native of San Diego County, she had rarely been farther north than metropolitan Los Angeles. Charity's parents and grandparents had migrated south before she was born. They lived on a reservation set aside for the Indians of Southern California, although their people had originated in the rugged mountains far to the north. She knew from stories told and retold by her grandfather that their people never had been very numerous, even in the old days. They were, as far as she knew, the only survivors of the Kern River Tribe.

Sometime near her ninth or tenth birthday the great American Influenza racked the country, and in a little over two weeks' time Charity found herself orphaned. Mother, father, two younger brothers, an infant sister, and grandparents all died and left her completely alone, bewildered and weakened by her own battle with the disease.

After that a smattering of years in a church orphanage followed by work as a menial in a state institution for incorrigibles completed the narrow scope of her existence.

She had never married but had loved a man, then lost

him in an automobile accident when she was eighteen. The other car had come boring in at them out of the night. Just before impact she felt her lover tug at her arm, pulling her away as the door buckled inward, shattering the window. One headlight survived the crash, and in its reflected light, Charity could just make out her young man's smile as he lay, head in her lap, looking up into her face.

It was a bare minute before she was aware of anything wrong—long enough to feel the thick warmth of something soaking through her skirt. His eyes had glazed before she found the glittering shard protruding from his neck. Gently she removed it from the flaccid artery and clutched its sticky sharpness in her fist.

She had not known even him, nor could she ever yield to any man after he had violated her loins with such a rape of blood. Charity kept the little arrowhead of glass for a long time until one day she dropped it and it broke. She had remained taciturn all the years since, and though she had had many friends, the relationships were always one-sided—and ultimately given up by the others when she would not let them in.

People who worked with her quickly realized that she was cooperative and energetic, but there was a side of her personality where she lived privately that they could not penetrate.

She seldom thought in words and had lost a primer grasp of reading. Yet her mind burned with picture images, and on occasion words would cross her mind in a strange but pleasant language remembered from her childhood. An anthropologist would have recognized the syntax and vocabulary of the Tubatulabal, a Nahuatl dialect of the Kern River people. But she had never seen the Kern and wondered often why she had been named "Flower of the Great White Mountain."

One day, when she was nearly fifty, she had been pressed into service as a temporary chaperone to replace a regular staff counselor on an overnight field trip for some of the better-behaved inmates where she worked.

The bus ride took them hundreds of miles north through the Mojave Desert and into the higher elevations of the Eastern Sierras. It was black dark in the hour before dawn with only the lights of an occasional onrushing truck to relieve the tedium of a night desert crossing.

Charity sat stiffly erect, all her senses strangely attuned to the new, yet somehow familiar environment. The smells dominated, of course, what with the darkness and the racket of the swaying bus. Tangy scents of creosote brush wafted in from the hot night, and as the road rose imperceptibly with their passage, the pleasanter fragrance of sage dominated. Gradually the temperature began dropping and Charity quickened with a strange expectancy, peering to the left and right for some sign that the dawn would soon wash out the stars and light the landscape.

Soon they rounded a long, gentle, rising curve and the bus slowed, eased into the graveled clearing of a rest area, and rolled to a stop. Charity shivered, noting for the first time how chilly the air had become. Several passengers began to stir, and Charity rose and picked her way to the front of the vehicle. As she stepped down from the open door, she breathed a long clear draught of crisp air pungent with wildflowers and the sweetness of flowing fresh water.

"Welcome to Inyo County, ma'm."

She turned to see their bus driver standing a few feet away. He continued to speak—quiet words drifting past her awareness.

"Inyo," she thought. "Inyo!" The word was music as the vision of her grandfather came clearly to her again. He

was telling the history of her people. Always the same
words, with the precision and intonation that had been
faithfully repeated for countless generations of the tribe.

"Inyo," he had used the word, "Dwelling place of the
Great Spirit."

She was moved to turn and look up. It was at that point
she saw the towering peak, glowing snow-capped and
majestic in the first light two miles higher than where she
stood. Charity watched spellbound, the vista of sunrise on
the eastern slope of the massive glacial crag lighting her
eyes.

"That one there's Mount Whitney," said the voice behind her. But she had not heard. The knowledge was
singing in her brain and she smiled up at the Great White
Mountain.

With instant conviction Charity knew she was looking
at the very peak whose name she bore. Somewhere on the
other side of that massive ridge was the place of her
people. Someday, she vowed, she would return to find that
spot.

So twenty-three years later she had left her retirement
rooms and again boarded a bus for Inyo County, taking
with her only those supplies and equipment she felt able to
carry on her trek along the two-mile-high trail. She had
notified no one of her intent. It had not seemed necessary.
After all, she was going home!

It had taken her four days of grueling effort to climb
the twenty miles to this spot where the trail led west to her
goal—the headwaters of the Kern River. Now the dream
seemed completely out of reach. She had intended to go
on farther, to try to reach the River Place, but her animal
instincts for survival had turned her around at last. She felt
the storm approaching long before the sheet of clouds
would block out the sun.

Glancing apprehensively at the sky, she was startled to

see a birdlike shape inching its way across the violet-blue
expanse. She recognized it as an airplane before the faint
sound of its engines confirmed that fact belatedly to her
ears. The thought caused her some discomfort. The plane
seemed a trespass on her sacred solitude. She looked at the
departing speck as it cleared the mountaintops by about
1,000 feet.

"Inyo. Beware, foolish bird," she warned. Then she
mused, Would the great spirits mind being bested by a
man riding metal wings?

Something triggered a soft laugh, and she felt confused
to be caught so between cultures. She thought of the climb
facing her and secretly wished she might borrow the air-
man's magic for an hour.

Sitting against the boulder, she thrust her arms into the
pack strap loops and bent to take the load upon her back.
She stood facing west at the trail edge for a moment, then
turned left and east—toward people, town, safety.

The cougar lifted his head covertly to watch her go.
Without turning her head in his direction, Charity waved
an arm, saluting him farewell.

2

JACK LAIRD TURNED AWAY from the blue and white twin-engine airplane sitting on the deserted ramp, a light frost coating its wings, and crumpled the two plastic bags he carried into a tight wad. He paused to scoop up a small stepladder standing by the plane and strode briskly toward a small building with an outsized sign displaying the simple logo JACK'S AIRCRAFT. Laird was a big man, and he walked with an easy yet cautious power. As he approached his small office, he stopped beside a trash bin at the edge of the ramp, looked at the wad of plastic in his hand, then lobbed it easily into the open container. He shook a few drops of moisture off his fingers and walked the remaining distance to the office, pausing to prop the ladder against the building and to peer at a thermometer nailed to the door frame.

"Twenty-five degrees," he muttered and then nodded a tight affirmation of that bit of information with the air of one who had been checking the instrument with more than curious interest. He turned to glance at the airplane he had just left, and let his eyes drift up and down the rows of parked aircraft, their tiedown chains listless in the dead calm of the chill pre-dawn morning.

A sudden clanking whine startled him, and his blue eyes narrowed. Almost immediately the whine was replaced with a belching staccato roar, and Jack's shoulders relaxed. Bud Fallon's old 195, he thought. He must have driven in from the other end this morning.

He turned to focus on the corner of an old hangar to his left and traced the progress of the sputtering engine with his ears as it taxied down the far side of the building and finally moved into view, a venerable old taildragger making gentle S-turns on its way to the runway for takeoff.

Turning once more, he watched the rising ball of California sun as it burst over a hill and fanned a flat warm glow on the wingtips of the parked airplanes. Its radiance warmed him from the knees up, penetrating the soft weave of his leisure suit. He looked again at the fat twin parked with the other, smaller planes. The white film of hoarfrost had already melted into a slick that evaporated almost as soon as it was formed.

Jack Laird shuddered involuntarily, set his jaw grimly in the face of the warming sun, and entered his office, closing the door firmly behind him.

A few miles across town Ann Regan nudged her husband.

"It's six thirty."

His eyes popped open, closed briefly, then opened hard awake.

"Oh. OK, I'm up."

He lay there staring up at her face. She was sitting on the edge of the bed, propped on her arm, gazing down at him, tracing languid circles on his shoulder with the fingers of her free hand.

"Why don't we stay in bed? Let me call and say you've changed your mind." Her eyes were serious. She had been awake for some time.

For a moment he considered, caught by his own erotic impulse and the appealing picture she presented, soft and fragrant in the dim light of morning. He leaned up, caught her gently, and kissed her lightly in the hollow of her shoulder. "Don't take advantage of my weakness."

He trotted to the bathroom and made the typical noisy splashing sounds of an awakening male trying to compensate for too little sleep, too much late-night discussion, and an insistent, warm, visceral ache in his groin.

She waited for a lull in the spigot, drain, flushing sounds, and spoke, more sharply this time, "Jim, please . . . "

He came back into the room and reached into a drawer, pulling out underwear and socks. "Whatcha say, Honey?" He looked at her as he hopped on one foot and pulled a sock on the other. He repeated this operation with the other foot, then stood flatfooted, naked except for the socks, and grinned at her crookedly. "Hey, what are you doing in my bed?" He leaped on the mattress.

She anticipated his lunge with preoccupied efficiency and stood facing him across the bed. "Please, I'm worried."

"But _why_ . . . ?"

"Jim, it's just not worth the risk. I don't like you to gamble like this."

"It isn't any gamble." His tone was condescending; they had been through all this the night before.

"You said yourself that right engine was running bad and needed overhaul."

"Look, I talked to Charlie last night, and he said the compression is all within limits. They pulled the sour jug two days ago."

"Charlie! I've heard you say you'd never let him work on *your* airplane."

He chuckled at the way she'd caught him in a trap. "Well, this is not *my* airplane."

"Oh, Jim, I don't appreciate being put off by funny statements."

"Hey, there's nothing funny about fifteen hundred bucks!"

"Well . . . that's certainly true. Why do you suppose tight-fisted Jack Laird would hand over that much money to ferry an airplane five hundred miles?"

"Because your talented husband's time and skill are worth that much," he winked at her, "and because I put the screws to him. He wanted me to do it for five, I refused, and he tripled the offer."

"Well, I can't see why he didn't try for somebody else. He usually flies the things himself to save all he can."

"This guy in Reno wants the plane by noon today or it's no deal. Jack couldn't go himself because he's got two prospects for another plane coming in from Phoenix, and there just was no time to get anybody else."

Ann left for the kitchen to get coffee while Jim rummaged through his small flight case. He withdrew a chart, opened it on the rumpled bed, and traced a course with his finger from a small dot in the foothills of southern California to another dot marked RENO. Damn, he thought, I'll be heading straight up the spine of the Sierras the whole trip.

He reached back into the case and withdrew two charts marked LOS ANGELES SECTIONAL and SAN FRANCISCO SECTIONAL. These he spread open on the floor and began making a series of straight lines with a felt pen, until all of the lines connected in a series of checkpoints leading from his point of origin east of Los Angeles to a small brown triangle near Reno marked SPARKS. Then he began making quick notes and computations. Finally satisfied, he picked up the bedside phone and called for a weather briefing.

The news from the briefer was reassuring. "Since you're leaving this morning you should have no problems. We are forecasting generally good conditions for visual flight rules until later in the afternoon along your entire planned route. Of course that will change dramatically by four or five this afternoon local time when that cold front moves in from the northwest. They are really getting nasty stuff in Seattle right now. You're not planning to return today, are you?"

"No, this is a one-way ferry trip," Jim replied, somewhat surprised at his own feeling of relief.

"Well, that's good. Even the heavies are having problems with this one. You may not be able to get a return flight on the airlines by tonight. They expect heavy snow as far south as the San Gabriels by tomorrow morning. Do you want to file now?"

Jim looked at his watch then replied, "No, I won't be off for an hour or so. I'll call you back for an update and file just before I start up." He thanked the specialist and replaced the receiver. While he was finishing his notes, Ann returned.

"Bad weather?"

She was standing in the doorway of the small bedroom, a cup of coffee in each hand. The cups were steaming in the early-morning chill. Her face was still puffy with sleep, and her auburn hair tousled yet pert with almost calculated disarray. She was wearing a simple light flannel gown, but even flannel could not hide her figure, which gave the cloth a substance that Jim now found particularly distracting. Her breasts lifted into erect little points from which the soft fabric draped.

He reached out and forced himself to aim instead for the coffee and grinned, "You're getting chilly." Then, seeing the serious look in her eyes, he remembered her question.

"Oh, no. There's a front moving in from the northwest, but it won't get to Reno till long after I arrive. The briefer said general VFR conditions should hold till the afternoon. I might have to use the bus to get home though. Unless there's a commercial flight leaving early in the afternoon."

Her hazel eyes turned dark. She started to say something, shrugged it off, and turned for the kitchen.

Jim watched her go, the half-smile fading from his lips. He know she was concerned about the weather. Fronts could move in unpredictably fast over the Sierras. But he wasn't really worried about the flight. Hell, he would be on the ground long before there was any turbulence over the mountains. And even if Charlie's work on the right engine was not the best, the twin he was flying had a single-engine altitude of over twelve thousand feet. That would be enough to limp east or west of the high terrain and land at a lower level strip or highway.

He had to confess, though, that he was somewhat puzzled by this assignment. Laird was not only a close dealer, he was nearly broke most of the time, and he allowed himself the shortcuts in aircraft repair most reputable firms avoided. Charlie Wise was a case in point. Charlie was a certified airframe and powerplant mechanic, but as Laird's only repairman, he had found himself forced to compromise his skills on more than one occasion. Reputations are built fast at a small airport. Before long nobody at Grant Field would let Charlie come close to his airplanes with even a screwdriver. But he was kept busy enough working on the planes Laird bought as distressed wholesale, and then repainted, recertified, and sold, largely to a non-local clientele. Most buyers were enchanted by Laird's personality, the appeal of low overhead, and finally, a below "Bluebook" selling price. They had one other thing in common: they never, never bought a plane from Jack Laird again.

That was what perplexed Jim. For a man who had no qualms about cutting corners, he seemed a bit quick to offer the extra money. On the other hand, he must be making a bundle on the sale, he mused. The used market of the twin must be close to three or four hundred thousand—depending on avionics and engine time. He knew Laird could not have paid more than half that figure to buy the damaged plane in Mexico on an insurance-salvage deal. Yes, he could be clearing quite a bit. . . . He needed to; that guy from the bank had been around just last week looking for Jack again.

Ann was standing at the kitchen window of their small apartment, watching the sun inch its way over the low hills to the east. It bathed her face in warm light, but as she turned to Jim, there was an anxiety in her eyes. She held out a paper sack. "Here's a lunch; be careful." When he took the bag, she turned again to watch the sun.

"Honey . . . , " he soothed.

She interrupted, "You'd better get going if you are going to beat that weather."

He stood for a moment looking silently at her profile. Then he kissed her and walked quickly out the front door.

3

THE AGING DODGE COMPACT threaded its way through mounting 7:15 Thursday traffic with an unhurried precision. Jim Regan never broke speed limits. At age twenty-five his auto-insurance computer would consider him qualified as a low-risk driver. He did not smoke, rarely drank except for an occasional glass of wine with dinner, had maintained a 3.2 GPA through college, was slightly underweight for his six-foot-one frame, and had an annual physical, which always attested to the good health his appearance suggested.

Midway in his second year of college he had begun flight training. It had been a hit-or-miss kind of program financed largely by "gofer" jobs around the airport in exchange for flying time. Much of this absorbed training came about through a long and pleasant association with Bud Fallon, a man in his middle fifties whose main activity these days was phasing himself out of a small airplane-parts business so that he could spend more time exercising a

Cessna 195, keeping it and himself in tune for monthly trips into bush country. Fallon had been flying since before the Big War and had piloted nearly every type of propeller airplane built. He had maintained his instructor's rating mostly out of habit—and to keep current with new developments. He had seen Jim Regan through all of his ratings, and was tickled that the youngster had passed him by, at least as far as legal qualifications were concerned. Bud was content to have helped his protege develop what he considered to be vital to pilot survival, a knowledge of and respect for machinery and Mother Nature.

None of these things was on Jim's mind as he guided the Dart off the freeway onto the nearly empty access road to Grant Field. The meager pay he earned as a flight instructor and part-time charter pilot barely paid his and Ann's living expenses. He had been building time, ratings, and education for six years to get a crack at an airline job. As a flight engineer he would make three times the salary he earned now.

He had applied for a position with most of the major carriers and had advanced through interviews and physicals with some. At the bottom line in each case he came up lacking either the rating or the total flight time. As a consequence he flew as often as he could, to build time and to earn extra cash to finance his way through flight engineer school.

Jim's thoughts were on the airline job as he turned the Dodge onto the narrow asphalt drive leading to the airport. He realized that he had little chance of being selected with his current qualifications, but this morning's ferry time would put him just that much closer to the rating and the job.

In a computer terminal room a thousand miles to the east, two technicians were setting up a priority program to be fed into U.S. Airlines' retrieval system for flight crew applicants.

"How is it coming?" Jill Cotter leaned over her assistant's shoulder to peer at the data sheet as he thoughtfully pecked out the new selection criteria on his keyboard. Her face was close enough to his for a wisp of her hair to brush tantalizingly across his left ear.

"OK. Another five minutes and you can check it." Frank Jordan turned his head to get her response. She continued reading, absorbed in the data sheet before them. Her full mouth was on a level with his eye, and he watched as she bit down thoughtfully on the lower lip. Her breath mingled with the smell of daily shampooed hair, and a clear female body perfume.

Suddenly she straightened. "Great, Frank! That can go as it is. Let me see the rest as soon as you set it up." She squeezed his shoulder and patted it with approval.

"What's the big rush for this anyway?" Frank was fighting for control, unwilling for her to leave, boss or not.

She came back and turned to face him as she leaned against the console. "It came down at oh eight hundred, the first thing. The Public Utilities Commission gave the line those new routes. All the furloughed pilots were picked up last month to fill in for retirement vacancies, so now we have to dig into the younger pilot apps. That's why we had to reprogram and adjust hiring parameters. They're doubling staff for the simulator trainer and reactivating flight engineer school."

Frank could care less about hiring trends for the airline, but the discussion was keeping Jill comfortably close. "That means some young pilots will be pleasantly surprised."

"Thirty, to be exact," she smiled warmly, pleased that this young tech was interested in something beyond his keyboard.

After she left, Frank made three errors in the repro-
gramming operation. He found and corrected two of
them. Mostly he was wondering if two could live comfortably on a programmer's salary, or if a thirty-one-year-
old divorcee would be interested in marriage to a
nineteen-year-old, if she also happened to be his boss.

Thirty minutes later Jill had approved the program—
including Frank's small error regarding flight time; it was
fed into the computer, and almost instantly profile sheets
began to issue on the printout.

Thad Monte sometimes regretted the disorderly nature of airplane insurance underwriting. He was fully
awake by the time he pulled into the parking lot behind
Jack Laird's office, but getting up this early to cover a
last-minute ferry policy was not the way he liked to do
business. He sighed resignedly as he picked up a briefcase
from the seat beside him and stepped out of the car. Oh
well, the commission on these short-term policies was
good, and that offset the erratic work schedule.

He was mildly concerned that Laird's call had come too
late for him to verify coverage with the central office, but
at least he had had the foresight to insist on a cash payment
of the premium before issuing the policy on his own. His
client had agreed quickly over the phone, adding that he
would like to offer payment in currency because of some
extra cash on hand. "You'll save me a trip to the bank,
Thad," the ebullient plane salesman had declared.

Neither man had any delusions about the game being
played. It saddened Thad, however, because he liked Jack
despite his reputation, and he didn't like to see him scraping bottom. Where he got the cash was anybody's guess; he
certainly had no credit left in town. Perhaps the sale of the
twin would bring him some level of solvency, though he

could hardly believe that any buyer in his right mind would be paying the nearly half-million Jack had quoted as the sales figure.

Jack's Mercedes was not in the lot, and Thad was surprised when the burly Laird greeted him at the door.

"Thought I beat you here, Jack. Didn't see your car." He reached out with the habitual insuranceman handshake.

"It's in the shop. Ignition. Those damned things are as finicky as Swiss watches. I should have a car like ole Jim's here," Laird said, sweeping a hand in the direction of the young pilot. "It may not look swanky, but it never lets him down. . . . You two know each other? Jim's takin' the bird to my buyer."

"Hi, Jim. How's Ann?" Thad was pleased that a competent pilot was going to ferry the plane his company would insure.

"Fine, Thad. How's the family?" Jim acknowledged, adding, "I guess you two have business. I'm gonna pre-flight the airplane." He paused at the door. "When I get back we'll have to get together for dinner. You free this weekend?"

"I think so, Jim. How about if I check with Shirley and have her call Ann? I can't seem to keep my weekends straight." Thad was pleased that they might have a chance to get together again. Shirley would certainly welcome a night out away from the kids.

Jim waved agreement and walked out of the office.

Laird and Monte watched him go, then sat down at the desk and settled into their transaction. After he had looked over the papers Thad had spread before him, Jack opened a drawer and withdrew a thick envelope. "Yeah. Well, look, I've got six hundred fifty here in cash." He counted out the new bills into neat piles on the desk. "That

takes care of the ferry hull and liability on the Dauphin and
gets me current on liability and hull for the other six planes
on the ground. Right?"

Thad consulted his notebook and nodded. "What
about the Phoenix people? Aren't you going to want
moving coverage for them when they try out the other
plane you are selling?"

"Who?" Jack looked at him blankly. "Oh, yeah. Well,
they are looking at a couple. . . . Say, I'm not too sure
which ones they might want to demo. How about if I call
you for a verbal binder when they get here?"

"That's OK, Jack. Just give me a call. Here, let me give
you a receipt for all this green stuff." He sat in an armchair
beside Laird and wrote out a receipt. "I'm sorry the premium is so high on the Dauphin, but this piecemeal stuff is
really expensive." He paused, looked up from his writing,
and added, "Also the sale price is above book, and you
know how sticky the underwriters are about that."

"Yeah, yeah. Someday I'll be big enough for you guys
to write me a blanket policy on the whole fleet—tied
down, rented, moving, or flying. In the meantime I'll just
have to bite the bullet."

Looking across at the insurance agent, Jack Laird beamed
his old public-relations smile under slate gray eyes which
remained inscrutable as always.

Jim had completed his preflight of N7695R and was
reasonably satisfied that the eight-seat executive twin was
ready for flight. The damage it had incurred because of a
wheels-up landing in Mexico some months before had
caused mainly cosmetic wrinkling, and this had been repaired quite nicely by Charlie Wise. Charlie might not be
the most conscientious mechanic, but in this case his work
seemed sound.

Jim ran his hand over the now-smooth underbelly with

its new coat of paint and admired the slick repair Charlie had made, though he had probably not replaced the aluminum skin as he should have. Under the paint there were probably several thicknesses of automobile body putty. It was not legal, and it could be dangerous where structure or center of gravity could be affected. In this case it was a coverup for a visual blemish and did nothing more serious than add ten or twenty pounds to the overall weight of the airplane.

"Charlie did a neat job there, eh, Jim?" He had not heard Jack Laird approach. Jim straightened up and turned to face the older man, who was leaning with an arm carelessly resting on the polished spinner of the left engine.

"Yeah, Charlie can hide a lot of things with a paint sprayer," Jim retorted. "I hope he used new parts when he pulled that bad cylinder," he added, pointing to the gleaming engine nacelle behind Laird's arm.

"Well, you checked the logbooks yesterday, Jim." Laird appeared unruffled by the attack on his mechanic as he pulled an invoice from his pocket. "Here, this is the parts list from Acme Aero." He handed the paper to Jim, who read down a long list of parts and machine-shop procedures.

Laird smiled and added, "You'll notice we replaced the whole cylinder assembly, not just the cracked piston and rings."

Jim was surprised. The procedure was first class and expensive, both criteria normally anathema to Laird.

He handed the paper back. "I'll be grateful for that about the time I pass by Mount Whitney. Thanks for relieving my mind, Jack." Inwardly he felt a touch of remorse for having judged the pair of flaky operators too harshly.

"You're going direct, then. I'm glad of that. I was afraid I would have to talk you out of the longer trip up the valleys. I just now talked to the guy in Reno. He asked that you get there pronto because there has been a change of plans, and some of the other parties in the sale have to get to Sacramento by one this afternoon. He thought they might as well use the new bird." He added, "They said you could fly with them. That will get you to the airline terminal faster and save the cost of a commuter flight out of Sparks. You could be home by five."

Jim looked at his watch. The thought of getting back to Ann before nightfall was most appealing. "I'd better get a move on if I want to be off by eight thirty. Let's call the gas truck." He climbed into the cabin to summon the fueler on the ground-frequency radio.

"Maybe it would be better to gas up at the pumps," Laird said. "I don't trust that truck stuff after a cold night. We had a lot of frost, you know. I'll taxi over with you."

"OK, I just thought it might save some time." He settled into his seat, opened a small window and called out to the deserted ramp, "Clear left!" In a few seconds the left propeller began to crank slowly. It had not completed one revolution before it caught with a healthy rumble. The right engine followed suit and the heavy airplane slowly ambled out of its tiedown space and headed for the pumps.

4

OVERHEAD A FLASH of low-angle sunlight winked off the polished aluminum wing of an arriving airplane. As it crossed the small runway at right angles, the heavy engine sounds increased in frequency as the pilot moved the prop into flat pitch and reduced power. "Grant Unicom, Cessna two four two four Pop, overhead for downwind, two-niner."

No one answered Bud Fallon as he replaced the microphone. Grant Field was an uncontrolled airport, as are most of the airports in use in the United States, but common practice called for transmitting on a "unicom" frequency to advise others in the air and on the ground that an aircraft was intending to land and what its location was.

Fallon squinted as he swiveled his head searching for other traffic in the pattern. Satisfied, he banked the big 195's cantilevered wings and turned left on his downwind leg for Runway 29. As the runway boundary passed to his left 800 feet under him, he saw the twin rolling toward the gas pumps.

He turned a close final, lined up carefully adjusting for a slight crosswind, and just as the fence slid under the plane, he pulled the big nose up and eased the tires onto the asphalt. An instant later the tail settled, and he had to find his way by looking out the side windows. With her tail down, only the radial engine and a slice of sky were visible through the windshield of the taxiing Cessna.

Just short of midfield he kicked the tail around and let the plane roll gently to a stop near a concrete pad in whose center stood a cluster of vintage gas pumps.

As he climbed down, Bud smiled at a man ten years his junior who was busy unsnarling a tangled static ground wire near one of the pumps. "Whatcha doin' here so early, George? Naomi kick you out of bed?"

"Normal starting time, Bud. My boss is a believer in the old school—twelve-hour work days, six days a week, no over time, below-minimum wage, and no pay for vacations."

George Feister could call the shots pretty much as he wanted, because the "boss" he referred to was himself—or rather he and Naomi. They owned the small area of the field on which the pumps and a small building were located, as well as the tanks in the ground and the pumps themselves.

Bud and the diminutive gas man watched as Laird's executive twin turned off the taxiway and nosed toward the pump island.

"You got a big sale comin', George."

"Hah!" George snorted. "Probably he'll buy one quart of oil and ask me to put half in each engine. Then Naomi will clean his windshield before I can stop her." As if on cue his wife stepped out of the office and walked toward them.

The twin's propellers clanked to a stop, and the door stairway fell open. Jim Regan stepped out, followed by Jack Laird. The big salesman waved. "Hi, George, Bud."

The two men returned his greeting and waved to the young pilot who was walking toward Naomi.

"Got the pot on yet, Mrs. Feister?" Jim had grown up at the airport and was not yet able to address her by her given name. Everyone else over the age of sixteen who knew them did, but the old amenities were hard for Jim to shake.

"Oh, sure, Jimmy," she answered warmly, "but you'd better hurry before Charlie drinks the whole thing himself." There was no mistaking her dislike for the mechanic.

Jim grinned. "So that's where he's holed up. I knew he'd find a warm spot this morning until the sun got serious."

Jack Laird took the 100-octane hose and dragged it toward the wingtip tank. "You get the static wire, George. I want to top these off myself."

After filling both tip tanks, he returned the hose.

"What did it take?" asked Feister.

Laird looked at the meter. "Thirty-eight even."

"Are you sure?" Feister seemed surprised. "I thought those tanks held forty."

Bud Fallon raised his eyebrows in an unspoken question. Laird said quickly, "Oh, yeah. Charlie must have put a gallon in each tank to make sure the quick drains weren't damaged in the belly landing. Well, I'm gonna check the pumps myself to make sure ole George's gas is OK." He took a small glass tube from his pocket, drew several ounces of fuel from each of the pumps, and held them up to check for water contamination. Apparently satisfied with each sample, he cast the last batch in a sweeping arc which evaporated quickly on the concrete apron.

Although he encouraged everyone to check for water,

particularly when filling tanks that had stood cold and empty overnight, George was a trifle rankled at the remark about his gas. He could not resist setting a barb.

"You know, Jack, you could have saved fifty cents by taking gas from the truck. That stuff in the ground tanks is sixty degrees the year round. After last night, the gas in the truck must be about thirty degrees. The stuff expands, you know. If you had put cold gas in those tip tanks, you would have got more energy per gallon."

He got more of a reaction than he bargained for. Laird spun around with a strange look in his eyes, then quickly recovered.

"Well, that about makes it even, then. By the time the plane flies fifty miles the gas would have heated up and gone out the vent anyway," he rejoined.

Bud Fallon jumped in, supporting George. "No, you're wrong, Jack. By the time you get fifty miles you'll be up where it's cold and the fuel would keep its low temperature. So you wouldn't lose it after all." Bud turned away and strode with Naomi back to her office for a cup of strong black coffee.

"You want to put any in the main tanks?" George, too, had withdrawn from the game.

"No, there must be two hours' worth there already. The flight should only take about two hours total. He's got enough for a round trip with the tips full." Laird seemed anxious to get off the subject.

"You want to charge your account?"

"No, George, I want to pay cash if you don't mind. Oh, I will need a receipt, though, for the office. By the way, make sure the registration number is legible. My accountant has been complaining about not knowing which plane was fueled when."

George nodded silently and wrote out the receipt, handing the original to the other man.

Laird looked at it carefully, then placed it in his pocket with the invoice for the newly installed cylinder assembly.

Charlie Wise had just finished his third coffee and was thinking of having half a cup more when he rejected the idea. From the window of the small office he could see Bud Fallon approaching with Naomi. Fallon was a licensed mechanic himself and had once told Charlie that if he did not shape up and improve his performance, he would report him to the FAA. Charlie had avoided Fallon assiduously since. Gritting his teeth as he recalled the humiliating experience, he turned from the window and crumpled the styrofoam cup, tossing it into a wastebasket. "See ya," he mumbled in Jim's direction as he attempted to get out the door and away before Bud and Naomi got any closer.

He was not quick enough. Bud called out practically as he opened the door, "Oh, Charlie, see you a minute?"

Charlie stepped outside the building and stood waiting with no response, gazing sullenly at some distant object on the field.

Naomi walked past Charlie into the office and closed the door behind her.

"Whatcha need, Bud?" Charlie continued staring off into the distance.

Fallon came quickly to the point. "We don't have time to beat around the bush, Charlie. I know you are a good mechanic when you want to be"—he did not pause as Charlie shot a look of black dislike at him—"and I hope you have been *wanting* to be a good mechanic lately. I want a straight answer. How good is that twin Laird is sending up to Reno?"

Charlie almost laughed out loud. So the old man is wet-nursing his Golden Boy. Afraid he might bust his precious ass on a ferry flight. For two cents I should give him something to worry about.

Fortunately for Charlie's physical well-being, he kept his thoughts to himself. He knew that Fallon was all business, and serious comportment was advised. Besides, he thought, the airplane was truly as sound as a new one.

"It's a tight bird. The guy who buys it won't find anything wrong with *that* airframe. The engines are both good, too. We put a new jug in when we did all the metal work." Charlie laughed without humor as he watched Jack Laird moving around the plane in question. "Though I sure as hell won't say that buyer is getting a good deal. He must need a tax writeoff real bad to pay what he agreed to for that plane. It must be priced fifty thousand over market."

Fallon was not getting the assurances he wanted. "I'm not interested in whether somebody I don't know is getting a 'good deal.' How safe is it?"

"Oh, don't get me wrong, Fallon. The plane is like new mechanically. Christ, I don't know what's got into Laird. He must thrown away a couple of grand on that thing. I mean money he didn't *have* to spend. Even *you* couldn't complain about the work we put into that bird. I mean, well, the critical engine had a cracked piston, you see, but the rings didn't even break. The cylinder was fine, not a mark on it, but what does Laird do? He orders a whole new jug assembly from Acme Aero."

An almost breathless enthusiasm possessed Charlie as he continued, "Another thing. I dunno whether you seen the belly of that thing when we brought her in from Mexico. Well, it was hardly dented. Most of the damage was cosmetic. I told Jack I could practically give her a heavy coat of paint—with maybe some filler,—but Jack said, 'No, rip off the skin and replace any bent formers.' I mean that stuff I replaced could have been left in there *legally*. He was spending bucks like it was his own plane. Then he fussed over the logbooks. At one point he was gonna have another A & P come in to supervise—so he

could get him to sign it off, I guess." Charlie's eyes darkened. "That really pissed me off. Here I am doing all this
shitty half-legal stuff for him and putting *my* ass in a sling
because he is too cheap to let me do things right, and now,
when he gets this new religion or whatever bug is up his
gazooch, suddenly my signature over my work is not clean
enough for these goddam logs!"

"Maybe Jack has changed, Charlie." Somehow Bud did
not truly believe this.

"I know this," Charlie looked at him with a fierce
pride, "I gave that sucker what he wanted. The belly and
gear doors are better than they were new. They could take
that belly section to paint and metal schools to show them
how it should be done."

Inside the office Jim Regan was making ineffectual
protests at Naomi's ministrations. He had already accepted
a morning donut and now she was forcing various
foodstuffs on him as provender for his trip.

"My gosh, Mrs. Feister, I couldn't eat all this in a
week!" He looked into the huge sack laden with several
cans of soda, candy bars, fruit, two tuna sandwiches, and a
dozen donuts.

"Just throw out what you can't eat, Jimmy. You'll be
doing George and me a favor," she said, laughing and
pointing at her rounded midsection. "I can spare the
calories."

Naomi pushed Jim out the door just as Bud and Charlie were parting. Bud fell in step with Jim as he walked out
to the waiting plane.

"Naomi is still afraid you might starve, I see." Bud
chuckled to see that Jim was mildly embarrassed by the
woman's motherly attention, but he did not press the opportunity for fun. "Have you checked weather?"

"Yes, it looks good all the way. Might get dirty this

afternoon, but that will be somebody else's problem. I'll
just sit back in economy and let some airline pilot do the
worrying for me. *If* I can get away from here before
lunchtime," he teased.

"That frontal system is moving in fast. Are you going
up the valley and then over?"

Jim reflected a moment. "No I'm going right up the
razorback all the way. I'll save time that way. I don't want
to get stuck in Reno if it does snow heavily."

Bud frowned. "You won't save that much time. Not
over fifteen minutes." He hated to see a pilot let time
force any decision.

"Well, I wouldn't consider that route if I hadn't had
such excellent mountain flying instruction," Jim replied
drily.

"Look, Jim, I don't want you to think I'm an alarmist,
but these early-season storms can get tricky. One thing
I've learned—the only thing dependable about mountain
weather is that it's *un*dependable." He paused. "If that
front does move in, you might want to take the Inyo passage."

Jim nodded. He had flown the route with Bud before.
It was a bit out of the way, but protected on the west by
the Sierra wall, and it followed the broad valley of the
Owens River for a hundred miles. He decided to keep it as
an alternative plan.

They had reached the parked twin and Jim swung the
heavy sack into the open door. Jack Laird came over as
they were saying goodbyes.

"Oh, Jim, don't forget to take off on the main tanks.
After you are airborne for an hour, switch to the tips. You
have about two hours in the mains and about two more in
the tip tanks. I wouldn't burn too much out of the tips,
because you'll be better off with some weight out there at
the wing ends. You have to save enough in the mains for

landing though. This model is placarded for takeoff and landing with the mains only."

Jim laughed and shook his head. "I haven't had so much advice before a flight since my first student cross-country. Really, Jack, I have flown these before, and I do read the checklists. I must look younger than I thought. No wonder the airlines have been shy."

Bud Fallon, who had gone to his plane on the other side of the pumps when Laird walked up, returned to the door of the twin. He was carrying a canvas survival kit that looked like an infantry haversack. Its zipper was sealed shut with a wire loop and lead disc much like the ones used on home electric meter boxes to prevent tampering.

"Here, Hotshot, take this along for good luck. At eight pounds it shouldn't upset your weight and balance. Bring it back with you tonight, please."

"Yes, Mother," Jim took the satchel and placed it on the seat nearest the door. "Gee, this weighs as much as Naomi's Care package. You won't feel hurt if I eat out of hers first, will you?"

"You'd better not even break the seal on that zipper, if you value your manhood. I want that thing back tonight unviolated, you hear? I never fly without it, and I get awful nasty when I can't fly for a spell."

Jim realized with a start that he had forgotten to call Ann. He was about to climb down from the plane when he looked at his watch. He had told Flight Service to expect to activate his VFR flight plan at about 8:15, and it was nearly 8:30. He had to get going.

"Say, Bud, do me a favor and call Ann? Tell her I'll call collect when I get to a phone in Reno."

Bud nodded as he moved to the front of the plane to help Jack and George Feister push the big craft away from the pumps.

As he pulled the lower half of the clamshell door into

place, Jim added, "Thanks, Buddy, she's kinda upset about this one." He closed the top half of the door, latched it, and moved up the narrow aisle to the pilot's seat and strapped himself in. Then he began the checklist ritual and finally started the engines.

The plane began to taxi slowly to the end of the field. Bud Fallon went into the office to get his coffee and to mooch a dime so he could call Ann Regan. Well, he smiled, at least that would be a bit of a nice thing. What a lovely lass that Jimbo had got for himself!

Jack Laird retraced his earlier steps to the back entry of his office. He did not notice Charlie Wise working on a balky magneto at his workbench in the open maintenance shed. He turned once to look back toward the runway as Jim completed the runup check before takeoff. As he passed the trash bin, he reached into a pocket and removed a length of belt similar to the kind one would find driving the accessories under the hood of an automobile. It looked brand new. Jack tossed it into the bin, and it fell on a pair of crumpled-up, wet plastic bags. The vee belt uncoiled slowly, like a rattlesnake numbed with the cold. The ends would match perfectly if rejoined where they had been neatly cut apart. Laird pulled its mate from another pocket and sent it squirming after the first.

Seated back at his desk, Jack Laird withdrew the invoices from his pocket and filed them in a fat jacket marked N7695R. He reached into his trouser pocket, leaning sideways to ease the movement, and pulled out a pair of seven-inch diagonal cutters. These he placed in the bottom drawer of his desk, all the way in back. Getting up, he walked to a small refrigerator beside the filing cabinet, opened it and took out a bottle of beer. He unscrewed the cap and held it up, noting the slushy cylinder of ice floating inside. He reached back into the box and turned the thermostat to a warmer setting. When he sucked at the cold beer the icicle jabbed softly at his tongue. But it did not relieve the dryness in his throat and the liquid was bile in his mouth.

In his cockpit Jim made two minor errors. One he was not aware of, the other he was. He did not notice that the ammeter needle was fixed in a slightly discharged position. He did note that the test light for a break in the alternator circuit was inoperative, but he chose to ignore it. "Probably burned out," he mumbled; "those damned idiot lights always go for no reason." Well, he thought, there is no point in getting a new one. On a VFR flight of only two hours I won't need to worry anyway.

Satisfied that he was ready to go, he made his call on unicom, got a reply from a small plane in the traffic pattern, rolled onto the runway, and locked the brakes. Boy, this bird felt good! He applied power smoothly, released the brakes and N7695R lunged powerfully into the wind.

Out at the wingtips the sudden lurch sent 25 pounds of icecubes in each fuel pod clattering against the rear of the tanks. Jim could not hear that sound of course. In fact, the ice was already beginning to melt from the warmth of the gasoline, which, until Jack Laird pumped it in 15 minutes ago, had been stored securely underground at 60 degrees.

In the midwestern United States Jill Cotter looked up from her desk as that nice young tech came in holding a stack of cards.

"Here they are, Boss, all thirty of them. Arranged alphabetically from Burnside, L.," Frank cocked his head, riffling the cards to read the last one in the stack, "to Regan, J."

Then he put his hands down on Jill's desk, and mustering all the savoir-faire of his nineteen years, looked her straight in the eyes. His voice was husky with insinuation. "Now, lady, how about a date tonight?"

And that was the fourth error Frank Jordan made that day.

5

ANN REGAN WAS NOT aware of how long she had sat at the breakfast table until she sipped at her half-empty cup and discovered the coffee was cold. Pushing aside the textbook she had been reading, she rose and refilled the earthenware mug and lit her fifth cigaret of the morning.

She had read several chapters since Jim left, but had absorbed nothing. Midterm exams were scheduled for the following week in this her final year of study toward a BS in Nursing, and she was finding it more difficult to concentrate as she got closer to the degree. Suppressing an urge to quit for the morning, she sipped from the steaming cup and resumed her reading. The determination paid off as the material gradually absorbed her attention.

At twenty-three, Ann was a few years older than her classmates at the University Hospital a few blocks away from their apartment. She had started training after two years of varied work to, as she put it, "find out where my

head was before setting any goals." In the process she had
uncovered an unexpected interest in medicine and had
met Jim. After a relatively short period of assessment she
resolved to have both.

Ann's special interest in nursing gradually centered on
obstetrical care. Part of the reason for her preference was
due to a liking for the chief gynecologist, Mildred Yancey.
Dr. Yancey in turn regarded the younger woman with
unabashed admiration.

Yancey claimed that Ann was the best medical student
she had ever worked with. "That woman is good for all of
us," she declared once at a staff meeting. "She has a drive
to learn. Besides that she is beautiful and intelligent without appearing to notice. Why, she has those old roosters in
my service eating out of her hand, and the young residents
practically fall over themselves when she's on the ward."
But Dr. Yancey had also voiced a concern: "I just wish she
could learn to ease up once in a while."

As Ann sat poring over the psychology text in her
kitchen, she too was becoming aware of the need for a
letup. Unfortunately the simple economics of her situation
pressured her to get the degree and begin earning something to supplement Jim's modest income as an instructor.
It was not that they had to go hungry, though an occasional
check was written at the grocery after banking hours to
bridge insolvent periods. They were reasonably content;
satisfied to wait for whatever rewards professional careers
might return.

For the second time that morning Ann discovered she
was following words instead of ideas. This time she closed
the text and pushed it away. Her cigaret with drooping ash
was squashed between her fingers. Soft gray ribbons of
smoke lazed past her ear and lost themselves in the fine
brown waves at her temple. "My hair probably reeks," she
thought.

She stubbed out the butt and took another look at the clock. Why hadn't he called? She looked at the cheddar block still resting where she had sliced a portion to make Jim's sandwich over an hour before. "I'll make the bed," she thought and started down the tiny hall.

Switching off a small study light brought Jim to mind again. Just a few days ago he had been concerned about all the extra work she had been putting in on the hospital classes.

"You are trying to learn the whole darned school of medicine," he had scolded one morning at three A.M. upon awakening to find her still plugging away at the books in their kitchen. "Look, you have a three-point-eight average already. You know you have an A wrapped up for this class. Why spend any more time on it? You're like a battery hooked up to a charger."

Taking him by the hand, Ann had turned off the kitchen light and led him back to bed. She began to run her finger around the elastic waistband of his pajama bottoms. "I think I could stand a little charging right now."

With her free hand she untied the sash of her velveteen robe and let it slip completely off her shoulders. She continued teasing his waist and abdomen, working the elastic even lower until the pajama bottoms slipped to the floor. Then she laid her cheek against his chest and began making idle circles around his excited nipple with her index finger.

"Boy," he croaked, "you really know how to change the subject." He began sleep-clumsy caresses of her soft shoulder and back.

"It was *your* analogy, dear," she said softly. With that she slipped free of him and with exaggerated nymph steps danced to the bed.

He took a step to follow, unmindful of the pajamas about his feet, and crashed in a tangled heap somewhat short of the bed. Ann peered over the edge of the mattress, alarmed at the terrific thump when he hit the thinly carpeted floor. "Did you hurt yourself?" she murmured.

"Only my pride, I think," he groused sheepishly. "Come here."

She slid from the bed and walked tentatively to his side. "Are you sure you're all right?" In answer he reached out his hands for her.

Softly she stepped to his feet and stood one foot on either side of his calves. He could just feel her ankles touch the skin. Her hands were on her hips and her head tilted to one side as she appraised him. He could not make out her face. She was a softly defined silhouette in the half-light of the door. Then she sank to kneel astride his hips and with deliberate slowness slipped upon him, continuing her downward movement till her breasts touched his chest and her full lips were on his mouth.

Thinking of that now gave Ann a sensuous delight. She made up the bed without being aware of the physical operations involved, and stooped to pick up their clothes, scattered from undressing the night before. After sorting clothes for laundering she pulled the nightgown over her head and cast it on the pile.

She turned to look at herself in a full-length mirror set in the bedroom closet door. She posed at different angles, wondering what stance was most provocative to men, to Jim especially. I wonder what he likes about me most, she mused.

Like many persons gifted by Nature, Ann was not fully aware of nor concerned about her degree of beauty. These private moments of self-appraisal were infrequent. She felt a twinge of embarrassed self-consciousness and tried to douse it with flippancy.

"Well, ole bod, you were good enough to get our

Jimmy worked up this morning, weren't you?" She winked at her image in the glass. "Almost made him forget his airplane."

She went into the bathroom to take a shower and wash the smoke out of her hair. Suddenly she wanted him with a desire stronger than she had ever known possible. The phone rang just as she had shampooed her hair.

The way Ann Regan answered his call left no doubt in Bud Fallon's mind that she had expected Jim to be on the other end. All she said was "Hello," but her delivery gave it an intimate quality obviously intended for her husband. Bud saved them both embarrassment by shouting over an imaginary poor connection on the line.

"That you, Ann? Bud Fallon."

"Oh, hello, Bud," Ann faltered, then added apologetically, "I was expecting Jim to call."

Bud grimaced as he continued the gentle ruse, his voice sliding down to a normal modulation. "There, I can hear you OK now . . . bad switching on the connection, I guess. Ann, the reason I'm calling is to give you a message from Jim."

"Oh, yes, Bud." Her voice was pleasant but disappointed.

"Yes, well, he wanted to call you himself to let you know when he took off, but he got bogged down with some last-minute stuff and he was running late so he asked me to do the honors."

"Thanks, Bud. I'm glad you called. I *was* waiting. When did he take off?"

"Just now. If you listen real hard you'll be able to hear him climbing out over town." Bud pushed the receiver away from his ear as he turned half away from the pole-mounted pay phone and squinted at the disappearing

speck of Jim's airplane climbing swiftly toward the foothills to the north. "I watched him leave. It sounded good
and strong."

"Thanks, Bud. Did he tell you what time he would
arrive?"

"In about two hours, I guess. Did he say he'd call?"

"He always does."

"Right." Bud paused a moment, caught in a flashback
to those times when there had been someone he too had
needed to call. He brushed the feeling aside.

Ann ended the call with a request for the "N" number
of the airplane and the destination airport. It was a good
idea to have the information handy as a precaution in the
event that Jim could not get through by phone after he
landed. She could then expedite information-gathering if it
were necessary to call Flight Service for information on his
arrival.

Ann replaced the receiver on its cradle by the bed,
picked up the soapy-wet towel she had been standing on
throughout the conversation, and rushed back to the
shower to rinse the drying suds from her hair.

The needle jets of warm water drove the last of the
tension from muscles in the nape of her neck, and she felt
more relaxed than she had in the last twenty-four hours.

6

NOVEMBER 7695 Romeo climbed powerfully out over the north end of the tiny community of Grant, California, its turbocharged engines pulling the lightly loaded plane in a cruise climb of 1500 feet per minute. Jim delighted in the craft's performance, in distinct contrast to the labored characteristics of the trainers he worked in as an instructor. The plush accommodations of the year-old cabin-class twin and the corresponding sophistication of its professional instrument panel filled him with a deep sense of achievement. There was a tinge of envy, too. This temporary reprieve from the frequent tedium and occasional terror of basic flight instructing served to emphasize the yearning he had to "get on" with the airlines.

He looked out the side window to watch how fast the familiar hills were slipping by under his wing even as he gained altitude. Now that he was high enough to pick up the ground signal for his navigation radios, the needles showing his position snapped alive. He checked to be sure that the weak-signal warning flags on the VOR receivers were fully retracted, assuring him of reliable course information.

"Better open my flight plan," he murmured aloud. He switched radio frequencies, glanced at his watch, and listened for a few seconds before he spoke.

"Los Angeles radio, seven six niner five Romeo on two point three." Although he was miles from that city, remote radio facilities linking federal control and information centers would respond.

A female voice responded almost at once in his lightweight earplug phone, "November seven six niner five Romeo, this is Los Angeles, over."

"Los Angeles, niner five Romeo is a VFR flight from Grant Field to Sparks, Nevada. Will you open my flight plan please, at fifty-six after the hour?"

"Roger, niner five Romeo. We will open your flight plan. Thought maybe you had decided not to go."

"Thank you, LA. I was delayed a bit. Time enroute is still two hours. Nine five Romeo."

"Roger, nine five Romeo, have you had a weather update since you filed?"

Jim's second sense opened a valve to his adrenals, and he snapped alert. "Negative on the update; something up? Nine five."

"Affirmative, nine five, suggest you contact Flight Watch on one two two point zero for weather along your route. That front is picking up speed. If you want to amend your plan, call me back on this frequency. Over."

"Thanks, Los Angeles, I'll call back if I need to change anything. Nine five Romeo."

Jim had been hand-flying the large airplane, simply because it was such a pleasure to handle. Now that he was becoming preoccupied with other things, he decided to engage the autopilot. By letting the "black box" do the flying, he could concentrate on a visual scan for other aircraft while completing his communications with flight service personnel.

He switched frequencies and depressed the thumb button on the control yoke. "Los Angeles Flight Watch, seven six niner five Romeo, over."

He had to repeat the transmission twice, adding his location to enable the answering agency to respond over a remote transmitter close by. Finally they answered.

Jim responded with his type aircraft and route and requested weather advisories along the route.

The specialist drawled back a heavy Dixie weather briefing, "Yuh'll be gettin' into some high stratus pretty soon, but that won't bother yuh. Too high. The real problem will come at the end of the route. That system forecast for late this PM has really speeded up. Yuh should be all right, though. The squall line won't hit Reno til about noon. Yer arrival is about eleven, so you should be curled up around a hamburger by then. You plannin' a return trip?"

"Yes on the ETA at eleven. Negative on the return trip. I was planning to pick up passengers and go back as far as Sacramento. Will the ridge be clear enough to cross? Nine five."

"Ah doubt it. The way this thing has been movin' in they expect the Bay Area to go below minimums about twelve thirty local time. Sacramento will go under about the same time. You might be able to get in legally IFR, but it will be iffy. Ovah."

"OK Flight Watch, I'll figure that out on the ground at Sparks. My compliments to your crew for keeping me on the ball. Niner five Romeo."

The specialist did not come back promptly and when he did there was a marked decrease in the volume of transmission. "Thank you for the compliment, suh. And be advised your transmissions are weak and breakin' up. Good flight, and good day."

Jim clicked his mike button twice to acknowledge, and mulled over this new situation. The transmission fade-out was not alarming. In hilly country, transmissions were often blocked for a minute or two. As far as his current flight was concerned, there was no change. The route was clear all the way from where he was to his destination, Sparks Airport. The buyer for the plane might not get his ride to Sacramento, but that was not his problem. Also, Jim might not be able to get a commercial flight out of Reno. By the time he bummed or bought a ride the fifteen miles back to Reno, which had commercial flights south, the weather might have soured to the point that he would not be able to get off. He might have to wait the night until the frontal system blew on through.

Switching off the autopilot as the plane reached cruising altitude, he settled down to old-fashioned contact navigation and hand-flying. He picked up his sectional chart, which was folded along his course line, and began a delightful half-hour of testing his ability to estimate ground speed with checkpoints on the chart and on the ground as he bore steadily north, deeper into the mountains the Spaniards had named Sierra Nevada, "the snow-covered range," which contained the highest peak within the continental United States, Mount Whitney, 14,495 feet above sea level.

Concentrating as he was on basic aeronautical skill and delighting in the majesty of the rising peaks, he did not notice the tiny red flags coming up on the faces of his radios. Under the cowling of each engine the alternators, without belts to drive their pulleys, sat with armatures motionless on their shafts. As the reserve charge of each battery drained away, the radios quietly went to sleep.

The engines droned on, unaffected by the electrical failure. Each power plant had its own magneto system, a double redundancy that would keep them firing independently of each other and of the airplane's electrical structure.

Jim removed his headset to scratch an itchy ear. When he put it back on he did not notice any reduction of amplitude in the signal. These were such fine radios that not a whisper of static or "hash" would come to his ear.

Of course, with dead batteries nothing else would either.

7

BUZZ TAGLIO DECIDED on the number-two breakfast special for a dollar ninety-nine. He gave the order to his waitress and nodded as she gestured with a steaming coffee carafe. She filled the cup at his elbow and swished away to minister to four other arrivals on the 9:40 commuter from Sacramento.

Buzz sampled the coffee and looked around the small cafe, noticing that the booths had been reupholstered since the last time he had been here. Remembering his purpose in making this trip to Sparks, he signaled his waitress to indicate that he was moving to a table by the window from which he could see the runway easily. A glance at the clock confirmed that the big twin should be arriving soon. Jack Laird had said that the plane would come in at ten or a little after. Taglio reached into the inside pocket of his lightweight plaid blazer and withdrew a slender document file. Among other papers he located a small notesheet with "7695R" scribbled diagonally across. Below that were the words "Blue on white."

Taglio was interrupted at his paperwork by the appearance of a platter deftly slipped in front of him by the rushed waitress, who held a pot of steaming brew in her free hand.

"More coffee?"

"Yeah, thanks." Buzz drained the last of his cup and raised it; he then considered his meal of sunnyside-up eggs and hashbrowns which returned his examination with a wet yellow stare of its own. Picking up a knife and fork, he began to tackle the plate with deliberation, his mind on other things.

This deal with Laird was strange, he thought; almost too simple. Only two days before Laird had asked Buzz by phone to broker the plane for him in Nevada. There was some reason for using an intermediary. He was not too clear on that—something to do with bypassing California sales and personal property tax. Apparently the buyer, whom Taglio was acting for, wished to remain anonymous at this point. Taglio had put together many deals with provisions for "John Doe" parties, but in this particular transaction, he would be acting more as a contact than as an agent. Laird had said he would take care of all the paperwork after the airplane had been delivered. All Buzz would need to do would be take possession of the plane, arrange for its safekeeping, and sign an acceptance of the merchandise on behalf of the new owner—or owners, he wasn't sure which. The whole thing was to be subject to their approval later in the week. Laird wanted him to stay in Sparks until contacted by the principals.

Buzz smiled as he considered the commission that would be his after the sale. He had squeezed 2 percent out of Laird with an advance of five hundred to cover expenses. If the gaming tables in Reno didn't get to him, he would make close to ten grand on the deal. All he had to do was sign some papers and wait around an airport for a few days.

"Not bad, Buzz Taglio," he whispered to himself and winked conspiratorially at his transparent reflection in the window by his elbow.

Suddenly he peered past his ghostly image in the glass at a blue and white airplane that was just settling to the runway fifty yards away. He half rose in the booth, pressing his coat with one hand to keep it from dragging on his plate. As the twin rolled by, he squinted to read the numbers on its fuselage.

"Sorry, wrong number." His mimic was louder than he intended.

"Expecting a friend?" The smiling waitress was standing beside the table handing him the check.

"No, Honey, I'm waiting for my airplane." He allowed himself to slide back down into the seat. "And it looks like I may have a long wait. Got any more of that good coffee?"

8

THE TELETYPE OPERATOR at the National Weather Service center on the West Coast began pecking out the handwritten weather warning he had just been given.

"SIGMET" was the heading he chose to show that this was an urgent update affecting all aircraft. In the cryptic abbreviations peculiar to the science, the text followed:

SIGMET ALFA 1 FLT PRCTN. SW ORE TO SRN CA, SVR ICGIC, LTNG, BLZD, VIC MT RNGS, OCCL HLSTO, HVY SNW WRS, SVR DWNDFTS, MTS OBSCRD IN FOG AND SNW.

There was snow coming—lots of it. The frontal system had speeded up but it had deepened, moving around a low pressure area off Santa Barbara. Moisture-laden air from the Pacific was being swept over the entire Sierra Nevada, and as it chilled, it would dump all that wetness in snow and freezing rain along the entire range.

Jim was fifty-four minutes into his flight, and estimated he would be passing Mount Whitney in another five or six minutes. He was on the western side of the range and would not pass over the crest of the great ridge until as far north as Mammoth Lakes. As he neared the rising slopes he would increase his altitude to cruise at 12,500. At that height he would be able to negotiate the passes with altitude to spare.

Out the right side of the windshield he watched the looming mass of Whitney inch toward him as he skirted its western flank. Even the lesser peaks towered above him, and he was struck with the relative fragility of the airplane and himself. He had been here once before with Bud Fallon on a training flight, and now, all alone in the plane, he had a deeper appreciation of the respect Bud held for these mountains.

"The Indians say the Great Spirit lives here," Bud had mentioned on that occasion. "Most of them considered these high places off-limits. They didn't want to intrude on God, I guess."

As Jim gazed up at the glacial slopes, he agreed that they were awesome enough for heaven—and high enough, if one thought the place could be reached on foot.

Suddenly he gasped. He had been so entranced with the spectacle off to his right that he had not noticed the rapid advance of weather moving in from the west. Peering ahead he could see that the clouds had already reached the windward side of the mountains near the area west of Mammoth Mountain. He would have to take Bud's Inyo-Sierra passage.

He trimmed the airplane for climb. He would have to gain enough altitude to clear the ridges to his right, fly

across the ridge to the eastern side of the Sierras and continue north to Reno to parallel the fast-advancing front.
He checked his altimeter. Eleven thousand and climbing.
He needed 14,000-plus to barely scrape over that formi-
dable ridge. Common practice called for another 2,000 as
a safety margin to cope with downdrafts on the lee side of
the ridges, downdrafts that were always possible but probable right now because of the mass of unstable air being
pushed ahead of the approaching frontal mass.

"OK, Regan," he began talking himself through the
change in plan. A glance at the vertical-speed indicator
brought a smile to his lips. It registered a climb rate of 800
feet per minute. "Thank God for turbochargers! Should be
at fourteen in four minutes. I have six minutes before I get
to the really tall ones, so that will give me a tiny cushion."
He rechecked the computation just to be sure.

"I'd better start sucking oxygen soon. First call Flight
Service, report my position, and get an update. Then I'll
put on the mask."

As soon as he depressed the mike button he knew
something was wrong with the radio. He could not hear
the telltale click in his earphone when the button switched
in the transmitter. Swiftly he checked the on-off switches,
changed to the secondary radio, turned the volume full up.
He attempted the voice call even though he doubted that
any signal was being sent out on either transmitter.
"Fresno Radio, November seven six niner five Romeo, on
point two."

He repeated the call several times. During the last two
tries he added "Any station within range" to the callup,
hoping to raise anybody within hearing. The headset registered nothing, not even the usual long-range chatter he
would normally have had to squelch out.

Then he caught the red flags on the navigation dials. In
an instant reflex, his eyes flicked to the ammeter gauge and

its motionless needle, then over to the alternator warning light. It was not on. He pressed the light lens to activate the test circuitry to see if the warning system was functional.

In a flash of self-recrimination he remembered the pre-takeoff runup crosscheck. The light had not responded then either, but in the rush to become airborne he had assumed that the bulb had failed without really checking it out. The fact that the alternator had been functioning minutes before he had gone to the gas pumps had deluded him into thinking that the malfunction must have been in the test circuit and not in the generator circuit itself.

Under present conditions the situation was not serious. It was not mandatory that he provide position reports on a VFR flight plan. The engines with all their necessary accessories would continue to function. There would be the inconvenience of a faster landing, since he wouldn't have flaps to give him additional lift for a slower airspeed. The landing gear would extend since they would free-fall and lock when he moved the lever.

"Damn. I'll have to remember to close my flight plan by telephone after I get on the ground," he muttered. "I sure wish I could get a destination weather update."

He was not worried, only irritated at his own oversight. There were several airports on the eastern slopes of the Sierras that he could slip into if the weather up north turned nasty ahead of the forecast time.

He noted that Mount Whitney had slipped past his right wing and that the ridge he was approaching at a forty-five-degree angle to his front now appeared to be even with his own altitude. He check his watch and the airplane's altimeter.

"Right on," he smiled. "Two minutes to the ridge and I'm at fourteen thousand now. I'll make it easily."

Something began nibbling at the edge of his euphoria and with a shock he remembered the oxygen. At fourteen thousand feet, even with youth and a non-smoking habit in his favor, his brain was beginning to fuzz. He was not aware of any change, but he knew from long training that the pleasant unruffled way he was taking the minor obstacles encountered during the last few minutes indicated the complacency of an oxygen-cheated brain.

He strapped on the mask, turned on the valve, and took a few deep inhalations. Looking at his watch, he checked the time again to verify that he would be high enough to cross the craggy barrier looming four miles ahead. He would have to circle if he didn't have at least a 1500 bonus going over the top. Another look at the altimeter reassured him that it would not be necessary.

Another half-forgotten item, triggered probably by his second look at the time, interposed itself as part of the flight problem.

"Switch tanks!" He was twisting the lever almost as the command came from his mouth. Bending down, he visually checked the position of the fuel selector and verified its being locked solidly in the detent marked LEFT AND RIGHT TIP TANKS, BOTH ON. He looked at his watch a third time. "Nine fifty-eight. Not bad; two minutes late."

The plane was still climbing, but the onrushing ridge looked much higher than it should. Jim's eyes narrowed as he looked at the altimeter once again. Suddenly he wrenched the big plane into a left banking turn away from the mountain and jammed both throttles forward.

"Goddam altimeter setting, you nitwit!"

During the course of the flight, he now realized, he had been flying into an air space that was much colder than normal. As a result, his altimeter, which had been reset only once—at the time he had opened his flight plan—was now reading nearly 1300 feet higher than he actually was.

Had the radios been working he would have received altimeter setting corrections as a matter of routine each time he spoke with a flight specialist. As it was, the uncertain horizon of the mountains made "eyeball" estimates very difficult.

He had caught himself in a marginal situation and immediately withdrew to circle to a safer height. One climbing turn would give him the altitude he needed, but the engines, developing nearly maximum power because of the turbochargers, sucked thirstily at the fuel lines.

Exactly thirty-two seconds after Jim switched tanks, the first of the ice water from the tip tanks was shot under pressure into the hot cylinders. The effect was instantaneous. Both engines quit with a shuddering, steaming cough.

Jim's body lurched forward with the sudden deceleration. He was shocked by the silence of the cabin without the reassuring rumble of two engines. Only the muffled sighing of air slipping past the insulated skin of the plane reached him.

He reacted with hurt indignation. What was the idea? On a check ride they only pull *one* engine. What was a twin good for if you couldn't depend on at least one good power plant? He was stunned into inaction.

The sagging airplane did not indulge him more than a moment's incredulity, however; he had to react swiftly to gain back the airspeed that was winding down with the windmilling propellers. He rolled the trimwheel to ease the swiftly increasing pressure of the control yoke. The plane was still in a slight bank. He leveled it as the nose sank past the horizon. "Best glide speed . . . Sweet Jesus . . . what's the best glide speed . . . ninety-seven knots! That's it, ninety-seven . . . Is that dirty or clean? Can't get flaps. Don't want wheels. I think it's clean. Yeah, it's OK, it feels OK at this angle."

He focused for a split second on the terrain reaching

up to capture the gliding airplane. "Six hundred feet a minute—not much time . . . what've I got? About twelve hundred, thirteen at best. Jesus, Regan, you're gonna buy the farm."

Although he did not truly believe this—that he was going to die—there was no mistaking the slim chance he had of surviving. Even though the plane was headed roughly south toward lower terrain, there were ridges on all sides that would be higher than he was by the time he reached them. He spotted a lake two or three miles ahead and to his left and headed for it, reasoning that it might provide a stretch of beach clear enough to belly-in the plane and slow it enough to reduce the final shock when the skidding craft hit the inevitable tree or rock.

He rechecked the airspeed and committed himself to the lakeside landing. His emergency discipline was paying off. He did not afford himself further speculation as to his fate, but began a methodical, swift check of the cockpit in an attempt to restart the engines. The first move was to reposition the fuel selector on the main tanks. Maybe there was a stoppage in the lines from the tip tanks, he thought. Then he proceeded with the rest of his emergency effort. The entire operation consumed nearly a minute, and a glance outside was all he needed to confirm that he and the ground would meet before another minute was up.

Switching his transmitters to the international emergency frequency, he turned off all other electrical equipment and keyed the mike in the dim hope of being heard by someone who could report his position. "Mayday, mayday, mayday, seven six nine five Romeo, two miles southwest of Mount Whitney, landing imminent."

He repeated the call twice and thought ruefully that "crashing now" would be more accurate than the nerveless, official phraseology of his distress call. He had no more time anyhow; he spoke one final message, "I'm gonna try for a lake here; 'bye."

The adrenaline was taking over. He switched off the radio, located the master electrical switch and turned it off too. "I'll save the mags till the last," he muttered, and removed the oxygen mask, which he had pulled aside to make his last transmissions. Reaching down, he switched off the oxygen supply, and after a second's hesitation turned off the fuel selector. If by some miracle the engines caught, he could twist it on again. Fire was his immediate concern.

The lake was looming closer now, less than a quarter mile to its near shoreline. He would make it easily. The beach he had hoped for did not materialize, however; the stunted trees at this timberline altitude reached within a few yards of the edge. What narrow open stretches there were were strewn with boulders.

Suddenly two things caught his attention. He had been concentrating on the shoreline with such desperation that until now he had not realized that the lake was frozen over! This had barely registered when he saw a narrow trail almost directly under him. He might be able to twist the plane around to try for the trail, which was running ninety degrees to his flight path. It would be chancy though, because he had not had time to see if it was wide enough or level enough to set down on, and he would run the risk of going into the trees and rocks before reaching it.

The frozen surface of the lake was not necessarily a better alternative. He could not tell how thick the ice was. If it would support the airframe, he could land the ship with virtually no damage, and he would be a highly visible target for search planes. If not, he would have little chance of getting from the sinking wreck to undisturbed ice and the beach beyond.

The narrow trail appeared again at the trailing edge of his left wing.

"Choose!" He shouted the command to rouse himself to action.

He chose the lake.

He felt a heady acceleration of images: treetops rushing, actually brushing, under his wings; the tilting picture of the lake as he lined up for touchdown; a boulder flashing by, inches from his wingtip and higher than his eye. Then the edge of the lake flicked past and he was settling gently toward the ice.

He was still over 100 feet above the surface, but he fought the urge to slip the plane sideways to lose altitude. The far side of the lake loomed closer; if he touched down now he would slide to a halt long before striking the far side. Despite the instinct to put it down where he was, he reasoned that if he held it off longer the plane might hydroplane to the beach even if the ice did not hold.

When he was below 50 feet he clicked off the magnetos to both engines, trimmed the elevators to the airplane's slowest flying speed, and let the blue and white craft settle to the ice.

With the barest of gentle bumps, the newly painted belly gave up its rounded contours and flattened as it yielded to the weight of the airframe. The propellers, barely turning in the slow airflow at touchdown, suddenly stopped, the lower blade of each turning back against the ice. Two plumes of shaved ice streamed back from the engines as the plane catapulted toward the shoreline.

Inside the cabin Jim fought to keep directional control with a barely effective rudder. He knew the instant of touchdown that the ice would not break and that he should have put down earlier. No snow had fallen since the lake had frozen over, and the crystal skin was smooth as plate glass, with no roughness to slow his 8000-pound machine. The winged bobsled skated toward destruction at 70 miles per hour.

He was less than 100 yards from the beach and managed to aim for a spot relatively free of rocks. The beach was narrow but it pitched up in a gravel ramp before giving way to the treeline. As the nose of the fuselage shot to the edge of the ice, Jim kicked the right rudder pedal in a futile attempt to swing the plane between the two closest trees. It would not turn. He was not prepared for the terrific smash as the nose rammed into the gravel bank. The metal crumpled back like a stepped-on aluminum beer can, spewing a cascade of rubble high over its back. He did not feel the bone snap in his right leg as the rudder bar jabbed viciously back as if in retribution for his last desperate kick to gain control. Jim was not even aware that the crescent dent that suddenly appeared in the glareshield exactly matched a welling gash across his brow. He felt the plane bound into the air a few feet. With the detached interest of one slipping into shock, he noted that the cabin would miss the two trees after all. He watched them weaving toward him, and wondered which tree would be the first to tag its wing.

The left tree won. It caught the wing at its root, inches from the fuselage, clipping it off the plane intact with its engine. The right tree imbedded itself outboard of the right engine, caught fast in a furrow of torn aluminum. With a terrible groan the dying plane spun halfway round the trembling old pine and came to rest beneath its cracked and swaying limbs.

In his twisted pilot seat, Jim sat staring through the incongruously unbroken windshield, his hands folded on his lap. His head lolled like a child's fighting off sleep.

"Oh, Ann!" The contrite whisper was all the remorse he could manage. A darkness was edging in around his peripheral vision, and he felt a deep exhaustion made more frightening because he was alone. With a resignation that would have been terror had he not been so profoundly drained, he realized that he had not been heard, that he would not be missed for hours, that he was miles off his course, and it would soon begin to snow.

He was unconscious before his nerves sent stabbing, urgent messages of pain from the flesh of his twisted leg. A spreading crimson film oozed from the gash in his forehead.

Inside the metal skin of the vertical tail behind the cabin, a small electronics package had been at work since its inertia switch had been closed by the crash impact. No larger than a can of chicken soup, the emergency locator transmitter, or ELT, had its own battery to broadcast a distress signal on the emergency frequency. Aircraft monitoring 121.5 MHz would be alerted to the tone and could home in on the signal. The transmitter sent out the alarm, emitting its tiny impulses through a short antenna sticking out of the top of the undamaged rear fuselage. It would operate automatically without interruption for as long as forty-eight hours.

High above and to the west, a dark pair of gracefully tapered wings were silhouetted against the clouding sky. They approached the crash site and, when directly overhead, pivoted suddenly in a graceful turn. A sharp unblinking eye caught fragments of unfamiliar shapes through openings in the pines. The California condor sensed some strange intruder in his sanctuary. He circled twice; then, with unerring ease, the old buzzard wheeled into an updraft and rode it toward his aerie in the solitude of the great white peak.

9

BY 9:25 ANN HAD ALL but completed her morning cleanup chores. She was placing the small block of cheese in the refrigerator when the phone rang for the second time that morning. She walked back to the bedroom to answer it before the second ring, unwrapping a towel from her head as she went. Picking up the receiver, she shook out her still-damp hair with a quick flip of her head and placed the standard-black instrument to her ear.

"Ann? Mildred. Are you free this morning?"

Ann smiled at Dr. Yancey's direct manner. A sharp wit with gentle barbs was her normal and expeditious method of getting a human response, and she wasted no words.

"Hello, Mildred. Yes." Ann paused. "For most of the morning, anyway. I'm expecting a call from Jim sometime after eleven."

"Good. Come on over to the staff lounge. I have that new psychology book on birth trauma you were interested in, and there is something I want to talk to you about. You can be home by ten fifteen."

"Oh, great. Give me fifteen minutes to fix my hair."

"Fine. If I'm not in the lounge, look for me in OB." The line clicked off and Dr. Yancey's crisp voice was replaced by a dial tone.

Ann replaced the receiver and did a quick step to the dresser to pick up her hairbrush. The book was a real surprise. She had not expected to get a copy until next month at the earliest. She had long felt that there was a need to tie in obstetric, new-born and pediatric nursing. Frequently the birth process became a coldly efficient procedure wherein the mother was relieved of the child-burden and post-natal care was an apartheid procedure foreign to the nursery and the pediatrician. Ann felt that there was a need to integrate medical care so that the personnel involved would consider mother-child as intimate entities before, during and after the delivery. Since obstetrics and pediatrics demanded such diverse specialization, for the doctors the key seemed to be a nursing team who could coordinate the two with a program sensitive to all aspects of the procreative phenomena. "And the father should be involved, too," she had declared on several occasions. "All the way!"

Her scalp tingled with the stimulation of the brushing. Finally satisfied, she put aside the brush and tied the burnished auburn curls back into a reluctant ponytail. Picking up her purse, she marched to the door.

On the landing outside their apartment Ann looked up at the sky, which was laced with thin cirrus clouds. Her hands brushed the curled, peeling paint of the handrail as she moved lightly down the weathered steps.

She strode along, enjoying the prospect of a walk to the university hospital. Each step was gracefully athletic, and she made herself feel each muscle pull its share. The experience gave her an almost sensuous pleasure, of sinew gliding under the tight control of satin skin.

The doctors' lounge was in the basement of the hospital at the rear. She chose to enter through the emergency room door because it was closer. The ward was empty. "That won't last," she thought, grimly surveying the waiting gurneys; "they'll be bringing in the freeway rejects soon enough."

"I'm meeting Dr. Yancey in the lounge," she said in answer to the questioning look of a secretary in the outer office. The polished mahogany door to the lounge whispered open to her touch, and on her entrance a rather dumpy little woman in a green scrub gown looked up from a document-strewn conference table. Smiling at Ann, Dr. Mildred Yancey rose and walked around to the young nursing student. As usual, she wasted no time with small talk.

"Here's that book you wanted," she said, handing it to Ann.

Ann thanked her and was about to ask how she managed to get it so quickly, but Mildred Yancey was already into another subject.

"Ann, you have applied for a position here after June graduation. Well, you have the job, of course." She waved Ann silent before she had a chance to formulate a thankful answer. "What I'm really after," she continued, "is something a bit more specific . . . and complicated." She paused briefly to let that sink in, then continued the monologue.

"I want you to work directly with me in OB-GYN as my assistant, while you, and this is the tough part, go on with your master's-degree work." With that the shorter woman fell silent, cocking her head slightly as she kept her eyes locked on Ann's, waiting for her reply. A faint smile betrayed her impish liking for surprises—in other people.

Ann was flabbergasted. To have the director of a medical service at the university hospital ask someone to be an assistant was flattery enough. That it was extended to a

fourth-year student was too much. There was a catch—
she would have to continue course work—and Ann was
beginning to wonder if she and Jim could swing it. Mildred
Yancey second-guessed the question before Ann could
speak.

"I've arranged a fellowship that should take care of the
school expenses, and you will be paid as a full-time R.N."

Yancey smiled and walked briskly back around the
conference table. Ann stood in the middle of the room
holding her book and realized she had not yet said a word
since her first "Thank you." She stammered out the same
two words, but the doctor cut her off again.

"Now you talk it over with that pilot of yours and let
me know. There's no rush. We have a whole semester
before you graduate." With that she began sorting through
the papers and waved Ann toward the door.

"Oh, Ann, another thing," she said. "This is no favor to
you. Please understand that. I only work with profession-
als. I think you're the best we have turned out."

By the time she was on her way down the corridor
toward the emergency room exit and the short walk home,
Ann was euphoric.

She was not prepared therefore for the sight of the
cadaver being rolled from the ER to the morgue. Although
it was draped decorously and being rolled expeditiously to
the freight elevator by two technicians, she had just a
glimpse of a lifeless hand protruding from the sheet. The
curling black hairs on the back of his hand caught her
glance, and she shuddered not with horror, but with a deep
sense of compassion and loneliness. She wondered where
his parents were and what their grief would be—or
perhaps his wife.

Pushing the thought from her mind, she hurried out
the door. It was nearly eleven. She would have to hurry to
be home when Jim called.

10

CHARITY WHITEFLOWER had seen the plane as it droned past the great peak, climbing toward the ridge several miles north. She gave it a casual glance, not interested beyond the fact that it was an uncomfortable reminder of the world she was returning to. She was fighting a strange inner conflict that left her more despondent with each step she took along the trail that would bring her to warm shelter before the day was over. Although she could not hope to reach the town nearly twenty direct miles away today, she knew that she had passed a ranger's cabin not more than 5 or 6 miles farther along the trail, where the road to town began. The next few miles would be difficult for, although the trail was clear, there was a slight upgrade of about 1000 feet that would sap her strength.

She could feel the approach of snow without looking for the signs in the clouding sky. The crippling aches in all her bones would worsen as the day progressed. At her age exercise no longer limbered up her stiffened joints.

Her depression was not one of physical discomfort or even pain. It was the thought of reaching the safety of the cabin that gave her unease. The thing that had driven her here was tugging fiercely at her, to turn back, to circle past her camp of last night to find what was so close she could almost feel it, palpable on the thin air.

It would be forever gone when she finally reached the ranger's haven. There would be questions, and phone calls, and forms filled out . . . and then the cloying press of social caring would strip her of her life and brief flash of solitary independence. She tried not to think of the long bus ride back, escorted this time by a concerned agency person who would be quietly efficient in these matters.

Yet she could not turn back. The long years had taught her conservation of her allotted time, an achievement of actuarial length if not depth. She must take care of herself—her body—and deny the spirit.

Foolish woman, she thought, using words this time, why do you want to call back something you never knew lived? You do not even know what you are searching for. To make the point she spat a frothy lump of saliva to the gravel inching backward to her feet. But the non-words, the music almost, inside her head denied the argument—without the need of counterargument. She groaned a sigh and plodded on.

The sudden whispering sound stopped her then. It came upon her from behind, sending a thrill to her breast that tightened on her heart. The sound increased in volume and diversity. She could hear several whistling notes as they attached themselves to the great central core of hurtling wind. By the time she had turned to face it, the sound had come upon her, rocketing downward across the trail not fifty feet above her head, flickering silver, flashing blue and white, gliding hawklike toward the lake below. Was this a spirit sign, her rendezvous?

With disappointment bordering on despair she recognized it as the plane she had seen earlier.

She trembled as she watched it glide across the frozen lake, shaken that she had been so neatly taken in by an object so mundane. She shook her head sadly, reflecting that perhaps her mind was not as sharp as she had thought and said, aloud this time, "Foolish old woman!"

Something about the behavior of the plane kept her from continuing her trek upslope. The plane was landing on the ice. She watched it touch, saw smoky plumes of powdered ice trail out behind. Through narrowed eyelids she willed her vision clear and gasped to see the blue-white speck slide off the ice, slash into the trees, and disappear.

She stared transfixed. The rending screech of impact and the muffled final groan of anguished metal echoed off the ice and mated with another sound that crashed up through the long years and roared again in her head.

Turning to the mountain, Charity shrieked a protest she had clutched in silence fifty years.

Before her scream had spent its angled bouncing through the hills, Charity pivoted like a martinet, eyes fixed on the lake, and began a shambling jog toward the plane.

"Want to take it for a while, Mr. Kemp?" The young pilot turned to his middle-aged, distinguished-looking passenger in the right seat of the cockpit.

"Thanks; not today, Bruce." The older man had turned briefly to give his answer and then resumed looking out the right window of the sleek, pressurized company plane. His face was drawn with fatigue. He sat or rather slumped in the copilot's seat looking morosely at the jagged topography of the land below.

Bruce Logan knew, like a barber good at his trade, that conversation was not the order of the day. He'll have to sort it out for himself, like always, he thought. He stole a sidewise glance at his employer, crisp as ever in his neatly tailored gray wool suit and unstylish starched white shirt, to which was pinned a conservative tie with maroon and gray diagonal stripes. His hair was full but gray also, combed in the severe military style of the late thirties. A straight part gleamed like a pink incision rather high on the left side, near the middle of his head.

Noting the slouched position of his employer, Bruce speculated on this unusual lapse in his decorum. He certainly was not looking well. Damned shame, and small wonder. That no good son of his would probably kill the old man, given time. Why is it that some kids screw up so badly?

Kid! That's a laugh. The bastard is thirty-five and still hasn't grown out of diapers. The more Bruce thought about Leo Kemp's only son, the more his temper rose.

They had just left the Mammoth Lakes resort area. Things had been quiet there because fishing was played out for the season, and the ski lodges were quietly going broke as they had been for the last three snowless winters.

Well, the exchange he had just witnessed between father and son was certainly not quiet. The elder Kemp had flown out of his way to remind Larry that his family connection to the company did not entitle him to take unannounced week-long vacations on the average of one a month. These times off were more than an embarrassment to Kemp personally; because of his position as Director of Finance and Accounting, Larry's frequent absences were causing definite harm to the organization.

The situation was even more galling in that Larry was good at his job. Senior members of his department considered him something of a genius with modern banking systems. Some of the innovations he had been responsible for, computer programs particularly, were so sophisticated that the old-timers had difficulty keeping current. The system needed his guiding hand on a regular basis.

There had been talk, too, about his gambling habits. A free-spending bachelor, Larry had trouble living within his generous corporate salary.

Well, Bruce thought, his days may be numbered. Leo Kemp had made that clear to his sulking offspring in their brief but explosive meeting at Mammoth Airport.

He glanced again at his boss, who was still morose and oblivious of the beautiful moutain scenery slipping under their wings. Bruce sighed and pushed in the autopilot. The last leg of their trip to San Diego promised no conversation.

A loud undulating wail suddenly filled the cabin and snapped both men from their reveries. The sound howled a grating tone until Bruce reached up and turned down the volume on one of the radios set in a stack on the panel. Leo looked at him, an eyebrow raised, more curious than alarmed.

"Nothing to worry about. Just an ELT signal somewhere." He went on to explain, "That's an automatic transmitter that sends out a homing signal from an airplane if it crashes or makes a hard landing."

Leo Kemp looked out the window and down at the valley below them. He turned to Bruce, "Do you think . . . ?"

Bruce looked at his watch. "No," he grinned, "probably some radio shop testing their equipment." He held out his left wrist. "See? It's three minutes after ten. FAA regs allow testing on the hour till five after." He pulled out his noteboard with the flight plan attached and jotted down the time. "Let's see. I'll try to get a bearing with the ADF."

He tuned the directional receiver to 243.0 Mhz, a companion frequency for the emergency locator, and listened for the eerie alarm tone. When it came in clear, he watched the directional needle swing to the right and settle. "There it is!" Bruce noted with pleasure that his boss was completely absorbed in the problem. Some color had returned to his face, and he watched intently, nodding occasionally as Bruce explained each step in the homing process.

They remained on course. After he had determined the bearing from which the signal was coming, Bruce picked up a chart and located their position along the course line he had been following since leaving Mammoth. Marking a small X through the line at their position, he used a protractor-like plotting ruler to establish another line representing the direction of the ELT signal.

He grinned and handed the chart to Leo. "See that line? That's the direction the transmitter is from us. You'll notice the line crosses the airport at Bishop."

"You mean the signal is coming from the airport?"

"Well, I don't know for sure. It could be coming from anywhere along that line. If it keeps up I'll plot another bearing and get a fix from the two lines."

They flew on another two minutes, the silence of the cabin broken only by the hushed rumble of the engines outside the soundproofed, pressurized hull and the muted complaint of the ELT signal. Leo alternately scrutinized the chart, the swinging needle, and—through the side window,—the approaching airport, which rolled toward them on the valley floor two miles below. In a corner of his mind he savored the merciful distraction and felt knotted muscles along his spine to the base of his skull begin to uncoil.

As suddenly as it began the signal faded and disappeared. They had not yet reached the airport. Bruce jotted down the time and location again, including the last steady bearing shown on the ADF.

"Well, I guess that's it," he said looking intently at his boss. "Must have been a test. False alarm."

Their plane bore steadily south-southeast, heading for the still-clear skies of the Mojave Desert. Leo Kemp still clutched the chart in his hand. His thumbnail rested at the end of the hastily drawn bearing line. There was a slight squiggle where Bruce's pencil had gone off the end of the plotter. It circumscribed the magenta W in the tiny letters spelling out "Mount Whitney." One-eighth of an inch below the trailing-off pencil mark was a tiny irregular circle colored light blue. Beside the blue dot a brown hairline ran an inch or so and disappeared under Leo's right thumb. If he had been interested, he could have lifted that digit to uncover a black dot with the small identifier "Ranger Station."

"Mind if I take it for a while?"

A slow smile brightened the pilot's face. In answer to the request, he switched the autopilot off and clapped his hands once above his head, a signal reminiscent of the old days when pilots communicated relinquished control by the "hands off" gesture. Leo put the chart aside, rolled his seat forward a few inches and, careful not to upset the trimmed airplane, grasped the yoke lightly with one hand.

They had flown for about six minutes, making gentle left and right turns along their course, when the wail of the ELT broke into the cabin again. This time the signal was considerably weaker, and Bruce turned up the volume to its maximum power. Although he responded to the alarm, there was a marked decrease in the urgency it had manifested when they first heard it, eight minutes before. He routinely recorded the bearing of the signal, checked and recorded their position, and looked again at his watch.

"Uh-oh!" he snorted, jotting down the time.

"Anything wrong?" Leo looked at Bruce, mildly curious.

"Not really. That radio shop could get into trouble back there though. It's ten minutes after ten. They aren't supposed to test except during the five minutes after the hour." He frowned briefly, then paused to look at the ADF needle. It was swinging slowly in oscillations centering on a relative bearing of 90 degrees. "The signal ought to be behind us," he murmured. "I'd better check the ADF when we get home." He studied the instrument for a few seconds. "The signal is pretty weak though; probably it's just not strong enough to get an accurate bearing." To himself he dismissed the erratic indications partly on the evidence that his boss was not really flying a constant heading. He left the receiver tuned to the frequency.

"Shouldn't you report the signal to somebody?"

Bruce mulled over Leo's question before he answered.

"Yes. Strictly speaking, all of those should be reported, but I'm sure it is coming from some electronics shop at the airport. Some guy is trying to get one of those things working and has lost track of the time. I'd hate to get him in hot water; get the Feds on his case, y'know. Maybe lose his license."

"But suppose it really is . . . . " Leo was on unfamiliar ground and was hesitant to intrude on Bruce's realm of expertise.

"Oh, we'll monitor the frequency for a few minutes. If it stays bleeping, I'll call somebody for sure. I'd hate to think somebody was down in the moutains with that front moving in over there." Bruce was inwardly delighted at the continued diversions, which held Kemp's private woes at bay.

They flew on, the mournful call of the beacon in their ears.

Fifteen miles away, directly off their right wing and a few thousand feet below, the first gusts of the approaching blizzard whipped at the creaking limbs of an old pine. One branch near the top was particularly distressed, having been severely wrenched some minutes before by a terrific smash somewhere down below its numb awareness. The vibrations from that impact had only just stopped before the wind began. Until now the graceful rhythm of the tree had absorbed the storm's mounting energy, but a sudden lull broke the pattern, and when the next gust struck in backswing, the tortured limb felt the heartwood snap. Slowly it yielded to a half-century's arm wrestling with the pull of earth and swung in a great arc swishing unheard in the howling wind, a great pendulum snapping free at six o'clock, and crashing nearly horizontal as it carried through the swing and landed crosswise on the aluminum tail of the airplane sprawled below.

It did little further damage to the plane, merely bending the vertical fin at a grotesque angle. A small wire threaded through the inner formers of the fin, and leading to a whip antenna at its tip, was snapped. A minor break. The frayed ends of the wire lay a scant inch apart on the inside of the rumpled duralumin skin. A man could twist them together with thumb and forefinger in a moment. An invisible pulsing wave was being transmitted from the lower end of the severed cable, but encased as it was by the aluminum shell, it spent its energy bouncing around inside.

"There it goes." The ululating, downswept tone abruptly stopped. Bruce noted the time—a token concession to habitual record-keeping.

"Do you think we just got out of range?"

"No, sir. It was coming in too strong for that right at the end." Bruce chuckled and looked at Kemp. "No, it sounds to me more like the boss came into his shop and pulled the plug. Either that or some pilot is trying to explain to all the people around his tied-down plane how he accidentally set off his ELT and didn't check the frequency before turning off and locking up."

"Is that sort of thing fairly common?" Leo Kemp was becoming his old self again, Bruce noted with pleasure.

"Well, yessir, I'm afraid it is. They are easy to set off; a hard landing will do it. But my guess is a radio shop. Boy, I'll bet somebody's face is red!" He laughed out loud with more mirth than the ELT incident would warrant.

Leo Kemp looked at him and knew. Why couldn't you have been a little like him, Larry, he thought, and mourned the loss of his son as though dead.

Inside the hulk of 7695 Romeo the tiny ELT kept screaming its alarm, unaware that its larynx had been cut.

11

THE SAME GUST OF WIND that had unlimbed the old pine now buffeted Charity Whiteflower. She had stepped onto the frozen lake just as the heavy branch toppled from the tree, but she could not see or hear it because of the surge of cold air roiling across the mile-long sheet of ice before her. Rheumy tear lenses blurred her vision, but she was able to keep a constant direction by simply heading into the chilly blast. Something from her genetic past, a revived instinct, was guiding her now. She knew that the snow would fall shortly, that the wind would let up briefly just before the flakes came, and that the storm would be heavy and long.

She was thankful for the heavy pack because it gave her spare frame stability, a reserve momentum that kept her track arrow-straight across the ice. For perhaps ten or eleven minutes she kept up a quick-step shuffle, her feet barely lifting from the surface as she plowed into the near gale.

When she was halfway across, the wind suddenly stopped. As if on cue she immediately began a methodical pattern of left and right diagonal sweeps crisscrossing her base direction. Now she hunted, head down, eyes cleared in the respite from the blowing chill, keeping the frenzied pace as before. On the third zigzag leg she found the two gouged furrows in the glazed lake skin. Without a sign of satisfaction that her efforts had been rewarded, she continued her shuffle not missing a step, keeping the opaque lines on either side as she strained for the far side of the lake.

She covered the mile in twenty-two minutes. By the time she had gained the gravel beach her breath was coming in grinding sobs. Something inside shifted into low gear and slowed her down a heartbeat short of collapse, but she did not feel the fatigue. She attacked the gouged sloping beach like some fantastic orange-humpbacked quadruped clawing slowly toward the trees.

Snow began to fall as she scrabbled up the ramp, a blinding torrent of hard pellets, nearly hail, cascaded around her. She was hard pressed to keep going up the incline, and when she finally reached relatively level ground, she remained on all fours to follow the trail of ripped earth and aircraft debris. So intense was the snow shower that she did not see the wreck until she had crawled completely under its sagging tail.

Pausing a moment to get her bearings in the shelter of the protective aluminum panels, she set out again to find a means of gaining entry to the cabin. Standing erect in the downpouring snow, which had become true flakes falling in a dizzying swirl, she felt her way along the right side of the fuselage in a fruitless search for a door or hatchway. She wasted precious time and energy by climbing up on the wing to try the windows.

When she had reached the forwardmost pane of

plexiglass she rubbed away enough snow to peer into the cockpit. It was very dim inside but she caught sight of a slumped figure in the far seat, and the glistening wet of blood coating the upturned palms resting in his lap.

A keening wail rolled from deep inside her. She turned in a frenzy to get down and try the other side, and slipped, falling headlong to the trailing edge of the wing. Jagged edges of metal ripped at her left arm, tearing the heavy sleeve and, she knew, her flesh as well. Unmindful of the hurt, she scrambled to the left side of the plane and frantically repeated the blind, pawing search for a way in.

The hatch swung open before she was conscious of turning the countersunk handle, and the lower clamshell door swung down, giving her shins a painful scraping bark. She paid this injury no more heed than she had her bleeding arm as she stumbled into the warm shelter of the aft cabin.

Pausing to let her eyes adjust to the gloom, she let the heavy pack and bundled sleeping bag slip to the floor. In a moment she had negotiated the narrow aisle and was crouched over the inert form of the young man in the pilot's seat. Snatching off mittens and hat with a flurry of snow, Charity thrust her left ear against his chest. A fluttering rapid pulse rewarded her rapt, breathless examination.

Tenderly she cupped his chin in her hand and rolled it back against the headrest. Gentle soothing sounds floated from her lips as she released the seat-belt buckle and tried to ease him into a more comfortable position. With exploring fingers she discovered the unnatural twist in his lower right leg, and a gasp interposed itself on her still labored breathing.

Remembering something, she swung back through the cabin again and wrestled with the doors, finally succeeding in getting them securely latched. Then she stripped off her heavy jacket and, bending over the backpack, rummaged through its contents.

Back in the cockpit once again, she tucked the jacket around the young man's unconscious form and began to clean the wound already purpled and scabbing on his brow. Every once in a while she would cast a rueful look at the twisted leg as though trying to recall a solution to a puzzle mastered long ago but now nearly forgotten.

After a time her eyes brightened and she looked at the leg with smug assurance. Carefully she arranged the blood-soaked swabs in a neat bundle on the vacant right seat.

"All's well, my love," she murmured softly in his ear. "Sleep out your mend. Your flower waits and tends you."

Jim's coma blotted out all hearing, and the soft blur of kisses on his cheek went unfelt. He would not have understood the words in any case; they sprang from ancient Tubatulabal. Probably they would not have been understood by the man to whom Charity thought she spoke, her lover fifty winters in his grave.

12

AT 11:15 THE Flight Service Station at Reno began a routine inquiry into the whereabouts of N7695R, which was now twenty minutes overdue on its flight from southern California. The specialist sorting flight plans for planes arriving in his area of responsibility noted that except for one position report early in the flight there were no notes of further communication with the plane. There was no cause for concern. Pilots sometimes forgot to close out their flight plans on arrival until someone on the ground reminded them or they saw one of the signs posted near the telephones in every pilots' lounge all over the country: DID YOU CLOSE YOUR FLIGHT PLAN?

Usually the callup time was predicated on several factors: a delay enroute because of unanticipated headwinds, a quick rush to the toilet, making arrangements for securing the airplane in its tiedown, and finally the usual trigger, that walk to the phone to get a cab or a room or both. That was when they would see the sign ... and remember. About twenty minutes late.

"Uh, yeah. This is Piper one two three four Xray, from Sacramento to Bishop. Ah, did you close my flight plan? I may have forgotten to call on the way in."

Sometimes it would be longer. Then the specialist would get on the land lines, telephone lines connecting the major centers, to pick up any news of the delayed arrival. The normal report at tower-controlled destination airports would be "Mooney four five six seven Alfa? Yeah, he landed thirty minutes ago." And the great search machinery would not be disturbed. Occasionally some pilot would land at an airport other than his declared destination, forget to notify *anybody* of his change of plan, tie the bird down in the weeds, hitch a ride to town, and sleep out the nasty weather that had sent him there in the first place. That kind really gave the FSS people gray hairs—and the search-and-rescue pilots hairy duty. The whole thing would be called off when the sleepy pilot would call an FSS somewhere to get weather for his continued flight. The penalty for this kind of forgetfulness was a rather stiff and humorless inquiry.

The specialist at Reno decided not to wait on this one. He knew about the messy weather that had moved across 95 Romeo's intended course about two hours ahead of forecast. The plan showed only the pilot aboard. That made the lack of radio transmissions significant. Lone pilots usually called up more frequently than those with company in the cockpit, especially over the mountains. Besides, he would have to have been blind not to have seen all that busted forecast messing up his VFR direct flight. That alone was reason for him to call with questions.

He made all the preliminary inquiries without success. No facility along the route of flight had received later information on the aircraft.

"Yeah, well, OK, thanks. I'll call the guys at Sparks. See if he landed and forgot to call. I'll bet he has a sick radio and drove right to the shop to see if they could figure it out. If I hear anything I'll be right back with you."

He dialed for an outside line and placed four calls to Sparks Airport: one to the radio shop, two to competing commercial airplane dealers, and finally to the airport coffee shop.

Twelve miles away from the FSS offices, Buzz Taglio was returning from his second trip to the men's room. He had passed four cups of coffee and was working on his most recent couple. Unfortunately the six cups had also been working on his stomach. This wait for Laird's airplane was taking its toll as well, in gastric complaints of sobering proportions. Maybe he *was* getting an ulcer as the doc had warned a few weeks ago.

He tore the end off a roll of antacid tablets as he stood watching his waitress ring up the check. When she handed him the change, he withdrew a bill from the pile and placed it on the counter beside the register.

He popped one of the chalky mints into his mouth and spoke around its alum dryness, "I'd like to wait at the table a while longer, if you don't mind." Rolling the tablet into the pouch of his cheek he added, "But please, no more coffee." An involuntary belch escaped to emphasize the point, and he swung away soured by yet another discomfort toward the plastic seat he had occupied for nearly two hours.

The waitress followed an entering couple to their table, scooping up silver for two and the coffee pitcher on the way. She had just handed them menus from the counter when the wall phone behind the register rang. Taglio watched her unwasted movements as she slipped behind the register and lifted the receiver before the second ring. Propping it with her shoulder, she carried on a brief ex-

change with the caller while her hands and eyes were occupied totaling up a customer's check.

Taglio was so absorbed in her efficiently unhurried
manner that he did not hear the question she was an-
nouncing to the cafe clientele until she repeated it.

"Anybody here come in on a Dauphin 7695 Romeo?"
She looked sharply around the room at the raised faces
looking at her. "That's 7695 Romeo, a blue on white
twin." Her voice took on a lightly deprecating tone. "The
'Federalees' are on the line; somebody forgot to close his
flight plan."

Suddenly Buzz Taglio reacted; he withdrew the scrap
of now-rumpled notebook paper from his jacket and read
the numbers. That's it, he thought. He looked back toward
the waitress raising his hand, waving the paper, not knowing what to do for a confused moment, because the girl had
turned back to the phone.

"Not here, Bill. Are you *sure* it was coming to Sparks?
Those luxury jobs usually go to Reno. All we get are
ragwings and tired Apaches." She was about to hang up
when she felt Taglio's minty breath on her neck.

"That's the plane . . ."—he felt curiously out of place,
uncomfortable in a world whose procedures he did not
quite grasp—" . . . the plane I'm expecting, I mean."

She told the FAA man to hold on and handed Buzz the
phone. A ripple of laughter escaped from the grinning
diners, who thought Buzz was the forgetful pilot. They
knew the feeling, empathized; it was a shared embarrassment most had had before.

Only the waitress remained serious. He could not be
the pilot. He had been here all morning. Was he family of
the pilot, a friend, or just waiting for a charter? The plane
was long overdue; of that she was sure. She watched her
customer nodding to questions put to him by Flight Service. He was shifting his weight from one foot to the other,

his body agitated but his face absorbed in the conversation. Well, I hope he gets good news before long, whoever he is.

She was shocked to realize, when she looked out the window toward the approach end of the runway, that it was snowing. There was even a thin sheet of snow covering the ramp and parked airplanes.

13

ANN COULD HEAR the muted complaint of the ringing phone as she pounded up the rickety stairway hung on the outside of their apartment. She plunged her hand into her purse for the key, glancing at her watch as her fingers probed the bottom reaches of the rucksack-size macrame pouch.

"Oh, my God, it's twenty after. Don't hang up, honey." This second sentence was shouted through the door as if Jim were inside, within hearing. The key came out at last, followed by two tissues, which wafted away on the wind, and a dime dropping sullenly to the wood landing.

Ann thrust the key into its way, turning it before it was fully home but managing to throw the bolt anyway. She made a mental note to come back later to retrieve the coin. Leaving the door ajar, she rushed down the short hall to the bedroom and the phone. She snatched the handpiece up quickly in mid-ring but did not answer until she had taken a second to sit on the edge of the bed and compose herself. Just wait 'til the big lug heard *her* news!

"Hello." For the second time in just over two hours she sent the message to the wrong ear.

"Hello?" The female voice on the line registered amused surprise at her reception. She was apparently a stranger. "This must be Mrs. Regan," the voice continued. "Is Mr. Regan there?"

"Yes, this is Ann Regan, and no, my husband is not here just now." Her tone was even, professional, the nurse on duty.

The voice on the phone laughed. "Well, I'm glad he's not. You're the one to give him the news; I can see that." The voice continued, "Will he be home sometime later in the day?"

Ann found that she was beginning to like this person, but she reserved some caution. "May I ask who is calling, please?"

"Oh, I'm sorry. This is the personnel center for U.S. Airways, and I'm Jill Cotter. We have some good news for your husband."

This information seeped into her brain slowly like ink following the circuitous capillary tracks of a blotter. A vague tissue-wrapped shape under the Christmas tree, hinting of a half-forgotten wish fulfilled. She was half afraid to believe her ears.

"Mrs. Regan?"

"Oh, yes," she fumbled, "I . . . I'm sorry. I'm a bit confused. . . . U.S. Airways did you say?"

"That's right, Mrs. Regan. Your husband made application to us some time ago, passed his interview and exams last year, and . . . "

"Oh, yes, yes . . . Please, it's Ann . . . Yes! I know. You have no idea how Jim and I have been hoping for this call. You said it was good news. Oh, I wish he were here!"

"I have some idea," Jill commented drily, "since I have made eight other calls to applicants today, you know. Flying an airliner seems to turn people on for some reason. I understand that the pay is not too bad either."

"Well, let's say that Jim and I would like to try a cut of meat you don't have to cook in loaves and patties." Ann laughed. "But please, don't keep me in suspense any longer!"

"Ann, if all goes well with his flight training, you and Mr. Regan will be ordering steak and lobster at the best joint in town just about six months from today." Her tone became hushed, conspiratorial. "You *will* have to live on our lousy probationary employee salary until he gets permanent status."

She waited a moment, then spoke more formally, "U.S. Airways is offering your husband immediate employment as a flight engineer trainee, based upon his exceptional qualifications and high performance in interviews and tests. Unless he has taken some other airline position, we would like him to report for training within the next two weeks." She dropped back into informality with "How does that sound, Ann? Think he'll go for it?"

Ann was jubilant. "I think he would go for it all the way to Oklahoma on his hands and knees! I can't wait 'till he calls."

"You know, I think I've been missing all the fun in this outfit," Jill commented thoughtfully. "All these years I have been feeding the computers, picking the candidates, and some PR type upstairs or out on the coast has been getting all the warm fuzzies. Ordinarily I don't do this sort of thing, but the brass put a rush on things to fill an extra class so they told me to contact the appointees directly. I'm beginning to feel like Santa Claus."

Ann's reply still reflected disbelief, "Well, you have just given us *our* Christmas. A month early, at that."

Jill suddenly remembered that she had two more calls to make in the Pacific Time Zone, and she gave Ann particulars as to how Jim should verify his acceptance. She promised full confirmation by mail in a few days. Each hung up knowing she would probably never speak to the other again and regretting that probability with some feeling.

Ann sat on the bed for several minutes smiling to herself at the news. She looked briefly at the cradled telephone, willing Jim to call. A glance at her watch told her it was twenty before twelve. He probably landed forty minutes ago. She was intrigued with the irony of U.S. Airways' call. Jim was probably trying to reach her at the very same time. She could see him pacing up and down by the phone booth in Sparks, getting madder by the minute. "Women!" She could almost see him muttering it in little puffs of frosted breath on the cold air. He would probably be slightly miffed when the call came through. She toyed with various ways of letting him know the news. Would his mood change fast! She remembered with a shiver that the door was still standing open.

As she approached the entry hall she noticed that black clouds had piled up, blotting out the sun. The weathered boards on the landing were spotted with dark splatters of the drought-breaking raindrops. How much like blood they seemed, irregular circles rusty in the otherwise silver weathered redwood.

She saw the dime she had dropped before, resting on one of the planks. As she reached for it, a fat drop splashed full in Franklin Roosevelt's upturned face. She picked it up and rubbed it dry with her fingertips. She was looking at it as she closed the door when a sudden impulse changed her mind. Swinging back the door, she took a running step to the outside landing and flung the tiny silver coin in a high arc to a weedy vacant lot across the street.

Hands on hips, she watched its trajectory until it disappeared. "Our miser days are over, dime," she called expansively. "I wish you were a quarter." The dead brown weeds swallowed up her profligate token and gave no answering sign. Maybe somebody who really needs a lift will pick you up, she thought. She returned to the telephone and sat on the bed again, knowing Jim would call in a moment or two.

14

JACK LAIRD HAD BEEN in his sales office all morning. Business was slack, a normal condition for a mid-week morning; most of his action occurred on weekends when the prospective buyers would drive out or fly in to the airport to look over his modest stock of used planes. Laird was usually quite active every day, however, working up prospective deals on the telephone. Today he made not one call, although he remained at his desk or close to it, tense and visibly agitated. At each ring of an incoming call he would rivet his attention to the phone but delay picking it up until after the third ring. His voice on these occasions would contrast sharply with his physical appearance, lilting with a cheerful, business-as-usual air. The conversations were ended more quickly today, however; the phone had to be free for a special call.

It came at 11:26, the local flight service office with routine inquiries.

"We have a flight plan filed for November seven six

nine five Romeo listing your company as its home base. Is that correct?"

"Yes, that's our plane. A . . . Dauphin, ah, blue and white." Laird was fighting to keep his voice casual, trying to allow enough curiosity to seep into his tone to seem natural.

"Well, sir, we list it as being overdue on a flight from Grant to Sparks. ETA was listed as eleven-oh-five local time. Have you heard from the flight; any enroute landings?" The specialist was probing gently. Like his Reno counterpart he too was aware of the severity of the weather in the mountains, and he was not sure of the level of objectivity with which he could discuss the problem with Laird. How close this stranger might be to the pilot. He would get all the information available before going into the special circumstances of weather, terrain, and absence of routine radio contact that were beginning to color this investigation other than rosy.

Laird's tone expressed cautious concern. "Why, no. Let's see; that was a ferry flight to the buyer. He left about nine this morning." Laird's voice trailed off. "What's up?"

"Was the pilot alone, or were there others aboard?" The flight plan indicated no other passengers or crew, but the specialist was making sure.

"No, Jim was alone. Say, what is . . ."

"What is your relationship to the pilot? Is he an employee? A friend or relative?" The specialist's voice slid full range from official to confessorial, soft at the end.

"Well, not exactly . . . not exactly an employee, I mean. He sometimes works for me part time, rents my airplanes to give instruction. He's a freelance CFI. I was paying him to ferry the Dauphin to a buyer in Nevada." Jack Laird had winced at the word "friend" and his answer avoided assiduously any reference to it.

Satisfied now that he could voice his concerns directly,

the caller filled Laird in with all the information—or, rather, lack of it—that had reached his desk. This included the talk with Buzz Taglio in Sparks.

"Yes, yes, Mr. Taglio was to take delivery of the plane and present a draft in exchange for the bill of sa . . . Oh, that's not important, What can I do to help?" He was beginning to let this morning's pent-up anxiety reflect in his speech.

"You might try asking around to see if the pilot has tried to contact acquaintances on the field by phone. Does he have any family in the local area?"

Suddenly the full impact of his guilt struck Jack Laird. Until now he had not allowed himself to think that Jim might be—probably would be—*killed*. He had contrived the scheme in such a way that the engines would fail over rugged terrain, virtually ensuring total destruction of the aircraft, but his plan illogically presumed pilot survival. With a chill he now realized that Jim's destruction had always been an ingredient in his subconscious intent. He remembered the sudden, last-minute decision to cut the alternator belts. That one act completed the setup; he had not wanted Jim to be around to testify at the inevitable inquiry, and cutting off his source of radio transmission power covered the remote possibility that Jim might suspect what really caused engine failure and broadcast his suspicions before the crash silenced him permanently.

"Hello? Are you still with me?" The specialist wondered if he had proceeded too fast. Maybe this *was* a close friend of the pilot. Damn!

"Oh, . . . yes. Sorry . . . I guess I'm getting concerned . . ." He trailed off in a voice that was shaking with real emotion. He struggled for control. Musn't overreact, he told himself, and viciously pushed down a wave of terror and self-recrimination. "Yes. His wife lives here in town; I have the number."

"Look, Mr. Laird, I hate to cut right through like this. I don't know how close you were to the pilot, but we may have a serious problem. The weather along his route of flight has really gone sour. The problem is that except for one call to activate his flight plan shortly after takeoff, he did not contact any station along the line. That means he missed the update and probably flew right into the stuff. What was his level of experience?"

"He wa—... is really sharp. Lots of multi-engine time, an instrument instructor. Had his interviews with the airlines. Good pilot, good pilot. That's why I picked him for the ferry." Laird's ebullience was beginning to bolster his performance.

"Well, that's good at least. Are there any kids? How old is he?" The voice paused. "Sorry, but it'll help to know if I have to call his wife."

"No, no children. He's young, early twenties." Beads of sweat had collected on Jack Laird's brow, and a tiny rivulet coursed down his temple. His mouth was cottony and he thought of the icy bottles of beer behind him in the refrigerator. Maybe one more after this goddam call was through; only one though. He'd have to keep a clear head for the next few days.

After the flight service specialist had completed his call to Jack Laird, he depressed the cutoff button on his phone and dialed an agency number. He pulled a bent cigaret from the rumpled pack on his desk, gently straightened it by rolling it with the fingers of his free hand. Satisfied, he put it in the corner of his mouth and lighted it with a flourished snap of an ancient Zippo lighter. His first words were muffled by the roll of exhaled smoke as he responded to the answering party.

"Simpson here. Joe, you got any more on that VFR, Grant to Sparks?" He slouched a bit in his armchair, swiveling idly back and forth, head propped by the receiver on one side and the heel of his smoking hand on the other; his eyes were closed as he listened. Then he sighed and leaned forward.

"Nuthin' but bad news, Joe. When are you ever gonna give me some *good* news, fer chrissakes." The wry smile he managed matched what must surely have been a tired joke between them for a long time. He twisted his head and looked at a clock on the wall with twenty-four numbers instead of twelve and a placard that read GREENWICH. He sighed again, cutting it off short. "Well, Joe, it's nineteen forty-five Zulu so I gotta do the shit detail." He paused for a moment, listening quietly. "Yeah, early twenties, married—but no kids, thank God. I'm gonna get it out of the way early, none of that 'no cause for alarm at this time' crap. I'm gonna have to hit her with it sooner or later on my shift; might as well get her prepared. I'll get back to you."

Giving himself no time to contemplate the task ahead, he glanced at the penciled notes before him and dialed the number quickly. Thanksgiving is a week from tomorrow, he thought glumly; I hope she hasn't bought the turkey yet. He listened as the relays clicked in and sent his signal to the Regan home.

He could not know that Ann was still talking to Jill Cotter about her husband's dreamed-of airline job, the one he thought he could not get without a little more multi-engine time.

All Flight Specialist Simpson knew was that the line was busy. He held the phone to his ear, savoring the discordant signal through eight or nine buzzes. Then he placed the receiver in its cradle slowly as if he were handling eggs.

"Thanks for the reprieve, Guvnuh," he muttered. "I owe yuh one."

15

FOR SEVERAL MINUTES after hanging up on his call from Flight Service, Jack Laird sat motionless in his upholstered chair, a curious piece of furniture that managed to conflict with itself by combining Swedish modern construction with country American patchwork cushions. He was a man of desperately mixed emotions at this moment.

The call from the FAA was a solid indication that, if things went according to plan, he would soon be in receipt of nearly a half-million dollars. Of course the insurance company had the option of repairing the plane if by some slim chance it had survived the forced landing with repairable damage, but the fact that there was no report of the plane's having made such a landing in a field or on some chance roadway pretty well excluded that possibility. Nor could suspicion that he had had any responsibility for the crash be proven. When, and if, the wreckage was ever located, examination of the engines would show fuel contaminated with water as the probable cause of the accident. Witnesses, including the underwriting agent himself, knew that the plane had been thoroughly preflighted before taking off. All the logs certifying painstaking repair, together with sublet work invoices from the most highly respected shops and the bill of sale for fuel from George Feister, had been carefully filed. A duly signed sales agreement executed by Buzz Taglio as agent for the buyer was in a separate folder. These documents would protect him from any suggestion that he had sabotaged the plane to collect the insurance.

As further guarantee, he knew that a half-million-dollar letter of credit backed up Buzz Taglio's signature for his proposed signing for and taking possession of the airplane.

Somehow all this assurance of the success of his plan was brass in his mouth. He could not get Ann Regan out of his mind. The idea that he had been the cause of another man's death did not grip him so fiercely as did the realization that he had put into motion events that would probably lead to her destruction as well.

In the manner of anyone whose code was based on getting what he wanted, Laird could actually believe he had intended Jim no harm, that his death was incidental to wrecking the plane. After all, he would reason if ever his conscience prodded, men have survived worse situations. Was he any different than the mining corporations who daily sent men into the pits knowing that statistics would inevitably take their toll in black lung and sudden death? For that matter, governments, his own included, sent thousands of military men, who were men after all, to their deaths every generation.

But he would have to face Ann Regan. The thought of that confrontation troubled him mightily. She had never liked him. He was sure of that although he had met her on only two or three occasions. She had the disturbing trait of ignoring his best facade; she seemed to be able to look into his brain. For some reason when she had looked at him those times, he had felt cheap and dishonest. She reminded him of his mother in that respect, which was a startling realization for him, because Ann was easily twenty years younger than he; and his mother, dead since his early teens, was a hazy memory stopped in middle age. There was something about her eyes, now that he thought about it. An uncomfortable hint of childhood guilt began to edge in at the corner of his mind, and he switched it off.

"Stupid!" The word was mumbled wetly around his fingernail, which he discovered he had gnawed nearly to the quick.

Well, he would have as little to do with her as possible. She undoubtedly knew about the fee he had promised to pay Jim for the ferry job. He would send her the balance with a note of deep regret. For a wild minute, until he caught himself at it, he entertained the idea that he did not really owe the money since the airplane had not been delivered according to the agreement. She would probably get something from the insurance policy for Jim anyway. He wondered what the death benefit for crew members was; probably he should check the policy in case she should ask.

No, leave that to Thad Monte. He was the agent. Let him tell her; apparently they were social friends anyway.

Thad Monte's name triggered another thought process. He began to speculate as to the proper time to let him know that the plane he had so cooperatively insured this morning was now missing.

He glanced at his watch: 11:55. Let's see, the plane had enough fuel for a three-hour flight—or was it four? The

FAA would not declare it officially down until after fuel exhaustion time, or until they got a confirmation by visual sighting, ground report, or ELT.

ELT! He shot bolt upright in the chair, eyes popping, and began to tremble. Jesus, he thought, I forgot the emergency locator transmitter!

He stood up so quickly that the swivel chair nearly overturned from the backward snap of his heavy calves. A cold knot of fear gripped his stomach, and he became slightly nauseated at the root of his tongue. A kaleidoscope of the morning's events spun through his mind so jumbled that he clamped his head between massive hands as he paced the office struggling to put his thoughts into order.

It was stupid to cut the goddamned alternator belts, he thought. Why the hell did I do it? There was no need. It really didn't matter if they knew he was going in; what difference would it make, after all? The whole plan was worked out so carefully that even Jim would hold me above suspicion. He might have suspected Charlie, think that Charlie had screwed up somewhere, but he could never blame me for the contaminated fuel.

The missing belts could cause problems, once they examined the wreck. There was little chance of a broken belt's falling out of the engine nacelle and away from the airplane during flight. Still, it was possible. Maybe they would not consider it important. They would trace it back to the warning light and find the burned-out bulb he had substituted for the good one after Jim had gotten out at the gas pumps. That had been easy, a few seconds' work to twist off the button and pop in the carefully cleaned old bulb.

He suddenly remembered that the good bulb, a tiny item smaller than the eraser tip of a pencil, was still in his pocket. He pulled it out, looked at it momentarily, then pulled open the file drawer of his desk and tossed it in. He heard it clink lightly when it hit the diagonal cutters he had placed in the back of the drawer earlier.

He had planned to louse up the ELT similarly but had completely forgotten to switch its fresh cell with a new, but carefully discharged, battery at the same time. The dead power unit was still sitting in the trunk of his car, at the garage where it was being repaired.

At any moment now some airline pilot or military crew would pick up the distress signal. They monitored the frequency as a matter of routine and flew at altitudes high enough to detect it at great distances.

Still, there apparently had been no reports, and the plane was surely down. Since Jim had not called from some farmhouse or out-of-the-way strip by now, Jack Laird was certain it had not been a soft landing. Maybe the locator signal had not been heard because the weather had grounded most flights in the area. He was on the point of calling for a recorded aviation weather update when the instrument jangled loudly under his outstretched hand.

Buzz Taglio heard Jack Laird accept his collect call and waited until the operator had said "Go ahead, please," in an automatically cheery tone, before he spoke up.

"Hello, Jack?" The questioning tilt was superfluous, he knew, but he felt unsure of himself and preferred to let Laird ask the questions.

"Hello, Buzz. Where are you?"

"I'm here; at Sparks Airport."

"Yeah, but where? At the cafe?"

"No, I'm in a phone booth outside. It was too noisy in the restaurant. I wanted to call you about. . . . "

"Yeah, I know. The FAA called me a few minutes ago, Buzz. We may have a problem."

Buzz relaxed a bit, feeling more security in the knowledge that Laird was privy to the call he had received. "They called me, too. Jesus! What's goin' on? I don't know how to move on this one, Jack." His voice took a more plaintive turn.

"Well, Buzz, it doesn't look too good." The voice on the line sounded funereal to Buzz. "I know you probably have not been involved in anything like this before, and I'm really sorry that it's working out the way it is. Planes are not quite like real estate, I'm afraid."

There was a pause. Buzz felt the need to fill it in. "Where do we go from here, Jack? I mean, about the buyer. Should I contact . . . "

"No, it's too early to get them involved." The voice continued reassuring and strong, like a strong member in a bereaved family, Buzz thought. "We're not absolutely sure that the plane went down. He may have landed some place en route. The weather is getting bad, I'm told."

"Yeah, it's snowin' heavy here now. Has been for the last twenty minutes or so."

"Look, why don't you check in at a motel. There is one near the airport, if I remember correctly, just across the street from the cafe. Just check in there so you won't have to wait by the phone all day." Laird paused for the briefest moment and went on forcefully, "After you get fixed up, call me back with your number so I can be in touch; OK?"

"Yeah," Buzz responded vacantly, "yeah, OK, Jack. Oh, yeah," he said craning his neck to look behind him out of the booth and up the street, "I can see the place. It's a Vacation Inn."

"That's the place. Now listen, Buzz, I'll pick up the tab for this . . . the whole shot, I mean. Get the receipts and send them to me—meals, cab, everything—I feel responsible for this wild goose chase I've brought you on."

Taglio was mildly grateful for these considerations, and would indeed send the tab to Laird, especially after the full reality of his lost commission took shape in his mind. The shock of having been privy to a probable air crash would soon wear off because he had never seen the pilot nor the aircraft he was brokering, and the harder truths of earning a living would take preference to emotional ones.

"Thanks, Jack," he began, "and when should I . . . . "

"Just sit tight," interrupted the voice on the phone. "Let me take care of everything from this end. I'll let you know as soon as I have anything definite. OK?"

Taglio nodded into the phone with a sigh that signaled more relief that responsibility had shifted than disappointment with a lost sale. "Whatever you say, Jack. You *will* call later today one way or the other, though. Won't you?"

"Right. Talk to you later then, Buzz."

After he had hung up, Buzz stepped out of the booth and angled his way up the street toward the Vacation Inn. His Italian loafers squeaked in the snow and he grimaced into the wind-borne swirling flakes. He had forgotten how cold it got up on this side of the Sierras. As he half-jogged across the nearly deserted roadway, he realized that his bladder was pressing badly for attention.

"That's all you need for a perfect afternoon, Taglio," he grumbled. "Piss your pants without a change of clothes!"

He was laughing to himself when he pushed open the door to the motel office. The desk clerk smiled amiably at his new guest, and reached back for a key. The clerk could spot a minimum-rate salesman when he saw one, but this guy must have hit a dollar slot on the way into town.

16

AFTER HE HAD REPLACED the phone on its wall hook, Bud Fallon scowled. He stepped around the littered counter of his modest aircraft-parts store, and walked toward the front door. The store was really a spartan arrangement filling a somewhat confined space in a corrugated-iron T-hangar. His place was on the end of a long row of identical spaces dovetailed back to back and side by side, in the configuration peculiar to small airplane shelters. Bud's floor plan differed slightly from the rest in that he had an extra cubicle in the back because of his end position in the building. This allowed him reasonable storage for stock, provided he kept the business within bounds.

He had been encouraged by many to expand his enterprise—and profits—by the simple expedient of leasing larger facilities. These offers of advice were usually met with a patient smile and a simple explanation: "No, this is as much as I want—all I can handle. This way I enjoy

the business, keep it all in my head. Don't need
employees. Anything sold in the store—I stand behind it
because I sold it. I make just enough money to keep me
and the airplane fueled up, and a little bit extra. Any more
extra and I'd get greedy—and miserable. No, I like the old
place just the way it is." The way he said it convinced even
the more obtuse kibitzers that the subject was pleasantly
closed.

As he reached the open door, he reversed a sign
standing in the adjacent window so that it read CLOSED.
The door held a framed sign with movable numbers, and
he picked at these until they read, 0100, the time promised for his return.

He looked at the sky after he had closed the door
behind him and started walking toward the fuel island a
few hundred yards away. His eyes swept the sky, taking in
a full circle of the horizon, and it was necessary for him to
pivot in mid-stride stepping backwards once as he moved
briskly along.

Everything he saw reinforced the worry he had felt
listening to the recorded aviation weather on the phone a
few minutes before. I should have called Flight Service
to see if he made it through to Sparks. The thought had
crossed his mind as he was listening to the updated record-
ings of nasty forecasts up and down the state. He had not
made the call for two reasons: first, for FAA personnel to
check on Jim's flight plan, and thereby relieve his anxiety,
would use up time and talent they probably needed else-
where on a day like this; second, such a request would give
concrete evidence of his acting like a mother hen with his
former student.

George Feister had invited Bud to join him and Naomi
for lunch at one of the restaurants in town, dutch, of
course, and he enjoyed their company, but right now he
wished he had decided to stay closer to a phone.

He snorted at his level of worry and tried to talk himself out of it. "My gosh," he rumbled, "that kid oughtta be old enough now to take care of himself." He strode purposefully toward the pumps and muttered, "Unless he does something stupid!"

If Bud was in a depressed mood when he sprinted the last twenty yards to escape the second shower of the storm, he was hard pressed to maintain the mood in Naomi Feister's company. She and George were hard at their normal banter, which to an outsider would seem to be the parting shots of an estranged couple on their way to the divorce courts. They were alone in their small office when Bud rushed in, slamming the door behind him. Naomi's face was flushed with the exertion of argument and her jaws were working marvelously.

"Put down that coffee now, George, can't you see that Bud is here and wants to go to lunch? Hello, Bud," she smiled affectionately in Bud's direction, then immediately reached out to the wall switch and turned it off, plunging the office into a gray gloom.

"Let's go," she said, and walked out the door, snatching a plastic umbrella from the corner as she left.

Bud chuckled as he watched George put down his full cup. "I guess I don't know what I'm missing, George. Shoulda got married again years ago."

George grinned back at him good-naturedly, slapping Bud on the back as he pushed him out the door.

The trio walked toward the gravel parking space behind the office, hunched together like drunken musketeers as the men on Naomi's flanks obeyed her repeated commands to get in under the protection of her tiny umbrella and save themselves from getting soaked.

After they had gained the dry comfort of his truck, Bud said, mumbling, "I want to stop off at Laird's on the way. Just want to make sure Jim landed OK." They drove in silence to the east end of the field where he pulled off and stopped in front of the office. Bud slipped out, leaving the engine running.

"I'll only be a minute," he said, jogging for Jack Laird's door. It opened for him, and they caught a glimpse of Laird as he let Bud in and motioned him to a chair. The door closed slowly, shutting off their view of the two men.

For a minute they sat, quietly watching the wipers sweep desultory drops from the windshield. Then something electric passed between them. George reached over his wife's lap and killed the idling engine. The wipers froze in mid-swipe. They both gazed back at the sullen office door, willing Bud to reappear.

The door stayed shut.

George placed a cracked and calloused hand on the truck door latch and popped it open. "C'mon, Nome," he murmured gruffly, "we'd best see what's keepin' Bud."

After she and George had stepped inside and closed the door softly behind them, Naomi had a sudden rush of anxiety. The quiet words of Bud Fallon sent the chill into her breast. She could not see Bud's face, but did not care to. His words were terrible enough, hissed in a near whisper, " . . . and I make you this promise, Jack; if he *is* down, and hurt, or . . . " he could not bring it out, " . . . or hurt badly, because of some sloppy shortcut you built into that plane, I'll blow you away." He stood like a boxer, Naomi thought, poised with his arms down, but coiled with pent-up rage. Somehow she found the right muscles in her legs, and propelled her heavy frame to the two men. George remained standing at the door.

"All right, Bud, let's use some common sense here!" She fixed Jack Laird with a no-nonsense look and continued, "What happened to that boy?"

Now that she was closer she could read the desperation in Laird's eyes. When he spoke his tone was uncharacteristically sad.

"About twenty minutes ago Flight Service called me that Jim has not closed out his flight plan. They don't know where he is. If he doesn't turn up in the next few minutes, they will declare him missing so that the search can get started." Laird was sweating, and he trembled so much that he had difficulty lighting a cigaret.

Naomi winced and felt the cold spot in her chest flare to real cramp. She sucked in a gulp of air, but the knot remained. "Has anyone told Ann?"

Laird exhaled a cloud of cigaret smoke and answered, "No. It may be a false alarm. There is nothing she could do. Why put her through this . . . ?" He added quietly, "At least not until we're certain."

"You said twenty minutes . . . . " she began, looking around the walls of the office for a clock. Cued by her half-voiced question, Bud Fallon moved over to the desk. He raised a bristling eyebrow toward Jack Laird as he picked up the phone. "I'll call Flight Service myself," he growled, and dialed the number. George and Naomi moved toward the desk and stopped a few feet from each other facing Fallon.

Jack Laird hung back in the shadowed corner of the room. Sweat loops were starting to darken the fabric under the arms of his beige leisure suit. As he drew again on his cigaret, the glowing tip illuminated his upper face. Twin red sparks reflected from his pupils as he studied the trio through watchful, hooded eyes.

As she rummaged through the sparse supplies in their tiny pantry, Ann's eyes sparkled. A quick inventory of the staples on hand today narrowed down the possibilities to two: macaroni and cheese casserole, or a three-egg cheese omelette with side dish of canned chile con carne.

"Not today, wolf-at-the-door," she hummed, slamming the single tin of chile back on its shelf and closing the cabinet. "Oh no, not today."

A reckless feeling of abandon surged through her as she trotted briskly back to the bedroom after her purse. Snatching it up from the floor by the telephone, she dumped its contents on the bed. She opened the checkbook and glanced at the last line in the deposit register. It was an entry from the previous day in the amount of five hundred dollars drawn on the account of Jack Laird Aircraft Sales Company. A quick computation in her head satisfied Ann that, considering the negative balance riding as a result of earlier checks still on their way to creditors, there was a safe four hundred dollars fattening their account.

What a dinner they would have! "It will have to be filet and lobster," she said with conviction, rearranging the heap of cosmetics, keys, tissues, pens and other odds and ends and absent-mindedly beginning to stuff them back into the purse. A small frown wrinkled her forehead when she remembered that she had never prepared lobster tail before. For that matter, she thought, I haven't cooked anything more exotic than an occasional sirloin. She began to speculate on whom to call for advice when a better idea dawned.

Why should I cook anyway? That big lug should take me out to the best restaurant in town. I have something to celebrate, too. She smiled at this decision and began to check off a mental list of the best dining locations in the area.

She rose from the bed, opened her wardrobe closet, and stood a long time making her decision on what to wear. She was not impeded by the great variety of selection available to her; the problem lay in what combination of limited outfits might work out aesthetically—and romantically—for this most special of celebrations.

She was glad the weather had turned cool. At least she could wear parts of the fall outfit she had not had on since the winter before. After laying out the basic ensemble on the bed, she made a careful selection of accessories. Finally satisfied that the effect would be passably captivating, she opened the drawer in the dresser to check for adequate underthings and hose. I really should get something delicate and nice to wear underneath, she thought. She began envisioning lacy and filmy things. She could skip out and buy some and be dressed, ready to go when he arrived—late this afternoon. Perfect. She would give him time to get cleaned up. After they got to the restaurant she would tell him the news—hers first, about Mildred Yancey's offer; then the big surprise, the call from U.S. Airways. She could almost see his reaction.

Then when they had both calmed down they would come home. She would undress very casually, watching his reaction when she got down to the new things.

Her eyes came into focus then and she caught her own eye in the mirror. She watched the provocative smile form on her reflected lips, and, caught in her own observation, began to blush hotly along the neckline of her blouse.

She winked at the face in the glass. "Down, girl!" she whispered wickedly. "Later."

17

AT THE RENO CENTER, Simpson had just finished another round of calls checking on five overdue flight plans. He had verified three of them, all flights that had landed short of their destinations because of the worsening weather. In each case the pilot had forgotten to close his altered plan after landing. He was not really worked up about one of the unaccounted-for flights, because it was only ten minutes over ETA, not unusual considering the stepped-up headwinds along the route. The other flight was Dauphin 7695 Romeo.

This time the call did not bounce back with a busy signal. He caught himself hoping she was not at home and was brought up short when she picked up after the first ring.

"Hello?" Her voice was excited, expectant. Damn! She thought this was the call from her husband. Simpson had had it happen many times before.

"Hello. Mrs. Regan?"

"Yes." Simpson pushed on with the messy job.

"Mrs. Regan, I'm Bill Simpson with the FAA, Flight Service. Now I don't want to alarm you unnecessarily, but we need to know some information on your husband's flight to Reno this morning." Simpson moved in with the briefest pause, not giving her a chance to react until he could get whatever information she might have. "His flight left about nine this morning. Have you heard from him since then?"

Simpson could hear her breathing on the line, and imagined her fighting for control. When she spoke her voice seemed almost clinical in tone.

"Jim's flight was from Grant to Sparks direct, no planned stops enroute. He probably went VFR. I'm sure he filed a flight plan . . . he was going up along the Sierras, which side I don't know. . . . Didn't he have a flight plan?"

"Yes, he did, Mrs. Regan. If you heard anything from him after nine o'clock it might help us out at this end." Simpson was deliberately vague, trying to pick her brain before the bad news clouded her thinking.

She was silent for a considerable time. Simpson was about to speak her name when she came back on. "Well, Mr. Simpson, I appreciate your roundabout way of trying to spare my feelings. It isn't necessary. I know now that you are calling to let me know that he hasn't closed out his flight plan. . . . That would make him about an hour overdue, wouldn't it? Please be direct."

Simpson's eyes were closed. When he spoke again his voice had slipped into the easy drawl he reserved for friends. "You are also a pilot, right?"

"Almost a pilot, yes."

"Well, Mrs. Regan, I'm gonna give it to you straight. He still has not shown up at Sparks—or anywhere else. We have no reports of downed aircraft along his route, and that's kinda good *and* bad. He might have landed in some out-of-the-way place, not near a phone, but to tell the truth we should have heard something by this time, Highway Patrol, CBer or something. On the good side is the fact that there have been negative reports on ELT signals—you know about ELTs?"

"Emergency locators, yes."

"You know, of course, that they are not always dependable. The plane your husband was flying had just had a complete airworthiness inspection so the ELT was probably in top shape when he took off."

"If anybody listens." Her tone had the slightest tinge of cynicism. "Jim always monitors one twenty-one point five when we are flying over rough country. I hope somebody out there is on the ball today."

"*If* he's down, Mrs. Regan; so far he's just overdue."

"I have a strong feeling you think he crashed, Mr. Simpson," she said quietly. "What other things should I know?" Simpson thought it best to sidestep her comment about his own feelings and give her the rest of the bleak prognosis.

"The weather is really getting bad. When your husband got his forecast, the entire route was expected to remain clear until late in the afternoon. There was a system expected to bring in snow and rain, but it was moving slowly. About nine o'clock it picked up speed and crossed his intended flight path at about ten."

"He must have monitored the Flightwatch frequency. When did you last hear from him?"

"That's the reason I wanted to know whether you had heard anything from him. You see, the only radio contact we have had was when he opened his flight plan shortly after takeoff. He got an amended forecast then, but it did not have the bad weather picture, which came in a few minutes later. We have no record of any further transmissions from the plane."

"My God! You mean he could be anywhere from San Diego to Reno!"

"I'm afraid that's right," he affirmed sadly. "Look, Mrs. Regan, I know things look real bad right now, but a call might come in any minute with good news. Just sit tight, and we'll get back to you the minute we hear anything. In the meantime I want you to jot down this number for you to call in case you hear anything that might help us locate that flier of yours." He waited a moment to give her time to get a pencil and then gave her the telephone number. "Just ask for Bill Simpson if I'm on another line at the time."

"Is there anything I can do in the meantime?" Her voice was beginning to lose its objective control, he noted, and he felt more deeply moved that she had taken every bit of bad news he had given her so stoically. He wished that he could give her hope—more than the fifty-fifty odds that were slipping away with every passing minute. To his credit he did not.

"You might call his pilot friends on the slim chance that he talked to them during the flight on the plane-to-plane frequency. Otherwise there isn't much except to stay near the phone." He had to give her something, so he mentioned that he had talked to Jack Laird, and that he too would be checking with others at Grant Field.

"Do you and your husband live with family or . . ." he could not quite bring off "alone."

"No, there's just the two of us," she said, suddenly remote. There was a pause, then her voice came back in focus once again, "I'll be all right. We have friends if . . . close by if I need anything."

"OK, then Mrs. Regan, I'll be in touch with you later. It might be an hour or two."

"I understand. Thank you, Mr. Simpson."

"I'll talk to you later, then. Goodbye." He waited for

her to break the connection, holding the receiver over the
cradle until he heard the click and droning dial tone before
letting it slip down on the buttons. It was wet where he had
gripped it.

The storm clouds over California whirled in a vast
cyclonic pool stretching from the Mexican border to
Mount Lassen above Sacramento. Television weathermen
were busy getting data together for the five o'clock news,
confident that programming would give them ample time
for a chance to really show their stuff. The breaking storm
promised to be the hottest news of the week, with harried
forecasters now openly suggesting that the storm would
probably break all known records for the state. The east-
ward momentum of the low-pressure area had stalled over
Point Conception on the coast and the huge system was
spinning counterclockwise, sweeping millions of tons of
moisture from the warm coastal waters of Baja California
and carrying the water-saturated air inland and north along
the western slopes of the Sierras. As it was pushed upslope
to colder altitudes, the air condensed out its unstable burden first as rainshowers and then as hail and heavy snow.
Finally wrung dry as it completed a three-hundred-mile
left turn, the gigantic air mass rushed south over the ocean,
warming to pick up moisture for another run up the eastern flank of the state.

In the Southland the sun would occasionally appear
through a hole in the overcast as the energy of massive
buildups sucked at adjacent cloud layers, pulling them
apart.

The slanting beam of late November sun stabbed brilliantly through Ann Regan's bedroom window, catching a
lazing ribbon of smoke rising from the forgotten cigaret in
her hand. She finally noticed the light striking her fingers
and shuddered, aware of the contrasting warmth of the

tiny shaft of light with the coldness in her body. She was dry-eyed but somber, not quite sure of what she felt now, five long minutes after the call. She turned her hands absently in the yellow bath of sunlight, and as she did, the light caught her wedding band, deep yellow gold, magnified it, polished the plain circlet so that it somehow seemed out of place, too new, unworn, a temporary costume, only make-believe.

Shaking her hair back behind her shoulders, she tossed the thought away and moved away from the sun just as it faded. Stooping over the night table she crushed out the unsmoked cigaret and tried to sort out some plan of action. Like nausea, tender thoughts were drifting around the periphery of her mind, and she knew she would not be able to handle them now. Somehow she had to keep a clear mind so that she could act without the confusion of grief—or fear.

By the time the pain reached her shoulder, Naomi Feister had realized that this was not another attack of arthritis but a spreading cramp from her right hand. She had been clutching her purse so tightly that the circulation had left her fingers and spasms of muscle fatigue were twitching along the top of her forearm.

She and George watched Bud Fallon as he listened on the phone, jotting notes, making barely audible rumbling comments in the mostly one-sided conversation. At last he straightened, replaced his pen in his shirt pocket, flipped closed the small spiralbound notepad, and hung up the telephone.

He turned back to face them.

"It ain't so good."

Naomi took a step toward him, looked quickly at her husband, then back at Bud, but said nothing.

"His only transmission was when he opened the flight

plan a few minutes after takeoff. After that nobody heard from him. They've had six or seven high-altitude commercial and military flights fly over the route monitoring the emergency frequency for the last hour or so, but nobody has picked up an ELT."

"What side of the range?" George Feister's voice cracked as he spoke, like a man just awakened from sleep.

"Both sides, George." Fallon stepped to a wall chart on the opposite side of Jack Laird's office. As he approached, Laird stepped easily to one side, moving to his desk to crush out his burned-down cigaret.

Bud ran his finger along the smudged paper. "A C141 out of Travis circled back over the route and continued as far south as Grant before doubling back to George at San Bernardino. They were at thirty thousand-plus, flying in and out of the tops. The others were transports from northern cities on their way to Phoenix or San Diego."

"Did they cover the Bishop side of the ridge?" George asked, his tilted nose inches from the chart as he peered intently through the bottom halves of his bifocals.

"Yeah." Bud was absorbed in positioning a course line tape between Reno and Grant Field. "At the altitude they were flying it probably doesn't matter; they had a line-of-sight range of any transmitter on either side. Even so," he added, "two of those commercial flights spaced themselves so they could fly parallel courses down both sides of the range at the same time."

He fell silent a moment, studying the terrain, measuring the tape. "No, they didn't miss anything. If there was an ELT signal, they'd have heard it."

Bud dropped the tape, letting it snap back on the pressure of its spring. He described a small circle with his fingertip on the grimy patch of the map near Grant Field. "This is where he was when he talked to Flight Service. After that—nothing."

"Bud, dear, does she know?" The voice behind him was small and anguished.

"I'm sorry, Naomi," Bud replied, taking her arm as he turned away from the wall and looked at the round face staring up at him. "Yes, she knows. The guy I talked to had just finished giving her the news." He shook his head. "Said she took it very well. Made it harder on him somehow; he said he felt that he couldn't give her any assurance at all. She would have known, he said."

"I don't think that we should call."

"No, she's probably hanging on every ring."

"Well, then I'm going over to stay with her until we find out—something. Let's go, George." Some of her old self was beginning to stiffen Naomi again.

"Just a minute, Naomi," Bud interrupted, "Ann will probably need the car. Why don't you take my rig and George can follow in Jim's car. He usually leaves the keys."

Jack Laird used the opportunity to escape momentarily by saying he would check the car for keys. After he had left, Naomi asked, "Aren't you coming, Bud? You're closer to them than we are."

"I'll look in on her later, Naomi," he replied, peering out the open door at the lowering clouds. "One thing that I didn't mention in that phone call is that they will not be able to start the air search until the storm has passed. The weather north of here is terrible, zero ceilings and visibility in the mountains from Tehachapi all the way to Reno. It's getting worse by the hour."

George looked at him hard. "So what are you thinking about?"

Bud returned the look and smiled. "Well, pardner, it's still possible to fly under the stuff until I get to San Bernardino or thereabouts. I want to get in one look-see while they're organizing the search pattern."

Naomi narrowed her eyes. "Bud Fallon, just because you're old is not an excuse for getting foolish. Don't take any chances."

"Naomi, you are just saying that because you want George to keep on pumping gas into my thirsty ole one ninety-five." Then he added with serious reassurance, "Don't worry; I'm not about to turn this into a search for *two* pilots. Jim will need all the help we can spare."

Bud walked them out and watched with Laird as they drove away. The two men reentered the office and stood together awkwardly staring at the wall chart. Fallon broke the silence.

"Jack, we've no time for anger, accusation, or personal grievances. I'd appreciate it if you'd forget what I said a few minutes ago." His tone was businesslike and even—anything but humble.

Laird nodded, considerably relieved.

Bud retraced his finger along the chart. "I'm gonna call Flight Service after I get up, and I'll request radar following wherever I can, but this is where I'm going so you will know." He looked at Laird. "Just in case."

After Jack Laird had driven him back to his store, Bud went inside and picked up the most expensive survival kit on his shelves. Tucking it under his arm, he left the shop and walked briskly toward his rain-lacquered airplane.

Less than a minute after he had climbed into the high cabin of the meticulously cared-for machine, the polished aluminum propeller swung through half an arc, then spun in a gleaming blur. A cloud of black belched from the exhaust stack, and the big radial engine roared to life.

He swung the plane toward the taxiway and trundled in the S-turning track peculiar to nose-high, tailwheeled aircraft until he reached the takeoff end of the active runway. Here he completed his engine runup and takeoff checklist. He did not let the pressures of emotion hurry him.

Finally satisfied that everything was in order, he increased power and pivoted the large craft in a complete circle so that he could scan the sky for other aircraft in the landing pattern.

He was about to roll onto the runway proper when the sight of his own truck braking to a skidding stop beside the fence caught his eye. A small figure leaped out and ran toward the plane.

"Jesus Christ, Ann," he yelled pointlessly in the closed cockpit as he pulled the mixture knob to kill the rumbling engine, "don't run into the blasted prop!"

She was panting breathlessly, hair all awry, and her lip was trembling, he noticed, as he opened the door and helped her climb aboard.

"I'm sorry, Bud, but I had to come along. I feel so . . . useless!" Her teeth were clenched and her throat was working hard.

"I figured," he said, trying to sound exasperated. "Well, don't just sit there. Put your belt on."

He could see her fumbling for the belt she couldn't see because the tears had finally started. The prop swung again and the engine coughed to life, grumbling at the delay. He checked everything again before he spoke, leaning close to her face to be heard above the noisy engine.

"You sure you want to do this, Ann? Could be dangerous, you know." He watched her wipe her eyes with the back of a hand as he turned the plane again to look for other traffic.

Leaning close to her ear once more, his eyes twinkling with an impish impudence, he added, "Y'know, the sky is no place for a *woman*!"

Her head jerked around instantly. She caught the jibe at once, though, and settled back in her seat.

The plane rolled out onto the runway finally, and

turned its upturned beefy nose into the wind. Ann touched Bud's arm, and he turned to her and winked.

The engine two feet ahead of their knees thundered as Bud pushed the throttle home and yelled above the din, "Now that you're ready, lady, let's go round up your favorite stray!"

18

SHORTLY AFTER he had cleared the pattern, Fallon radioed the Flight Service facility in his area. His conversation was lost on Ann because Bud had long since given up on speakers in the noisy cabin of his antique. Instead he had installed rather elaborate headsets and intercom to match the modern avionics he had bought for the otherwise "stock" old airplane.

"I'll keep up this heading as long as I can, and advise you folks as to the weather along the way. If you need to raise me later, I'll be listening on one twenty-one point five all the time as well."

"Roger, two four Pop. Check in with us once in a while. It looks like the search is gonna be limited to ground parties until this thing is over. Be careful. Over."

"OK. Thanks. Two four Pop, out."

"Ah, two four Pop, are you a friend of the pilot?"

Fallon paused a moment before answering, too many memories beginning to push in, mellowing, hurting . . . .

"Yeah, Friend." The mike switch clicked off, then on again; he heard his own voice in the headset as he added, "And a student of mine—for a long time now."

"Understand, two four Poppa. Good hunting." The Flight Watch operator also came back as an afterthought, "Listen, it really gets bad farther north, don't get carried away. Be careful, please."

Bud Fallon smiled at the concern voiced over this usually all-business frequency and gave the mike button a double click in acknowledgement of the message.

He sat for a few moments hand-flying the airplane as it climbed to his cruising altitude. Soon he pushed the nose down to a level attitude and reduced power. He trimmed the plane for level flight and, when it was stabilized, turned again to Ann and spoke. She could hear him more easily now over the decreased rumble of the engine.

"Hold this heading for a while." She grasped the yoke lightly, and he turned back in his seat and pulled an extra headset out of the pocket behind her seat. He plugged it into a jack on the panel and handed it to her. After she had put it on, he turned a small selector switch near the radios and spoke into his microphone. She heard his voice clearly in her earphones.

"That better?" He saw her nod and say something although no sound came over the line.

"You have to press your mike switch . . . there on the yoke," he said, adding, "It's OK; you won't be transmitting. I have it set on intercom."

She found the button with her thumb and tried again. "Can you hear me now, Bud?"

"Gotcha. Loud and clear."

A look of concern crossed her face and she spoke again, "What if we miss the ELT signal, or one of their transmissions?"

He explained, pointing at a series of switches, "Oh, we

are still receiving on both one twenty-two point zero and one twenty-one point five. We'll hear anything that comes along. I just have the transmit mode switched off. When I need to call anybody, I'll let you know."

He pawed around blindly behind his own seat for a few seconds, grunting with the exertion caused by his contorted position. At last he straightened up, pulling with him a small set of binoculars. He handed them to her.

"Use these to check out anything that looks suspicious. Use a regular pattern with your eyes, try to cover as much of our ground track as possible. Don't forget to look *under* us. It helps sometimes to visualize that you are painting a wide strip with your eyes, straight ahead and on your side." He gestured with his hands, blocking out a rectangular pattern.

"Where will we join the other search planes?" Ann asked after nodding confirmation that she understood his instructions.

Bud took a moment to scan the expanse of lowering ceiling a few hundred feet above them before he answered. Then he turned to look her squarely in the eye. "There are no other search planes, Ann. We are doing this on our own, although the Feds know what we're doing. You see, they can't send out the air search people because the weather is getting so bad."

She was startled at this news, and the dismay she felt registered in her voice. "But the visibility is so *good*. If we are able to get up and look, why can't others?"

"Because the time margin is too close," he said. "The air search takes hours of coordination. This storm"—he nodded for emphasis at the purpling sky pressing down on them—"is already down to zero-zero over most of the search area. The search aircraft will have to wait till the front passes before they can do anything."

Another look in her direction was enough for him to

realize that his explanation left her in doubt as to why they were up here themselves. Dammit, he thought, if I was honest with myself I would have to admit that I'm doing it more for my own relief than for any real hope of finding Jim.

"Look, Ann," he tried again lamely, "the odds against our finding him on this flight are about a million to one. That stuff up ahead will probably drive us back in another ten minutes or so. That will put us about ten to fifteen miles north of where he was when made his last radio contact with Flight Watch. Chances are he actually went farther before he got into trouble. I'm gambling on the slight chance that he had to force-land," he chose this term deliberately, "just after talking on the radio."

He noted that she accepted his frank admission of slim hope with silent resignation and attentive ground scrutiny.

"Ann?"

"Yes, Bud?" she acknowledged without taking her eyes off the ground.

"Remember that we're still piloting an airplane. Keep your eyes peeled out that side for other traffic between ground sweeps."

"OK," she said quietly.

They flew on in silence for several minutes, each absorbed in the task. Occasional wisps of scud appeared beside and below them, and the great mass of black overcast appeared to be canted downward to a point several miles ahead where it met the rising terrain of the Sierra foothills. Bud knew the airspace through which they were flying would soon be solid cloud. Although filing for and flying an instrument approach back to Grant Field was within his and the plane's capability, he had no desire to be forced to that alternative. Flying a search pattern would be an exercise in futility if they could not see the ground.

He gave a position report, including observed weather,

and advised that they would be turning to fly the return heading to Grant. The return track would parallel their outbound course about two miles farther west. In this way they would be able to cover fresh ground.

"Sorry, Ann," he rumbled into the mike, "no more room. We have to go back." She looked at him and nodded again, lips pressed tightly together. "Keep looking though. This will be ground we haven't been over before."

Their hearts were not in the work, however. Each had the conviction, carefully hidden from the other, that they would not find Jim anywhere near this place. Once Ann stole a rueful look back toward the cloud-shrouded peaks to the north as though they were somehow competitors from whom she fled, hopelessly outmatched in her struggle to repossess the prize.

It was nearly two in the afternoon when they finally made their way back to the home field. It appeared to be much later because the heavy skies gave a late twilight effect to the chilly, wet afternoon. Bud swung off the runway and taxied to the gas pumps to refuel before tying down the plane. Naomi Feister stood in the open doorway of her office twisting her wedding ring nervously. She watched as they climbed down from the high cabin door and waved them over to the office.

She had not expected good news, though she had hoped for some. However, there was nothing in their walk, she noted, to help dispel the morbid gloom of this miserable day.

A little after three that afternoon, Thad Monte braked his small station wagon to a halt in front of a small ranch-style house in an older but neatly maintained tract. It was raining fiercely, and he debated waiting in the car till the downpour slackened or sprinting for the front door and risking an almost inevitable soaking. He liked the rain.

There was a certain excitement in the change from the tedium of a normally arid climate. If the weather persisted he might take Shirley and the kids up to the snow over the weekend. He wondered if they could scrape together enough jackets and gloves for all of them. Probably not. They would certainly have to buy a pair of boots or two; it had been two years since snow had fallen in the local mountains, and the larger items would now shift down to the younger children.

He decided to make a dash for it. Gripping his attache case firmly, he shouldered open the car door and sprinted through the puddles and slanting rain toward the front entrance. The short overhang gave him little protection from the wet so he slowed only to wrench open the heavy paneled door and plunged into the front hallway like an eager child.

His wife had just completed a call on the telephone in the kitchen. He watched her hang up deliberately and walk toward him, a strange expression on her face. Feeling foolish as he shook the rainwater from his arms and stamped it from his shoes, he greeted her a bit sheepishly.

"Sorry about your tile, Hon; I'll get the mop in a sec."

"That was Ann Regan, Thad." His wife seemed ill at ease, he thought.

"They can't make it for dinner?"

When she didn't answer, he turned to look at her, dislodging a tangle of wire hangers which fell musically to the bottom of the closet. He suddenly knew that there was something very wrong with his wife and that it had nothing to do with a wet spot on the floor or a messy closet. She literally sagged against him.

Lifting her chin gently with a finger he looked into her eyes and waited.

"Jim has crashed somewhere ... they don't know where ... out in that awful storm," she whispered.

It was his turn to be speechless. He listened to her, not quite grasping it at first, feeling his exhilaration of a moment ago slip from him.

"God, I felt so terrible, calling like that . . . giving her the invitation to dinner—jabbering on like a fool, saying we wouldn't accept *any* excuse."

She had taken Thad's hand and was drawing him after her into the living room, to the couch.

They sat down together, close, not realizing they had traversed the room.

"Oh my God, Thad, it was so awful. She was so patient, and polite, and . . . calm! She *apologized* to me for not being able to come, and then she said, almost like he was going to be out of town on business, that Jim had not made it through the storm on a flight to Reno, and they were afraid he might be down somewhere in the mountains.

"The terrible thing is that he could be *anywhere*. He didn't use the radio except when he took off, so they don't know where to begin searching. And now the storm is all over the place, and they don't expect it to stop for hours. Dear God, and she just has to sit there and *wait*!"

Suddenly spent, she let her head fall back against the couch and stared helplessly at the ceiling.

"Is anyone with her now?" he asked quietly.

She nodded, "Naomi Feister and Bud Fallon."

"Did she happen to say when he was due in Reno?"

"Yes, she did. It was about noon, I think."

Thad took his wife's hands between his own and held them for a minute before he spoke again. "Let me get you a drink. I think I could use one, too." He paused, then added, "I'll make a few calls . . . see what I can find out."

He left for the kitchen and returned shortly with a scotch and water for each of them. They sipped in silence, looking at each other.

"Do you think I should go over?" she asked.

He nodded. "Yes, see if you can get someone to stay with the kids. We both should go." He was thoughtful, running his index finger around the wet top of the glass, making it vibrate with a low moaning tone. "It's gonna be partly business, Hon. You see, we insured that airplane."

Shirley looked up, startled.

He grimaced as he spoke. "I hope the whole thing is a false alarm. If—if it isn't, I want to make sure that she gets everything the damned policy provides."

19

SHORTLY BEFORE five o'clock that afternoon, Jack Laird stood looking out his office window at the puddled ramp behind the building. The odd assortment of used airplanes he had for sale drooped at their tiedowns like chickens caught in the rainy twilight without a covered roost. The empty space marking the twin's location gave him a twinge of remorse, and he turned away agitated and lit a cigaret.

The sudden jangling of his telephone sent a new charge of adrenaline into his nearly exhausted system, and he again had to force himself to wait for the third ring before picking it up.

"Jack Laird Aircraft, Laird speaking."

"Hi, Jack. What's the word?"

It was Larry Kemp. Recognition of his caller's identity filled Laird with a rush of anger. "Where are you calling from, Larry?" he asked brusquely.

"My room. I'm still at Mammoth."

Laird's tone was impatient, irritated. "Look, Larry, I told you not to call here. The idea of making a long distance call from a hotel to my number is just plain stupid! Why couldn't you wait until tomorrow when you would be near a local pay phone?"

"No problem, Jack. Nobody is going to take the trouble to go through the phone records to check my long distance numbers. Besides, what if they did? Wouldn't it be perfectly natural for me to contact you if I'm the one who is supposed to be buying your airplane?"

If he thought it would have ended the conversation with no possibility of a callback, Laird would have hung up then and there. He decided it would be more prudent to explain.

I hope to Christ nobody has any reason to bug this stupid son-of-a-bitch's line, he thought. "The problem, Larry, is that you *aren't* the one who is buying the plane. Your father's *company* is the one who is buying the plane. Remember?" He paused long enough for this to sink in. "As long as you're on the line, I might as well tell you that the sale is off. The plane didn't make it to Reno."

"Oh, well, that's what I called about. I had to know if it would be reasonable to transfer the funds back tomorrow. Something happened this afternoon that might affect things a little."

Laird pressed his free hand to his head and smoothed his hair, expecting the worst. He waited.

Larry cleared his throat and resumed. "I had a little run-in with Dad today. He was quite upset about ... "

"Does he know about the money?" Laird's question cracked over the line like a whiplash.

"Oh, no ... no." Larry's voice gained a level of reassurance. "There isn't a chance of his finding out about that."

"Well?"

"It was a bit of the old thing about my taking so much time off . . . and the gambling lecture again."

Laird relaxed, relieved that it was nothing more serious than the old conflict with his father. He laughed into the phone. "What happened this time, Larry. Did the old man fire you?"

"Yes."

"Jesus Christ!"

"I honestly cannot see how he could do such a thing, Jack. His only *son*! Can you imagine! I admit he had *some* reason to be upset, but to treat me like an ordinary employee. . . . I mean, the company is partly mine, or will be some day. The man simply has no sense of family loyalty or . . . "

"When?"

"When, what, Jack?"

"When are you gonna be out on your ass, you nitwit!"

Laird regretted the comment immediately. He had to keep some semblance of good will.

"I think that was uncalled-for, Jack. Dad gave me until the first of the year to find something else."

Laird apologized contritely, giving concern over the plane as reason for being edgy. "Are you certain nobody will be checking out that credit transfer?"

Larry laughed confidently. "Listen, Jack, it will take me a month to train them in the system. I'm the only one who knows how to get the confidential stuff out of our computer."

"I'm sure you'll get things right with the old man, Larry."

"Yes. Well, enough of my troubles, Jack. You said the plane didn't make it to Reno. They didn't crash or anything, did they?"

"I don't think so, Larry. These missing aircraft reports

are fairly common." He lied easily, the words flowing like honey.

"Well, what have you told the 'pigeons' in our little game? They must be concerned that the plane has not shown up."

"Look, Larry, let's just say that they did check the Taglio account and are quite ready to buy. A little delay won't hurt much—maybe it'll whet their appetites. I think for your sake that the less you know about the deal the better off you'll be in the long run. These kinds of things are common practice—a kind of priming-the-pump to speed up slow buyers, but they *are* somewhat extra-legal. If it came to a hearing, not that it will, I wouldn't want you to get hurt. After all, you have more to lose."

The insinuation of the last comment was not entirely lost on his listener, but it was so gently put that he felt that Laird was indeed looking out for his best interests.

"Whatever you say, Jack. You know how to handle these things better than I." The voice paused and Laird waited for the next question.

"About our, ah, financial settlement, Jack. The delay in the plane's arrival won't, ah, affect our arrangement, will it? I mean, when will I get the balance of the forty thousand?"

Laird reassured him that he would get the agreed-upon cash just as soon as they could meet at a prearranged place close to Grant. Kemp was to call Laird as soon as he got into town the following week to set up the time.

"The cash is where I can lay my hands on it any time during working hours, Larry. It's yours as soon as you can come down and pick it up."

"Fine, fine. It will be a relief to get the money back into the firm. I have to admit that I was a bit nervous about it even though it was quite safe these past two days. I'll have it back as soon as the lines are open to transfer the credit tomorrow."

Jack Laird could not resist one last sales pitch on a sold customer. "Say, Larry, did you ever compute the interest I'm paying you just to keep your money in your bank under your name?" He chuckled. "Figure it out. Forty thou for two days' interest on half a million. What does that come to?"

Lawrence Kemp was silent a moment. "Why, it's exactly eight percent, Jack."

"Right, Larry, eight percent for two days. Figure out what the annual percentage rate would be on that!" He laughed into the telephone. "Don't worry, Larry, I'm not going to lodge a complaint with Consumer Affairs; just consider it a sales commission."

After he hung up, Jack Laird allowed himself a private laugh. Larry Kemp would probably wet his pants if he knew he was party to a conspiracy to sabotage, insurance fraud, grand larceny, and . . .

He could not quite think the word. Not manslaughter, nor homicide; certainly not murder. But the *idea* was clearly there, and it troubled him.

He looked at his watch. Better make one more call to Flight Service before he left for his apartment.

His anxious tone was duly noted by the answering specialist, who responded to Laird's queries with a solicitous but frank report. There was little doubt on the part of the FAA that the plane had crashed. The fact that six hours had elapsed since fuel exhaustion time, that the weather was the worst it had been in years, and that the plane in question was not apt to divert to a small airstrip and therefore park unnoticed, all pointed to the probability of calamity. Additionally, the absence of a phone call from the pilot, a professional who would take care to notify authorities in such an emergency, suggested that he had not survived.

Laird began to have second thoughts. Maybe Jim had managed to land the plane intact somewhere isolated from a telephone. Maybe this very minute he was tramping out of the wilds toward a highway with angry questions. He turned and fixed his stare at the wall chart Bud Fallon had been studying hours earlier. He heaved himself out of the chair and stepped over to it. With the precision of someone who had computed the problem many times before, he located the spot where fuel-tank switchover probably took place. Holding the spot with a fingertip, he reached for a pen in his breast pocket, and was on the point of marking a small X on the chart when he stopped and jabbed the pen back into his jacket. He peered intently at the spot on the map to memorize the location, then strode to his desk, pulled out a drawer, and rummaged around until he found a roll of masking tape. He unrolled a few inches of the wide strip, folded it in upon itself to form a sticky square, and returned to the chart. Using light pressure he fixed the wad over the spot he had located and stepped back. His eyes scanned a small area approximately 5 inches in diameter encircling the dot.

"Nothing but peaks and tree-filled ravines," he muttered. "He couldn't even put a helicopter down in there."

Turning away from the chart again, he walked over to his desk and dropped the masking tape by a file folder lying flat on the mahogany surface. He picked up the folder and stood leafing through its contents. When he came to a page marked CLAIMS, he ran his finger down the small print until he came to a sub-heading, HULL. He spread the policy open before him and continued reading.

Gradually a frown worked its way into his face, and he shifted his eyes back up the page to the phrase "Proof of loss." He could not find what he was looking for. Extending a fat forefinger, he read the troubling passage aloud as though it would yield the sense he so much desired if he heard the words, lifted from the page to his ears.

"When presented with proof of loss the company shall, at its discretion, either reimburse the insured for loss or assume the cost of repair."

Jesus Christ, he thought, what if they never find the goddam plane? How long will I have to wait?

Quite unexpectedly the door burst open, and Charlie Wise, dripping wet with the rain, his face white with fury, stood glaring down at Laird from across the desk.

"Why didn't you tell me, you bastard? Why did you let me walk into all of them cold?"

For a moment Laird could not imagine what he was talking about. Then he remembered that in all the turmoil, he had forgotten to tell Charlie about the plane's disappearance.

"Who did you talk to, Charlie?"

"Naomi and George!" He choked the names out. "And everybody else on this goddam airport! I wondered why it got so quiet in the coffee shop when I took my break at two thirty. Nobody even spoke to me." His voice was shrill.

"Jeez, Charlie, I'm sorry. I guess I just assumed that you had heard," Laird said, measuring his words carefully.

"Well, thanks a bunch! I think George would have brained me with a towbar if I hadn't left when I did."

Jack seized the moment. "Look, we both know that plane was in top shape, probably the best mechanical condition of any airplane we ever sold." He paused to let that sink in. When he resumed, he gripped the mechanic firmly by both shoulders and looked him full in the face. "Charlie, when they find that bird and do a teardown, they will find that it was in perfect shape before the accident."

Charlie knew that what Laird said was true. He, more than anyone else, could vouch for that. For some reason he could not quite explain, however, he did not believe Jack Laird despite the earnest look about his face. His shoulders felt chilled where his boss had gripped them, and he turned wordlessly away.

His eye caught the wad of masking tape stuck to the wall chart and he paused in front of it for a time to gather his composure.

A few steps behind him, Jack Laird watched him closely. Charlie was studying the chart. He pointed to the dot of tape and asked, "Is this where he went down?"

Laird's face darkened perceptibly at the question.

"What? Oh, that. No, that's nothing ... no connection."

Charlie was not sure what Laird said after that as he walked him to the door.

After he had closed the door on Charlie, Jack Laird returned to the map and reached up for the wad of masking tape. He plucked it away from the chart, cursing himself for being stupid, and flung the sticky square into the wastebasket. In a rush he scooped up the insurance folder and slammed it into a desk drawer. Snapping off the lights, he stepped into the heavy rain and darkness and slammed the door shut after him.

On the wall chart a tiny triangle of white gleamed in the darkened office. It matched exactly a torn fragment of magenta-tinted paper sticking to the tape in the bottom of the wastebasket.

20

AS SOON AS HE entered the lobby, Bud Fallon was uncomfortable. The smells, the chiming, muted intercom, gleaming linoleum floors, stainless steel wainscot bumpers down the corridors all swept back to him ten-year-old memories of the last time he had set foot in a hospital. Wisps of long vigils on plastic couches, holding a wasted hand beside a curtained bed, listening to the labored breathing, hoping for death to release her, and the crushing feeling of guilt when it did all brushed across his mind.

He followed the nurse's aide assigned to direct him to the staff offices, picking up the tempo of his walk to keep the rushing girl in sight. Her shoes squished softly as she trotted along. Why do they always seem to be in such a hurry? he thought as he sidestepped to avoid colliding with a huge rotary floor polisher moaning its whispery daylight rounds like some chromium snail leaving a glistening scalloped track on the waxed yellow surface of the corridor.

Down the hall a few paces the aide had stopped, holding a walnut-paneled door open for him.

"Just have a seat in here, sir. Dr. Yancey will be up in a minute."

He entered the room and turned to thank his guide, but she was gone. There were nearly a dozen comfortable-looking armchairs around a long dark table, but Fallon elected to stand. The prospect of sitting alone to wait again for a doctor in a hospital evoked a discomfort he chose to leave unanalyzed.

He walked to the windowed wall opposite and stared at nothing in the rain-slick darkness of the street.

"Hello, Bud Fallon."

He turned to acknowledge the speaker, a short, pleasant-faced woman smiling up at him with an impish light in her eye. He could not guess her age; forty to fifty was as close as he would speculate.

"Dr. Yancey?"

"Well, Bud, since I'm obstetrics, you don't qualify as a patient. So, you can be here for only one of two reasons: one, you want to sell your old airplane to a rich fool of a doctor; or two, you are short on students and you want to teach this old chick to fly!"

Fallon was completely taken aback by the peppery monolog. He swallowed and nearly stammered.

"I'm sorry, Doctor; I wasn't aware that we had met before. I should remem—. . . "

"We haven't—directly, that is—but Ann and Jim have told me enough tales about you for the past year to make me feel like I have. By the way, you look exactly like they described you." She cocked her head sidewise to give him a thorough up-and-down scrutiny. "Well, I'm not surprised—not pleased, mind you, but not disappointed either!"

Fallon discovered, to his mild chagrin, that his jaw was hanging slack. For some reason he felt an instant liking for this strange woman, whom he had known only vaguely as a good friend and boss of Ann Regan. It was apparent that she had not heard about Jim, and when she did, a little of that exuberance would be dampened for a long time.

"Dr. Yancey, I'm afraid. . . . "

"Please call me Mildred, Bud." Her tone had softened. She *is* quick, he thought; already she knows it's bad news.

He nodded. "OK, Mildred. The reason I'm here is for Annie. . . . " He stopped, aware that he had slipped into the diminutive form of her name.

Mildred ventured mildly, "You'd better not let her hear you call her that."

He laughed unhappily. "Guess I slipped. They seem so much like kids to me. Look, Mildred, Ann is gonna need some extra help for a while from you folks here at the hospital. You see, we think Jim may have gone in—up in the Sierras."

Fallon paused, allowing her time to absorb the shock. After a moment he knew it was not necessary. Mildred Yancey waited, silent, a professional listener, as he gave her all the information he had. All the while her attention never wavered, her expression never changed. But he could see the pain stab, from the start, deep within her eyes.

She said not a word throughout his entire briefing, nor after he had finished. She did pause a moment to lay her hand on his arm, which was tightly crossed with the other across his chest. He had not realized how tense he was until then, standing rigid, hugging his upper torso as though it bled. He felt her touch through the thickness of the jacket sleeve, and some of the tension slipped away.

She was on the phone then at the end of the room. "Randy? Mildred. Be a dear and cover me in ER for an hour or two? I'll call in when I get to a phone." She listened a moment then added, "I'm going in a friend's car, so mine will be here. That won't be a sign that I've returned. Thanks."

They were a block away from the parking lot before she spoke again, her eyes squinting through the truck windshield as though she, not he, were driving. "You don't like hospitals much, do you, Bud?"

Fallon turned a quizzical look in her direction. "I'm not qualified to judge. I haven't been in one for ten years."

"Was it a long illness?"

"Oh, it wasn't me. I haven't been sick much."

"I mean your wife. It was an ordeal for both of you, I take it." She met his startled eyes with a compassionate look.

"I remember Ann saying she had heard from someone at the airport that your wife had died some time ago. The rest I just sensed about you, that's all."

He eased the truck to the curb, set the brake, and killed the engine. Peering through the now-blurring windshield up to the second-floor flat where Jim ought to be, he answered, "More for her than for me. She was sick a long time—nearly six months. We both knew how it would end right at the start. I'd stay with her most of the time, especially toward the end when they took her in—to the hospital." He stopped, gritting his teeth to retain his objective tone.

"She would pretend to sleep for hours at a time, trying to give me a break, I guess, but I always knew she was just keeping still, fighting back the pain." Again he paused, biting at his lip. "Sometimes I would leave; she needed time to cry without the worry of its hurting me. But we both knew what was going on, right up to the end. We never could fool each other much, ever." He reached for the dash and pushed out the lights.

Then he turned to her and said, "I think we'd better go up and see what we can do for Ann."

"What was her name, Bud?"

"Sarah."

"Sarah. A strong name."

"Yes."

They were deep in thought as they climbed the rickety stairs to the Regan apartment. Strangely, neither was preoccupied with what they had been discussing. But both were somehow glad that now they could better cope with what would have to be done for Ann.

The woman who answered the door was a stranger to both Mildred and Bud. For an awkward moment the three were about to exchange social credentials when Ann broke off a conversation with Thad Monte and made introductions. Ann was halfway through the names when she realized she and Shirley were still blocking entry to the newcomers. Once they were sorted out, to the accompaniment of nervous, restrained laughter, Bud asked Ann, "Any new word?"

"No, Bud," she answered quietly. "I really don't expect to hear much of anything until daylight. Weather expects partial clearing sometime late tomorrow. Unless someone flying on top picks up an ELT, there isn't much to wait for."

Shirley Monte spoke up, her face reflecting a desperate hope, "I was telling Ann before you came in that Jim might have made a precautionary landing at some airport without a telephone. He might call any time now."

Bud remained silent. Ann looked at her old friend and smiled at his abstaining vote on Shirley's speculation. She continued looking at Bud though she spoke to Shirley, "No, Shirley, Jim would not let this much time go by. He would have notified somebody to get in touch with search and rescue by now, if it were humanly possible. He knows how much risk an overdue flight causes others." Bud Fallon gravely nodded his corroboration.

Ann looked back to Shirley and the others. "I think we must assume that Jim did crash-land somewhere—probably in the mountains, and work from there."

"Ann, I need to talk shop with you for a minute," Mildred Yancey broke in suddenly. "Let's go back to the bedroom. Excuse us, folks." It was definitely a command, and it was abrupt; but Mildred was one of those rare people who could take charge in an emergency without giving offense.

When they were alone she came directly to the point. "As of now you are on emergency leave from your nursing duties. Take as much time as you need. Also, you have just graduated from the program . . . don't interrupt, please . . . a month early. The exams are waived. They would just be a formality in your case anyway. Jim and I have been trying to get you to slow down in your greedy pursuit of knowledge, and this is as good a time as any." She took a breath and went on as though she were briefing an agent for an espionage assignment. "Beginning tomorrow you will commence drawing regular starting R.N. pay. The state license exam can be taken next spring. In the meantime you're hired as a Graduate Nurse; I'll make out and sign the certificate of graduation tonight."

When Mildred finally wound down and stopped, Ann was speechless. "Any questions?" the older woman asked.

Ann shook her head and countered, "Mildred, you can't do . . . "

"Never say 'can't,' especially to people like me—*and you*!" she snapped. "Now, if that nice Bud Fallon will take me back to the hospital, I'll get my things and my car and come back to spend the night. The couch will do nicely.

Randy Jacobs has agreed to cover my emergency room
stint."

Ann reached out to take her hand. "Thanks for that,
too, my friend, but I have to handle this one alone—at
least for now."

They returned to the living room to find that Shirley,
Thad, and Bud had switched on the television to catch the
seven o'clock news. The weather had preempted many
items and was, in this semi-desert ski-conscious community, the Big News. A bespectacled forecaster was animated almost to breathlessness as he rushed from chart to
tables to graphs to satellite pictures, piecing together a
glowing report of recreational snow on the ground with
the happy promise of more on the way.

Bud Fallon was more interested in the radar charts,
which showed areas of heavy precipitation, and in the satellite photos than he was in the commentator's monolog.
He was amazed at the extent of rain, and therefore snow,
activity. The storm had dumped massive amounts of
moisture from Tijuana, Mexico, to Mount Lassen in
northern California. When the hour-old space picture of
the West Coast was flashed on the small screen, he took
some comfort in noting that the cyclonic comma cloud had
already moved partly through the Sierra Nevadas. The
center of the low appeared to be positioned somewhat east
of the range. That would mean clearing sometime before
daylight. Maybe they would be able to begin searching the
grids at dawn tomorrow.

The commentator's voice broke in on his thoughts.
"And now, good viewers, here's the rest of our
Thanksgiving present to the snow bunnies. We will have a
short period of clearing—just enough to open up the roads
to all your favorite ski resorts . . . and *then*, folks," pointing
to a new photograph showing much of the Central Pacific
Ocean, "just look, will you, at all this weather coming in

starting day after tomorrow. It looks like we will be having snow every other day at least up 'til Thanksgiving."

Fallon nearly gasped. He had never seen such a procession of potentially evil weather outside of aerology textbooks. Tomorrow may be our only chance, he thought miserably. By tomorrow night—what's tomorrow?—Friday—by Saturday morning at the latest those peaks and valleys will be socked in until the following weekend. Damn! He almost said it aloud. As it was his lips were drawn back in a grimace over clenched teeth.

Too late he looked over at Ann. She had been watching him throughout the weathercast. She smiled sadly in his direction, almost as if she were feeling sorrier for him. Her voice was low, almost a whisper, but it rang clear over the babel from the TV, "It doesn't matter, Bud. He's alive, and I know that you will find him."

It was after nine o'clock before everyone left, reluctant, despite her protestations that she would be quite all right, to let Ann spend the night alone. Mildred Yancey and Bud Fallon discussed the matter while he drove her back to the hospital to resume her duty as the physician-in-charge of the emergency room. Both agreed that Ann was of the disposition and stability to handle the emergency alone. Jim's chances for survival were a different matter. Dr. Yancey was most concerned with getting as much frank opinion out of Bud as she could.

"What's the bottom line, Bud?" she asked finally.

Bud thought for a while before he answered. He had not really considered the odds—had not permitted himself to consider them would be more accurate. Finally he spoke in a voice graveled with the barest edge of emotion, "We always presume that there will be a survivor; it helps to keep us on our toes while involved in the search. Of course, the intellect pushes in sometimes insisting that one situation is more hopeless than another. There are times that the only thing that keeps us looking, wearing out our engines and eyeballs, is the hope that we can find the wreck and get the victims a decent burial—for the sake of surviving loved ones, you know." He paused again. "As far as Jim's chances are concerned, on the face of the information we have—weather, terrain, other things—I'd have to give him maybe a ten percent chance."

"Of survival?"

"Of survival."

"That's not much to go on," Mildred murmured almost to herself.

"No, it sure as hell isn't," he growled, using mild anger to keep deeper emotions from welling up. "And the odds will get worse with each hour that goes by until we can locate him."

"You are thinking about the weather—exposure. Has he had any experience in survival techniques?"

"Only the barest fundamentals; some stuff I showed him as part of his flight training. How much stuck in his head I can only guess at. I don't think he ever had much chance to camp as a boy. He's strictly a flatlander, born in the shadow of the Sierras but like so many kids in southern California, his exposure defenses are limited mostly to how much suntan oil to use at the beach."

"But if he stays with the airplane, surely that will give him some measure of protection."

Bud nodded. "If the cabin is not all broken up, if he can find enough to wrap up in to keep warm, and the biggest if—if he's not hurt much from the landing."

They fell silent, sitting in the nearly deserted hospital parking lot.

"Do you want to know what the official odds are for survival, according to the FAA?" he asked suddenly.

"I have the distinct feeling I should say 'No' at this point, but I'm hooked on gathering life statistics."

"Average time for an uninjured person is seventy-two hours. It is so low a survival time because exposure takes its toll. That figure includes crashes in all kinds of conditions, including balmy summer days."

"What is the time for a survivor who is injured in the crash?"

"Average life expectancy: twenty-four hours," he responded flatly.

"Dear God," she gasped.

Fallon lifted his wrist so that the street light fell on the face of his watch; it was quarter to ten.

"Jim has been in the snow for eleven hours already," he said quietly.

21

SHIRLEY MONTE SLIPPED INTO bed beside her husband and lay rigidly on her back. She smoothed the counterpane across her breasts and spoke to Thad via the ceiling of their night-lighted bedroom, "He's dead, isn't he, Thad?"

"I'm afraid so, Hon," he answered softly. "There is always a chance, but an unreported flight in this kind of weather almost always ends up that way."

"I have this unreasonable kind of anger—outrage— that it had to happen to such nice kids. My God, what did they do to deserve this kind of treatment? They were just getting started after all that hard work. Did you hear what she said about the airline call?"

"U.S. Airways?"

"Yes, I think so. . . . It's so goddam unfair! They worked themselves silly so that he could get a decent job with an airline. Then, of all days, the call that he's accepted has to come today."

"It's a shame, all right. Too bad they hadn't called last week, or even yesterday; he would probably still be here today."

"It's like God is just sitting up there setting us up to chop us down. I'd like to ask Reverend Barton about *that* this Sunday; how come the good kids take it in the chops while rich slobs have it easy."

"Cut it out, Hon."

"What do you mean, 'cut it out'? That's the way it is, isn't it?"

"I mean . . . cut it out because you are making me feel lousier than I already feel."

"Well, I'm thinking how poor Ann must feel. How is she going to face up to the fact that Jim is just some . . . thing, freezing in the snow God knows where. No amount of money is going to make up for losing her husband."

"There won't be any money either," he said grimly.

Shirley was silent for a moment, unsure of what he meant. Suddenly she feared she might have caught his drift. "Oh, my God, Thad, you don't mean that . . ."

"The pilot isn't covered by the insurance policy," he confessed miserably. "Only passengers."

His words struck her like a blow. She was faintly sick, but had to make the accusation. "You mean that the airplane was covered but not the crew? How could you in conscience write such a binder? God in Heaven, Thad, they are our *friends*!"

His voice was so low she knew it had been twisting in him all evening like a knife, ever since he had read the policy through, and she felt loving pity for him for his pain, but loathing for his omission. "The crew was covered only for medical care up to a thousand; no death benefit for an agent or employee. It is our standard policy," he finished lamely.

It was well into morning before the Montes succumbed

to sleep. During all those miserable intervening hours they never spoke . . . or touched.

At 11:30 Ann snapped off the TV, having watched with deepening apprehension a rehash of the weather forecast. She dialed the Flight Service number for the fifth time that day to see if there was any additional information for her to hang a hope on. The best they could do for her, however, was to confirm that the air search would begin at first light as long as the weather held clear. After thanking the specialist, who was a new man with whom she had not spoken before but a most understanding and supportive person, she hung up secure in the knowledge that they would call at any hour, good news or bad.

She picked up a wrinkled cigaret package off the night-stand and tried to shake out one more smoke before undressing for bed. When nothing but a few crumbs of tobacco rewarded her effort, she looked at the empty pack with disbelief. She could not remember ever smoking an entire pack of cigarets in one day.

Walking to the living room again, she snapped the lock on the door, switched off the only lighted lamp and circled back to the bedroom. She undressed and slipped on the flannel gown she had worn the night before. Vaguely she thought it would be time tomorrow to strip the bed and take the clothes to the laundromat. I'll shower in the morning, she thought, setting the alarm for five. She did not want to be asleep in case somebody called.

As she pulled down the covers on her side of the bed, she avoided looking across to the other side and slipped between the sheets quickly. She snapped off the lamp and lay on her right side staring at the blackness toward the unseen wall near the bed. It was totally dark, inky without perspective—and a bit frightening. She had forgotten to turn on the dim nightlight in the hallway through the door on Jim's side. Still supine, she closed her eyes, hoping that the darkness would seem normal and she would be able to drift off.

After several minutes, she flung off the covers, snapped on the bedside lamp, swung out her legs, stood, and marched purposefully to the hall and turned on the nightlight. As she strode back into the room, she kept her gaze fixed on the lamp but felt her head drawn to his side of the bed.

She turned out the lamp and lay flat on her back, waiting for her eyes to adjust to the darkened room, lightened now by the feeble glow from the hallway. As objects began materializing into familiar and comforting shapes, she relaxed a bit, allowing her muscles to yield to the lumpy support of the mattress.

She forced herself to dwell on practical, solvable things: when the air search would start, when she would do the laundry, remembering to put some gas in the car because, as usual, Jim had forgotten to . . . getting another pack of cigarets, going to the bank . . .

She closed her eyes again because they had adjusted so well to the dim room that she was beginning to see his lampshade out of the corner of her left eye.

It was a lost cause, and she knew it. She had never gone to sleep on her back in her entire life, and since they had married, she never slept on her right side unless they went to bed mad at each other. She put that out of her mind quickly. "This is ridiculous!" she said aloud and regretted immediately the sound of her own voice.

Turning deliberately on her left side, she willed herself to look directly at the still-unmussed side where he should have been. OK, she thought, see; he's not there now, but he will be tomorrow, so forgot it and get some sleep.

But she made the mistake of pulling up her knees and reaching out her arm to snuggle closer to the middle of the bed. For a devastating second she could almost feel the curve of his back against her breast and his buttocks in her lap. She smelled his fragrance then upon the sheets and pillow case, and suddenly her yearning drained away to an eviscerated repose.

Some moments later she reached out and slowly drew his pillow to her bosom. Half clutching, half caressing it, she wept.

22

WHY DIDN'T HE take the time to pull up his pants? He must have hit his head on the bed when he fell, legs all tangled in his pajama bottoms. God! They must be twisted tight around his leg. Stupid to fall asleep like that with the circulation all cut off. He lay there gasping with the pain that throbbed between his head and leg, somewhere. Where was the pain? He tried to concentrate his thoughts, tried to trace it down; his brain reached clumsy fingers out, running down the nerves, but he never got past his thigh before the effort caused his head to pound again. Then there were two pains pumping from opposite ends, out of synch . . .

Desperately he reached for the prop controls, little levered knobs sprouting from his chest. He'd have to squeeze those props in synch before the passengers complained. God! What a throbbing buzz! It was driving him crazy.

Where was Bud Fallon? Bud . . . Bud . . . Give me a
hand here, willya. Trim off the pressure on that right rudder. My God this is a terrible airplane . . . engines out of
synch and all rigged wrong. Help me, Bud . . . cramp in my
leg . . . more right rudder . . . left wing dropping . . . we're
going into a spin . . . God, I'm gettin' sick . . .

The pain blended in with giddy nausea and he slipped
backward into bed again, reaching for the drawstring of his
pajama pants. It was thick, and cold, and metal-hard, and
wrapped around his leg. Ann, please get your scissors and
cut this stupid cord.

He felt her stir beside him in the bed and wondered
why she was sleeping on his left. The effort of thinking
started up the headache once again and he let it go at that,
lying still to let the pounding lessen in his brain.

A rush of cold air brought him back. He pouted,
pushing out his closed lips a little, but they cracked and
stung. Why did she always throw the covers off like that
when she got up to do her shift at the hospital and freeze
him to death?

He felt her grab his foot. What was she doing? Not
tickle his right foot! Ann, Ann . . . She doesn't know about
the cord! Oh, be careful. Please don't move the leg until
you cut the cord. How cold her fingers felt, and thin. He
heard her grunt a funny, happy-sounding word he did not
understand, and when she zippered the quilt over him
again he let himself fall back to sleep.

Charity Whiteflower gently tucked the folds of the
down sleeping bag loosely under her sleeping patient,
making sure his face had a clear airway. She felt around the
carpeted floor of the airplane near the sleeping bag until
she found a stub of candle set into a collapsing metal
drinking cup. From a pants pocket she withdrew a packet
of wooden matches. With stiff fingers she selected one
and struck it alight on the match box. As she brought the

flame to the candle wick, its light reflected brilliantly from the foil walls of an improvised tent fashioned from several "space blankets."

Holding the light above Jim's face she inspected the bruise above his eyes and noted with satisfaction that the swelling had decreased somewhat from the day before. The cut that traversed the bruised and puffy flesh had begun to heal almost from the first day. It would barely leave a scar.

Fearful that she might disturb his rest, she lowered the candle and placed it on the floor a foot or so from where he slept. Near his feet she located a laced portion of the makeshift tent, undid the ties, and crawled on all fours into the colder open area of the passenger cabin.

It was dimly light inside the fuselage of the crippled plane, soft light barely visible through the side windows. She would have to open up the door again today, she thought. More snow must have fallen to cover the windows she had cleaned off the day before.

Yesterday she had had a moment of panic, when the door had refused to budge with its weight of snow. Her waning strength had not been enough to lift it. She had spent most of the morning struggling, fearful that they might lie trapped under a deepening layer of snow. In the end she had managed to pry it up, the upper half only, by using an axe she found in a canvas pack on one of the seats. Since then she had not latched the door. She was content to put up with the loss of heat as a fair trade to ensure access to the open air and essential ventilation.

This time the hatch swung up with little difficulty. It was still snowing lightly as she gazed from her tiny dutch doorway across the waist-high drifts to the far side of the lake.

Charity was content. He would recover with strength and beauty. In the first days she had not been certain. That

he was in the strong sleep so long was not good, but now
the sign that he would wake again was on him. True, he
had not made sign, nor words, nor even look-spoke to her
in all this time. That was because his mind was with the
Spirit to be healed, and would return when his swollen
head had room for it again. Just now he had tried to put it
back too soon, and it was squeezed and made his throat
make hurt-noise like the injured rabbit.

She smiled secretly to herself and turned shyly to look
at the tiny tipi where he slept. That would be her
strength-over-him which he would never know—that she
had heard his moan slip past the strong teeth of his manhood.

It was good!

Even his leg was straight and mending. She had pulled
it hard and felt the clicking of the broken part the first day
when he sent his mind away to heal. Now it would be true
as the sapling shaft she had found before the snow got
deep, and trimmed and bound to the leg to help the knit-
ting bones find their way to straightness.

Stepping to the foil-like enclosure she had rigged
over the sleeping bag she opened the seam again to look
at him and check that the burning candle was not in a
position to scorch either the bag or the tent. The small
flame burned low and steady, giving off a multiplied light
from the thousand facets of the wrinkled enclosure.
Memories of holy images crowded in on her, filling her
mind with conflicting moods. She stared at the light, so
like a votive candle in that church long ago, and she could
hear vague whispers of a choir, their melodies strangely
mixing in a fugue of joy and sadness, blending with the
cloying fumes of incense.

She looked again at the figure huddled asleep in the
oversize mummy bag and she was struck with the unset-

tling bier-like nature of the scene. Her mood switched sharply morose, and to satisfy herself she crawled within the tent to check the man's breathing and color.

Reassured that he was fine, she backed out on hands and knees and carefully closed the lacings once again.

Charity was amazed at how much colder it was outside the little tent. It must have been many degrees below freezing inside the airplane, colder than that outside, but that single candle flame, augmented by their body heat and insulated by the foil-layered walls of the shelter, had raised the temperature to the point of actual comfort.

An urgency now animated Charity's activities. She bustled about the confining space of the cabin with the enthusiasm of a twenty-year-old and the pace of a septuagenarian. It was a pathetic exercise played out by an old woman cast in the role of a debutant primping for an expected gentleman caller.

She completed her "dry-camp" toilet quickly, combing and then braiding her long hair carefully into two gray plaits, which hung over each ear and draped in front of her shoulders. Then, because the chill was beginning to penetrate her sleep-warmed body, she put on the heavy parka stowed on one of the forward seats. Her hands were beginning to ache with the cold, but she endured the discomfort, buoyed up by an inner warmth. After disposing of their accumulated waste by tossing it out the open hatch, she cleansed the container by swabbing it with snow.

Sorting through her own supplies and those she had found in the airplane she completed an inventory of the foodstuffs available to them. It was a reasonable collection, enough to keep them alive for many days as long as they were prudently rationed.

Some of the equipment was foreign to her experience.

There were items that smelled like fireworks, cylinders and tubes, and a gun-like thing with a fat, stubby barrel. Other hardware—fishing gear, tools, and assorted cables and polished metal items—did not interest her, but she stowed them carefully away in the knowledge that when he awoke he would find uses for them.

The food situation had begun to worry her. Her own small store of provisions was nearly exhausted. She had started out on her strange quest with only the lightest supply of simple fare, an odd assortment of basic cereals and fruits combined with commercial varieties of breakfast bars and dehydrated soups. There was a small packet of jerky which she found she could not chew, but occasionally cut up into bits to suck on or add as flavor to the soup.

Now a week had passed and these items were nearly depleted. As she squatted by the half-open door, sorting and repacking, she strained to think just where she had been heading seven days before. Try as she might, the thought slipped out of reach, blotted from her consciousness by the great marvel of her finding him again. The incongruities of her own age and the very airplane she was in contrasting with life so many years before simply never crossed her mind. It was as though the intervening time had slipped by in a month.

For two days now she had been able to feed him small quantities of broth. Charity managed this by spooning it into his mouth and massaging his throat until he swallowed. It was a tedious process made more difficult by her apprehension that he might choke, but she labored at it knowing that he must have nourishment or he would weaken further and she would lose him as before.

She was an imaginative and conservative camper almost by nature. Although there was a small primus stove in the survival pack she had found, she seemed not to know how to operate it, and opted for more primitive alternatives. The generous supply of stubby candles was a godsend, and she combined their use with some pine branches scavenged before the onset of the heavy fall of snow to build small cooking fires on a piece of torn wing panel. These she set before the cabin door opening, directly on the metal floor, which she had bared by cutting away a large circle of the light carpeting. The scrap of wing aluminum was actually a rude stove resembling a flower basket with a large flat handle formed from the ends of the piece and bent up over the firepot. She had crimped the ends of the pliable metal together, providing a fragile support for small containers directly over the scant flames.

Charity glanced at a neatly piled stack of deadwood sticks near the doorway. There were a few handfuls left, enough for cooking fires for two more days. Like her every other action, firemaking was a frugal undertaking. She contrived to use just enough fuel to complete the cooking task and no more. Without considering the comfortable alternative of building a fire large enough to warm herself as well, she applied practicality to the problem with the instinctive need to conserve what little she had managed to snatch from the storm. She would be warm enough if she kept busy, dry, and properly dressed, but the cooking fires were essential to the man's recovery.

She wondered if she might be able to get more branches from the broken limb and leaned out of the door, twisting her neck to look back and up to where it lay across the crumpled tail of the plane. There were some small branches about the thickness of her fingers which would be ideal, but they were far out of reach, even if she could manage to flounder through the waist-deep powder and climb upon the horizontal tail-plane. With displeasure creased into the lines of her wrinkled face, she grunted and shook the idea from her mind.

Later. There was much to do for now. The problem
would resolve itself in time. She placed it in the care of the
Great One of the Mountain. Let him worry about it! There
is enough for me to do anyway, she thought testily.

A low moan behind her brought her quickly back inside, and she scurried over to the cocoon-like tent. It took
longer to open the lacings this time, because her fingers
had become rubbery numb with the cold. Finally she was
able to open the seam and peer inside, taking pains to keep
the opening small to prevent the precious candle heat from
escaping.

From the far end of the enclosure two eyes, reflecting
the tranquil votive flame, glittered feverishly back at her.
She watched the pupils labor into focus and knew that he
was truly looking at her and not blinking rapidly as he had
before. There was no sign of recognition though, and,
suddenly embarrassed under his gaze, she wondered if she
should speak.

Her personal, and tribal, taciturnity prevailed and she
kept silent.

When he is one again he will want to speak, she
thought. It is the old way. I will wait for him to speak his
thoughts of me. After the hurt has left his head there will
be room for soft things he will want to tell me of.

She was at his feet kneeling on the floor in the partly
opened tent. Avoiding his eyes with averted glances, she
busied herself with the candle and the sleeping bag, tucking in loose ends around his legs. At last, satisfied that he
must be aware of her presence, she withdrew without a
look or sound and laced the seam snugly as before.

Before long the sound of a small twig-fire blended with
her soft crooning voice intoning a melody that had not
been heard near the Great Mountain for more than a
hundred years.

My, God, she has to quit that job! What were they doing to her? How she's aged. You don't have to push yourself so, Ann. Dear Ann, he choked on a sob. She floated over to him, reaching out to cut that goddam pajama cord, but she looked so haggard. Oh, close your mouth; he reached out tenderly with his hand to touch that dear chin. Where are all her beautiful teeth? Dear God, I've got to tell her that her teeth are falling out, she doesn't know, oh, don't go to that butcher dentist Charlie Wise, he'll ruin you for sure.

He felt hot again and saw Ann swirl backward in a silver whirlpool and vanish through a puckered little hole. He watched the shimmering silver-paneled sea and felt the left wing fall out again in a helpless wingover to a flat inverted spin. Let go of it! Let go! Let the stupid thing fly itself out this time. He watched his stomach whirling till at last it caught and slowed the spinning wings and he wasn't sick anymore. A gush of sweat released him so violently he could hear small tubes popping open in his brain.

He woke thinking a groan but caught a grip on it before it reached his throat, and very cautiously opened his eyes.

Jim had trouble focusing his eyes. Try as he might, he could not force them to work properly. He felt drugged, the circuitry between brain and eye somehow misrouted. He blinked to clear the fuzzy picture but it was no use. Somehow the incoming pictures could not be willed into sharp detail. He was trapped in a control room looking at a television screen whose cameraman had gone to sleep.

He stared upward at the covering above his head but could not make it out. His range of vision, even at the point of sharpest focus, was of a uniform gauze-diffused vagueness. The walls and ceiling seemed to glow softly with a thousand tiny lights muted and yellowish. A delicate

warm odor permeated the space and he thought incongruously of a crayon-hard slab of margarine melting in a frying
pan—more crayon than margarine. The vision of an
omelette filled his mind, fluffy eggs with bits and pieces of
broken crayon oozing red and green into melted puddles
dotting the yellow mass.

He had nearly become sick thinking about it when the
idea of melting wax pushed the image from his slowly
spinning brain and replaced it with the first logical thought
he had developed in nearly five days. The realization of
this fact, that he *was* thinking, was electrifying. He struggled to maintain consciousness by clutching at the idea and
holding it above the swirling vertigo that lay just behind
his eyelids.

"Hot wax," he whispered almost soundlessly and without articulation, deep in the back of his throat. Like a
one-year-old balancing blocks, he kept a fierce grip on that
concept as he groped for another that he could build on
and give it meaning. His eyes were begging to be closed;
each second of the baffling array of lights pumped up the
monster headache he must have had for years now. He
would not yield. To close them would release the clutch
and he would spin off again into a dizzy vortex of uncon-
trol.

"Candle!" He mouthed the word and nearly smiled in
triumph. "Candle," he repeated softly in agreement with
himself, pulling his chin down in an almost imperceptible
nod.

Another idea, one that excited him even as it was
forming, took shape. Jim nearly had it under enough control to examine when the sheer effort of concentration
became too much to bear. The eyelids dropped and he
groaned under the weight of his spinning nausea. Hating
himself for his weakness, he bowed to the inexorable pull
of insensibility and the release it offered from his pain.

This time however, a flickering knowledge that he would awaken again pulled the corners of his mouth up in triumph.

Then the great sprouting horror clump of pain was under him. It filled all the cavities of his mind and finally, mercifully, shorted out his brain.

23

SOMETIME DURING the night the wind had shifted. The great gray blanket of clouds was stretched thin and torn apart by the ragged white teeth of the leviathan range. As the storm moved east it trailed a tattered edge of harmless stratus fabric. Behind the retreating weather, blobs of fragile cumulus fought a delaying action against the clearing sky, racing like corvettes to gain the safety of the mother cloud before they were absorbed by the drying air of the pursuing high pressure system.

In the first graying of dawn, the great moutain looked like an active volcano spewing a banner of smoke nearly a mile downwind. Huge drifts of snow, piled in unstable terraced steps around the peak, were being undercut now by the reversing wind. As the light increased, the windspeed intensified, whipping huge scoops of powder into towering snow dervishes wildly dancing along the ridge. Occasionally a drift, weakened by the eroding currents of frigid air, would collapse in upon itself and trigger a series of avalanches. Then the eruption would take on the proportions of firestorm ripping tons of cold fuel from the mountain flanks and blasting the stuff into a giant cloud mushrooming into the raging wind.

At this great height, sunrise came earlier than in the meadows and along the lake shores thousands of feet lower. When the sun did finally strike the peak with its first rays, the spectacle from the darker elevations was truly breathtaking. The entire mountaintop and its gushing plume flamed scarlet, and at a distance its close-range violence was transformed into lazy, silent brilliance.

Had he not been a creature of scent, and therefore nearsighted, the cat might have been distracted from his discomfort by the scene. The narrow cave in which he had waited out the storm looked out upon the lake, the trail on the far side that he had crossed the week before, and in the distance the sun-bathed mountaintop.

He had stumbled upon the cave after the snow had become quite deep, and it was fortunate because he had not found so much as a bird to stave off the hunger which by now had turned ravenous. No more than a slit in the face of a tumbled wall of rock, the cave opened up to more generous dimensions inside, and it was floored with earth and trash. It had been used by other animals in the past, but his luck had held. He had not had to fight for its shelter by evicting existing tenants.

Throughout the storm the cougar had slept to conserve the scant fat on which he depended now. With the smell of clear weather he was up and eager for a kill.

Pausing at the opening, he seemed somewhat disconcerted by the immense white desolation, and he turned back once to look in upon the security and comfort of the rock-lined room. The hackles rose briefly along his spine in acknowledgement of the cold, then he carefully padded out, picking his way along the ridge from rock to rock. A few hundred yards from the cave where the elevated spur gave out, he paused. An easy, snow-dusted trail led off to the left, but after sniffing the air for a moment he chose instead the more heavily drifted course to his right. This latter path was upwind; the scent of any prey within range of his prowling would drift down to him long before it became aware of his presence. His choice was not thought out, of course; it was the net result of all the factors affecting him today: breeding, hunger, the cold and snow, instinct. He had not developed the individual hunting patterns sometimes found in older, shrewder mountain cats. These would find their way into his brain many seasons into the future—if he was able to survive the incidents that would be his learning environment.

Uninformed observers of the cougar floundering in the deep powder, snarling occasionally when he sagged into a particularly heavy drift, might have thought he was at play. He certainly displayed none of his customary grace as he pulled himself through the snow. It was a grim and serious business, though, and each time his head and shoulders popped up, the yellow eyes narrowed and black nostrils flared. When the first airborne message came, he would not miss it.

At one hundred sixty pounds the cat was heavier than average for his age, but underweight for his frame. By the next summer, after a game-plentiful spring guaranteed by this winter's bounteous snowpack, he should fill out to thirty pounds above his present weight. Even at his present size he was probably the largest mountain lion in the state.

For six hours he struggled upwind, bounding clumsily through the snow. The scent his nostrils yearned for was catalogued deep in the reflex-memory of his brain. Fleshed out, the specifications would detail a fat deer, on the smallish side; probably a doe weakened and slow after a week's exhausting forage in the bad weather.

Finally, something told him it was no use. He climbed onto a boulder that had been swept nearly clean of snow by the freshening wind and shook the snow powder from his rusty coat. With the fastidiousness of a Persian he leisurely gnawed away a few ice pellets from his foot pads and proceeded to wipe the wetness from his body with forepaws and tongue.

Finished with his grooming, he sat for a moment and surveyed the lower ground, which sloped away between a scattering of stunted trees and abruptly flattened out to the broad white surface of the frozen lake. The wind was beginning to worry the snow in that open area, driving it into occasional clouds that rolled up and then subsided into long, sweeping airborne ribbons snaking downwind across the blanketed ice.

The cat did not note this. What he was looking for did not appear and he growled petulantly and yawned. The chill of the wind at his back pushed him into action finally and he crouched forward on the boulder, inching lower over the rounded granite until forced to spring.

He landed in a shoulder-high drift and snarled disapproval. The snow would be lighter down near the lake where the small game lived. He plunged lower, picking the easier route now, because the wind was from his flank. Surprise would be gone, but it did not matter. He would simply follow tracks when he found them and easily run the smaller creatures down. There was no demeaning self-reproach in this lesser hunt. The beast was hungry and would not scorn any game as ignoble. To down a deer would have been more practical because it would have fed him for a week, after he had dragged it back to the cave for safekeeping. This business with rodents was time-consuming, a mere tradeoff of energy for nourishment, not his preferred livelihood.

On the way back toward the cave he worked the

shoreline methodically like a hound, keeping up a zigzag pattern to avoid missing any trail. Once he stumbled on a covey of birds huddled in the lee of a low bush. They surprised him with an explosion of snow and feathers as they scrambled frantically to become airborne almost under his nose. His reflex had been good. Leaping after the drumming wings, he managed to bat one a glancing sideways blow. Stunned, the quail foundered into a branch and tumbled to earth. In his eagerness for the kill, the cat misjudged his leap by inches and the bird literally brushed his nose as it fluttered into the air and darted to safety through the trees and blowing snow.

Rising from his compromised sprawl the cougar hissed a rasping, hateful sound in the bird's direction and resumed his hunt. The eyes which gleamed from slitted lids had paled to a more baleful cunning now than they had ever shone in his short life.

For several hours longer, well into twilight, he prowled along the lake edge. The wind had calmed somewhat and he sensed an urgency for stealth again. Burrowing things might venture now in the short evening respite from the blowing snow to strip some weighted branch of tender bark or nibble at the frozen tips of drifted bushes. He would have little time. Already the cold was settling in, and small animals would burrow deep until the morning sun made life above ground survivable again.

Even he had been trembling in the biting cold for some time. The exertion of his prowl provided little heat, because he was living off muscle now, not fat. The cave with its lure of relative warmth and bed of litter beckoned, and he swung left, away from the lake, in a surly gait toward higher ground and the security of his tumbled rocky ridge.

He nearly missed seeing the rabbit. It was downwind, off to his right. The big cat froze, the hackles rising behind his ears. In a fluid movement he turned and flattened himself in the snow. Once he had the animal in sight he locked on the target like a heat-seeking rocket. The rabbit was in distress. It was floundering in the snow, unable to make headway. The prospect of an easy kill did not affect the cougar's strategy; however, he moved with an intensity and stealth he had never exercised before. Saliva formed at the root of his tongue.

He was ill-humored, hungry, and he was learning.

As she waited through the long hours since she had set the snare, Charity cast frequent glances at the tent. A great confusion had settled over her since early morning when he had awakened. She had been sleeping in the confined space of the large bag with him as before. As before she had slept intermittently throughout the night. The difficulty of sharing his bed without disturbing him in the process had to be overcome at the cost of her own severe discomfort. It was necessary no matter how cramped and stiff the long nights left her. The cold was an adversary he could not possibly outfight alone, especially at night when the temperature plummeted and the chill pressed down upon them like death itself.

If the truth were known, she probably needed their mutual warmth as much as he. The headlong rush when she had seen the plane tear itself to pieces in the trees had undone her severely, and all the days since had taken their toll. She was not aware of her diminishing strength, however, because in the regressed timeless frame of her reference, those virtually meaningless years since the auto crash were blotted out. She had—rather, her mind had—performed a surgical resection of the bleeding ends of her existence, and she was at once young and old with no awareness of the incongruity.

She was confused.

This morning as they lay together in the bed, she felt a difference in his sleeping. She had been awake nearly an hour before his eyes flicked open. She had known that this time he would be fully conscious as he had not been before. His long look at her had upset her terribly; so much, in fact, that she hastily lifted her head from his chest and let herself out of the sleeping bag. Not a word passed between them, even when she brought him the cup of broth later.

Oh, he had nodded his thanks, but it was the unsure gratitude in his look that bothered her, as though she had been a stranger to whom he was in debt.

A terrible thought passed through her mind: "A piece of his mind, a part of yesterdays, has not come back!" She was shaken by the possibility. "Has the Spirit-of-the-Mountain kept part of him from me?" She shook her head against the idea. She could think of no reason why this could be so.

Charity had kept vigil outside the tent throughout the day, silent when he lapsed back into sleep, and giving increased quantities of nourishment during his brief periods of wakefulness. She smiled. So much like a baby he seemed, waking only to be fed or changed, then back to sleep again.

She frowned. There was one important difference. Unlike a babe, he did not smile. He accepted all her ministrations with grave and silent thanks.

Suddenly she brightened. "He feels himself not a man!" *That* would explain everything! He would want to put aside his helplessness and dependence on her once his strength returned. She nodded shrewdly to herself. "Ah, yes, my brave love. I can see your manhood hurting. You who danced on clouds with white wings. How foolish you must feel to be so helpless now."

So it was just a game to hide behind. Well, she could play. A loving smile creased her face at last.

The flying image fluttered round her mind, and she was briefly worried. She worried if he had flown as high as the Great White Mountain. It would not have been wise to do that. Someday she would ask him.

The sun had set. Charity watched the blowing snow flame atop Mount Whitney in the last rays. She could make out little else through the window by the seat in which she sat. The wind had scoured a portion of the plastic clear, but it was already dusk over the lake.

Shifting the cord she was holding to her left hand, she moved her body gently to a more comfortable position. It was getting very cold in the cabin. She would tend the snare a few minutes more before giving up for the night. How she wished she might trap a rabbit! Bits of fresh meat would not only be a luxury; in a day or two they might make the difference between starvation and survival. Perhaps it had been unwise to bait the snare with even snippets of dried vegetables from their rations, but she had decided to risk their loss.

All doubts and self-recrimination dissolved instantly when she felt a velvet vibration pass up the cord wrapped around her hand. Adrenaline flashed throughout her gaunt frame, giving it yet another vibrant shock. Her fatigue and chill replaced by hot concentration, she knelt and walked noiselessly on her knees the few feet to the hatch, winding up the slack of the cord smoothly as she went. When she reached the clamshell door, she faced it squarely, still on her knees, and peered through the narrow gap provided by the unlatched and cracked-open upper half.

The opening was nearly on a level with her eyes as she leaned forward, squinting over the riffled surface of the drifted snow. She nearly gasped when she saw the cotton-tail. A fat buck, the plump rabbit seemed disproportionately large. It was an illusion caused by his nearness, not over four feet from her face, and the fact that she was actually looking at him.

He was already well into the loop of the snare, having pushed aside the threads she had webbed it with to send the warning tug she had just felt. Holding her breath, Charity forced herself to wait an excruciating 15 seconds until the unsuspecting animal went deeper into the mouth of her snow burrow trap. When only his hindquarters protruded from the hold, she yanked the cord sharply.

He nearly got away. The snow-covered noose whipped tight around his loins, and he burst out of the snow with a desperate, kicking wiggle. The cord slipped past his narrow hips, its ever-tightening circlet working lower until one hind leg kicked free. Plunging wildly the frantic rabbit strained against the hardening knot. If he had run toward Charity, the noose would probably have fallen off. In his panic he tightened the loop.

Clutching the coiled line tightly in her left hand, Charity kept enough pressure against the tugging rabbit to prevent the slip knot from loosening. With her free arm she pressed out against the top-hinged upper hatch. She needed to open it wide to draw in her struggling prize.

The door would not budge. She pushed again from the awkward position on her knees. Nothing. Frantic that she might lose the contest now that it was nearly won, she pulled the rabbit closer to the opening and, taking the cord into her mouth, clamped it firmly with her toothless gums. Then rising to her feet in an awkward forward leaning crouch, she slammed both her forearms at the stubborn panel. It popped open with a sullen click.

She was still tottering, groping for the taut snare-line, when a tawny projectile exploded the snow into a cascade of white that nearly knocked her down. The cord was yanked from her mouth and burned her hand, but she held on, pulling it back, doggedly ignoring the erupting snow. Hand over hand the line came in, followed by a boiling commotion like some rusty torpedo lunging erratically toward the half-sunken airplane.

So frantically did she retrieve the line that the rabbit plopped against her chest and bounced to the floor at her feet. It lay there, still, and for a split second she marveled at the bloody rent along its side. Then the hair roots behind her ears convulsed erect, and she raised her eyes to look into the face of the cat.

The cougar's eyes blazed fury at her out of the snow, and his lips drew tight against saliva-glistened fangs. He was standing belly-deep in the disturbed powder, scarcely more than an arm's length from her position at the door. For a frozen two seconds he did nothing, did not snarl, did not move, did not even breathe. A glimmer of recognition tickled at his memory, a distraction; nothing more.

Charity acted without plan. She felt her bones begin to melt a rapid collapse upward from her feet. Only her head survived those terrifying few seconds; it floated independent of her vulnerability, masking her mounting terror for herself and her helpless lover in the tent. Her face was doing all the right things, dark eyes snapping anger, nose aloof, mouth disdainfully forming words of reproof. She might have been addressing an alley cat caught in her garbage.

"You, Puma," she used the ancient words, "go now. It is my rabbit."

Behind her sternly working jaws, collapse was imminent. Her head felt propped on the end of a swaying rubber spine. The cougar waited, uncowed but indecisive. He blinked a fluff of snow off his right eyelid and sucked in a breath of air.

That was enough for Charity. Her right hand stabbed at the air over his head, and she gambled. "Shame on you,

Puma, that you fight with the rabbit. Scat! Go and take the white-tail deer!"

Although his fangs were still bared, the great cat's ears unflattened slightly and his perplexed head tilted ever so slightly.

Charity's outstretched hand found the raised door handle, and with a desperate tug she tried to pull it down. It hung there, stubbornly resisting movement. She had forgotten to release the button on the sidebrace.

The cougar raged a deep metallic rasping snarl and tensed himself for the lunge. He could smell her fear now—her scent was strange but, seasoned with the sour signal of terror, she became simply a different kind of game. He screamed in panther triumph and sprang for her throat.

He was already in the air by the time she had fumbled the catch off. The door was halfway down when he crashed against it, ramming it completely closed. The force of his charge knocked her to her knees, but she hung on grimly, long enough to twist the handle, driving the locking pins in place.

Shuddering uncontrollably now, Charity sagged in a doubled heap, still on her knees, her head cocked awkwardly against the lower latch. She could hear the beast clawing at the door above her, and her eyes widened when his enraged shriek split the twilight calm.

Several minutes after he had gone away, she discovered that for the first time since childhood she had wet herself.

24

BUD FALLON DECIDED when he entered the landing pattern at Grant Field that he had been flying too long for his own good. He was off nearly 100 feet of altitude and too close in to make clean turns to the final approach. He looked sideways at George Feister, who was in the right seat. "Ten hours is too much for one day."

"It sure the hell is," George drawled, without looking at his friend, "especially for an *old* bastard like you."

Bud was too weary to rise to the baiting. "Look at this sloppy approach. Hell, I'd send me back to pattern work if I was my instructor."

"Jesus Christ, Fallon, you can't even talk straight. Look, if you want to see what your endurance is, how about doin' it solo. I'd just as soon not have you bust *my* ass when you hit your limit." He looked apprehensively out the window of the banking, turning 195. "You want I should land it for you?"

Bud laughed. "Nice try, George. Sorry, you'll *never* get your itchy palms on this bird."

Both men lapsed into silence then—reflective, sober.

As they passed the runway end on the downwind leg, Bud reduced power and touched a printed checklist on the panel. George nodded silently then followed the list with his eyes as Bud called off each item.

"You forgot 'Undercart,' old chap," George said brightly in a terrible attempt to mimic Oxford English. "Oh, that's right. This is a very *old* aircraft, isn't it. The tyres are always 'anging doon, ayn't they?"

Bud had heard this melange of British types many times before. He could never figure out if George really did not know that he was mixing things up or doing it deliberately. It struck him now that it was somehow soothing—an old-shoe kind of thing that he could depend on. The typically unclever banter distracted both of them from the dismal feeling of failure today's flight had produced.

After he had turned off the runway, Bud stole a glance at Ann in the back seat. She was rousing from the sleep into which she had retreated when they had given up the search over an hour before.

God! but he was tired. He rubbed the back of his head and neck to ease the ache. No use. Even a long hot shower would bring only temporary relief. Tiny muscles bunched like boils under the skin at the nape of his neck and down along his spine. Maybe he should see a chiropractor.

Even the thought of gassing up the plane before he tied it down for the night was a burden he considered skipping. He would not, of course. He'd need full tanks in the morning—full of gas, not water condensate sweating in the empty cells.

As they rolled to a stop at the gas pumps, George could see his wife peering anxiously out of lighted windows of their tiny office. From the darkened cockpit George watched Naomi on her little lighted stage as she acted out her unconscious mime. The slowing blades of the big prop cut her fluid standing, turning, walking to the door into a staccato sequence of freeze frames, jerked along like an old-time silent film run at the wrong speed. It was a curious effect, somewhat comical because she was a big woman, and appeared to pop along like a bewitched balloon.

George Feister loved his wife fiercely—and privately. Their public verbal battles were the *cause célèbre* at the airport and it was a rare day that someone did not drop in for lunch at the cafe with yet another tale of her shrilling criticisms and his comparatively quiet rejoinders, marvelous with profane images. The gossip was always friendly, borne with a delight tinged with awe—colossi testing each other. And such a Mutt 'n' Jeff; she eclipsed him physically, in height and girth. What a pair! The story would always wind down to the same conclusion. There would be a pause after the laughter, and someone in the group would add, "Y'know, it's funny, but I think they still got a crush on each other. Damnedest thing!" There would be a bobbing circle of nods.

He watched his wife approach as he stepped down from the high cabin of the old Cessna and kicked a stub of two-by-four to chock the wheel. George wished that he had been able to give her children; maybe then she wouldn't have become so attached to strays and their problems. His own gruff dismissal of Jim and Ann he knew was a mental retaliation of what their fix was doing to Naomi. He did not dwell on the sense of guilt that might arise from thinking such an unneighborly thing; he had enough to do worrying about his wife.

She puffed into the lighted circle of the island, arms crossed, tugging a chain-knitted pink mantilla across her

back and ample, bobbing bosom. Their eyes met across the
old gas pump from which George was unhooking the hose
nozzle. No question was needed, but she asked it
anyway—quietly.

"No sign at all? Didn't anybody? There must . . . "

"Dammit, no, Nome," he cut her off, but gently.
"There ain't much hope, you knew that."

She dropped her head, and he looked at her graying
crown pivot back and forth in a negative swing. He bled
for her.

"We're gonna try again, tomorrow," he said, not to
reassure her with hope, but to let her know that everything
possible was being done. It had taken on the shape of
ceremony, this ritual search. He banged the scarred starting lever with a calloused paw angrily and was rewarded
with the thump of the tired pump wheezing into life. He
handed the hose up to Bud who was standing on a ladder
ready to fill the wing tank.

"Watch yourself, Honey," he heard his wife chirp and
turned to see a sleep-dazed Ann place her foot tentatively
on the cabin step. "George!" she scolded, "help the poor
thing; she's apt t'fall."

But he was already there. She did not need help but
took the outstretched hand anyway, savoring the token
support.

"G'won in and have a cup of that diluted tar Naomi
thinks is coffee. It'll wake you up and get her off my back.
Bud and I will be in in a couple of minutes."

"Thanks, George, I will," she said. "Hi, Naomi. What
about it? Can you spare a cup for a weary traveler?"

"Of course, dear, you just come along with me," she
soothed, draping Ann's shoulder with most of the pink
shawl and hugging her close. They had gone a few steps
before she yelled back at her husband, "If you would ever
wash out that filthy cup of yours, George, you would be

surprised at the improvement in the taste!" She added to Ann, but loud enough to carry back to the men, "Honestly, I worry so that he will become diseased drinking all those germs. Some day the Board of Health will shut us down for that disgraceful cup."

George looked glumly at his coffee mug sitting on top of the squat 80-octane pump. It had been there all day since he put it there to ride shotgun with Bud. Picking it up tenderly, he peered inside with a hurt air. He knew Bud was watching from the ladder as he snapped down the filler cap on the full wing tank. Finally he hooked a finger through the handle and extended the cup toward his friend.

"Squirt a little gas in there to rinse 'er out, Bud. It sorta does look like the inside of your old oil scavenge tank, all right." He pulled the cup back and examined the inside more carefully. "On second thought, old chap, there cawnt be any germs in 'ere!" He took another peek. "Oi don't think *anything* could live in that muck!"

"For God's sake, George, have mercy. Put that damned cup down and move the ladder. I wanna top off the left tank, park this thing and get home. Tomorrow I promise to help you look up the address of a good acting school."

"What time we gettin' off tomorrow?"

Bud climbed the repositioned ladder as he answered, "I'd like to be off before first light—about five, I guess. That way we can work the assigned grids early and still have time to poke around in places of our own."

"How much longer will they keep it going?"

"Hard to tell; I think the weather will probably shut us down before they call it quits."

George was silent. The two friends stood looking at each other. They listened to the fuel splashing in the wing cell. The gallon marker chimed dully, measuring off their wait.

"What do *you* think, Bud?"

The shut-off valve abruptly closed, making the long hose jerk spasmodically once and then lie still. Bud handed down the nozzle and capped the tank before he answered. He looked like he might gag on the words.

"I think the boy's been dead for a week."

25

A PAIR OF SKIERS mustering their courage to begin a first try at an intermediate slope turned amber glances into the aching brilliance of clear winter sky. The throaty rumble of a 300-horsepower radial Jacobs racketed above them as the polished aluminum airplane caught them in its shadow. They waved and yelled, welcoming the chance to release some of the novice fears that had been building all the long way up on the chairlift. One of them laughed and pointed to the shadow racing under the climbing plane. The shadow bounced crazily down the slope, jerking over moguls, dropping into gullies, flicking up and down the sides of trees, like a mad leech sucking light in a hellbent scramble.

Ann smiled sadly, raising her hand to the window in a half-hearted salute. That is what we should be doing right now, she thought, instead of this grim business. Thoughts of snow now sickened her. There was no longer any beauty in the white stuff. Her head ached and her eyes burned with the constant surveillance, the mentally lifting the blanket from every unusual shape that poked a suggestion of aircraft wreckage to her weary brain. She had been airsick for most of the flight, too; the banking and turning while her eyes were fixed on the pivoting earth made her dizzy. Probably she was coming down with something. This morning the smell of day-old coffee warming on the stove had turned her stomach. She resolved to scour the pot; even now the memory of that brassy acid-oil odor made her shudder.

Out of the corner of her eye she caught Bud Fallon's concerned look. Pressing her intercom button she gave him a half-hearted grin and spoke, "I'll be OK. I think my morning coffee is still getting back at me."

Bud reached into his pocket and handed her a roll of antacid mints. "I thought only us old folks had that kind of problem. Maybe you should stop the heavy drinking and carousing."

Ann laughed in spite of her discomfort and sucked on the wafer. She looked out the window again, trying to concentrate on the job at hand, but an image of Jim's back flashed into her mind, and she could see her hands massaging the corded muscles of his neck and shoulders. His skin glistened with the liniment, satin smooth under her palms as she worked it in, passing her fingers out from the neck, across the scapula, gently caressing the turn of his strong shoulders, down the arms . . .

Well! Enough of that! She caught herself in time; the tightness was just beginning to grip her throat, and she blinked away the blur before she would have to admit—even to herself—that it was tears.

They were climbing. The angle was shallow as the low-flying single compensated for rising terrain. This would be the last search leg of the day; probably another hour. She looked across Bud's back, past the hunched, intent figure of George Feister peering down from the back seat, and checked the position of the setting winter sun. It would be twilight by the time they crossed the ridge at Lone Pine.

Ann forced back the throbbing in her temples to a remote corner of her mind and pressed all of her attention to terrain scan. It was becoming easier as the angle of the sun flattened, particularly on her side, looking downlight away from the glare. The shadows defined everything, giving objects a third dimension. Lengthening puddles of shade lay to the northeast of every tree and rock, every snowy hummock.

She tried to think how beautiful it was—not that the day was ending without a hope, that each shadow stretched grotesquely, staining out the sunlit snow with the spreading black of night.

This day had not been good to Charity Whiteflower. Oh, she had managed to accomplish many things in the way of providing for their survival needs. She had done much. She had skinned and cleaned the rabbit, and it was large. The day had warmed enough for her to open the door and make her way to the branch hanging over the tail of the airplane. This had been most difficult, for the snow was waist-deep and soft with the warmth of the strong sun. She had gotten wet in places where the snow soaked through her heavy trousers, but she would dry, and she had managed to get a rope around the branch to pull it down.

Much of the wood was resinous and dry, and she was able to gather a great armload of pine cones. A few slender limbs were still green, but she gathered them as well, because she knew them to be a strong herb; the tender needles could be chewed to give strength to heal cough and redness in the throat.

All the time she worked outside she worried about the cat. She knew he would be a threat until he killed some game. It was with great relief that she lugged in the last of the wood and cones and closed the hatch.

That noon she had built a rather large fire. She needed boiling water to stew the chunks of rabbit meat, and the smoky heat served double purpose in drying out her clothes. By the time the meat had been cooked, the inside of the cabin was steamy but stuffy with smoke. She had vented the door only enough to let in air to breathe, and at the floor level their quarters were quite comfortable.

No. Her difficulties were of a different quality.

He had been awake most of the day, and it was true—he did not know her. She was crushed with hurt disappointment. What if that part of him that knew her never returned! She was devastated at the thought, so much so that the prospect of their living apart cut through her stoicism and made her lip tremble.

He was watching her now as she prepared his cup of stewed meat and vegetables. The whole cabin was so warm from the cooking that she had tied back the folds of the foil-blanket shelter. As much as she could, she avoided meeting his eyes, now that she knew this thing about him. She ached to hear him call her name, to give her some sign that he knew, that they would be as one again. But she had looked so many times, so boldly into his eyes, and there had been nothing.

Sighing inaudibly, Charity gave the watery but fragrant stew a final stir and lifted it from the heat. She ladled a generous portion into one of the metal cups and rose with difficulty from her kneeling position by the nearly burned-out fire. Her lower legs were numb with the constriction of her former position, and she nearly fell.

"Agh!" The sound of disgust burst loose from her and she muttered in the old words, "Foolish old woman!" A

momentary confusion crossed her face, clouding the normally placid expression. She recovered quickly, however,
and shuffled over to his bed with the cup.

"Are you all right, ma'm?"

She froze in midstep. The voice was odd. She dared to
stare at him, trying to reconcile the sound with his face. It
was so distressing; she passed a hand over her face like one
reviving from a swoon. Her vision was not too clear, and
she knew it was not just because of the smoky gloom of
the cabin. She thought of all the work gathering branches
and thought idly that she would have to conserve her
strength, get some rest.

Shrugging aside her confusion she approached him,
kneeling slowly at his side.

He was sitting up! He reached out for the cup. She
held it out to him. Their hands met, his enclosed hers,
clumsily groping for a purchase on the cup. She was fasci-
nated by the hands! How white they were—and strong-
looking even in their present weakness. She withdrew one
of her own so that he could get a grip on the container, and
guided his large fingers to the warm metal.

Suddenly she caught the contrast. Their overlapping
hands caressed the cup and she saw her own—objectively,
at last—withered to leathery claws, clutching at his young
flesh.

Charity recoiled in horror, tearing herself away. The
precious cup of meat spun out of his grasp, and he fell back
against the bed. She was overcome with a great trembling
and huddled against the wall of the cabin, hiding her
averted face from him with a pitifully upraised hand. Great
spinning images shattered in her brain. A storm of broken
stained-glass windows, cracked and cascading fragments of
her love-collage, splintered to the floor of her skull, and
she was sane—and old—again.

A long time passed. She must have slept, because the

light seemed different in the plane, and she was chilled and stiff in her doubled-up position against the padded wall of the fuselage. She looked across to where the young man lay in her sleeping bag.

He was struggling to crawl over to her! Catching her eye, he spoke.

"It's all right," he said soothingly. "Please, can I help you? Are you OK?"

Charity scrambled to her feet. He must be careful of that leg! She helped him back into the makeshift bunk and tenderly pillowed his head with a seat cushion.

She noticed how haggard he seemed with a week's beard sprouting from the pale skin of his drawn face.

"Yes, yes," she answered him at last. "Now, you rest."

His emaciated appearance prompted her to gather up the chunk of meat and vegetable fragments from the carpet and put them in the righted cup. Retreating to her rude cookstove, she built a small fire, added broth from the larger pot to the salvaged stew parts, and began to heat the cup directly over the flame.

This time when she brought the cup to him, he laughed weakly and joked, "Thank you, ma'm. Shall we try it again?"

Charity responded with a light chuckle of her own and took pleasure in feeding her young patient. She even began to feel a strange tenderness for this wan youngster, forgetting the fact that he had been the instrument of the cruel trick her mind had played with her emotions.

What Charity did not forget, and never would, was that she could not rest until she was once again with *him*.

Half an hour later, after he had fallen into an exhausted sleep, she heard the plane approach. At first she did not make much of it, for there had been sounds of planes before, always high above the clouds, during the storms. By the time she realized that it was clear, that the plane sounded very low, and that it might be someone searching, the sound was almost directly overhead.

Charity lunged for the door and wrestled the handle until it popped open. She looked up through the overhanging branches of the trees and saw the exhaust-stained underbelly of the silver airplane. It was not more than a few hundred feet above them, and with the cabin door open, the racket from the straining engine was deafening.

She barely heard the weak voice crying out behind her, and she made a futile wave with a frail arm knowing that she could not be seen through the pines. She watched the plane climbing out over the lake toward the trail and pass beyond.

"That's Bud! That's Bud!" the voice behind her shouted weakly. "Get the flare gun . . . the flare gun!"

Dimly she remembered going through the strange packages in the large pack—the strange-looking pistol. She rushed to find it; to give it to him, to get the other parts he asked for. In the end of course, it was too late. The plane had disappeared and its engine sound silenced long before he had showed her how to fire it.

Strangely, he did not seem too distressed. "Don't worry; they'll be back," he said. "I know the man in that plane. He was my friend. He'll be back."

Charity was not so sure. Her young patient did not know that they had been here eight days, and this was the first plane that had even come close.

Darkness began to replace the short twilight, and she pulled the hatch closed for the night. Without comment she began to drape the bunk with blankets to save the warmth.

She thought he was asleep when she began to wrap herself in the single blanket on the floor beside him. The sound of a zipper startled her, and he spoke.

"Please get in the bag with me. If you don't I think we both will freeze tonight."

Grateful for the warmth, Charity struggled into the huge sleeping bag and lay still as he zipped it closed. The simple act of pulling the zipper must have exhausted him for he dropped off to sleep almost immediately. She fought the tremors as long as she could but finally let go, shivering convulsively until his young animal heat warmed her through. Then, finally, she too slept.

After refueling and getting a snack at Lone Pine, the exhausted searchers took off for the long flight down Owens Valley toward home. They had switched seats again, Ann taking the back bench, George up front riding copilot with Bud.

They were thirty minutes into the flight before either man spoke, and Ann was fast asleep.

"Bud, it gave me the creeps back there when we were letting down to land—what she said, I mean."

"When we were crossing the ridge?"

George nodded in the darkness. "Yeah. She kept looking out the window, saying, 'He's here. I can feel it.' She said, 'I know he's here, he's alive, and we'll find him.' I know you didn't hear her, Bud, because she was lookin' away and kinda whispered. But I could tell from her lips. She said, 'Wait for me, Jim, I'll come for you.'"

Bud turned to look at George, both their faces red-lighted in the dim cockpit.

"That's what she said; or close to it." George shook his head sadly. "Goddam, you're gonna have to watch that girl, Bud. I'm afraid she might crack and do something foolish!"

They were well past Mojave, boring steadily toward the San Bernardino Mountains, before George spoke again.

"Y'notice them rooster tails up high late this afternoon?"

"Cirrus? Yes, I did."

"Think another one's comin' in?"

"You could make book on it, George."

"Goddammit," he said, "I hoped *somebody* would find *somethin'* before more snow came. She"—he jerked his head toward the back seat—"should be able to get the boy buried, pick up the pieces, and start to make a new life. This lousy waitin' is enough to drive anybody wacko."

Bud looked at his watch and answered by tuning in the transcribed weather forecast. They listened on their headsets.

It was bad.

26

ALTHOUGH IT WAS pitch black inside the draped blanket enclosure, Charity snapped awake at dawn, anxious to prepare for the day. She did not, as she had done for the past eight mornings, light the heating candle in the tent. Instead she opened the blankets wide and set about building a fire for an early meal, using the heat to take the chill off the cabin as she cooked. She wanted to be ready this time in case another plane or rescue party appeared.

The inside of the cabin was bitterly cold, the panes of plexiglass frosted thickly with condensed vapor from their breathing. She wanted to look outside to see if it was clear, because the weak light filtering in gave no indication. It was not yet time for the sun, she was sure of that, and the only way to tell the weather was to look up at the sky. She elected to wait, however, contenting herself to open the hatch the barest crack for ventilation. After the fire had taken off the chill would be soon enough, she reasoned, and began the morning chores.

By the time she had cooked a gruel concocted of cereals and rabbit liquor, the cabin was reasonably comfortable, not too smoky, and the young man was awake. He was not as alert as he had been the night before, but he managed to feed himself and ate with more relish than ever.

After he had finished, Charity unzipped the sleeping bag and examined his lower leg. The swelling had gone down, and she was happy to note that the circulation was strong in his foot. It felt warm to the touch of her cold hands. She adjusted the bindings along the pine splint, tightening them slightly to the aluminum frame she had fashioned from her backpack. As the puffy lower leg shrank back to its normal dimensions, she had taken care to keep it adjusted tightly immobile while the bones rejoined. Her greatest fear had been that she might cut off the circulation, inviting frostbite or gangrene. On the other hand, loose bindings would risk rebreaking the fused fracture. Apparently the compromise had been successful; the leg looked good.

Noting that he was more alert now, she dragged the heavy canvas bag over to him. Pulling the Very pistol out, she handed it to him making signs and speaking monosyllables so that he would understand that he was to teach her how to use the flare device. After several demonstrations of loading, aiming, and firing steps, both seemed satisfied that she would be able to operate the launcher when the time came.

Exhausted again from his efforts, he dropped off into sleep. Charity sat by him a long time looking at this face, a wistful longing in her eyes. She had no delusions now, but his youth and vulnerability moved her deeply and she allowed herself to dwell on her golden eighteenth summer.

It was no use. All nostalgic side trips inevitably wound

their way back to that darkened, violent roadway, the somber church, clouds of incense smoke stabbed by slanting red and yellow light-arrows beaming from a flat Christ jigsawed on the window. She saw again the splattered beads of holy water draw themselves up in high-shouldered isolation on the too-shiny varnish of the box they laid him in.

She shook her head slowly. Strange, that she could bear thinking of it now. Perhaps it was good, she thought, but her heart was lead in her breast.

Some time later, when she finally realized that it was long past sunrise and she had not seen the welcome yellow light strike the cabin windows, she got up and opened the hatch enough to see the sky.

A blast of chilling air greeted her, and she shrank at the sight of gray clouds screening the ball of sun to a pale, haloed dot. Something stirred unpleasantly inside her trembling frame, cold, like death itself, and she grimaced knowing this would be a storm worse than the one they had barely survived.

Narrowing her eyes, she looked across the drifted flat that was the frozen lake, trying to pick out in the distance the notch in the far hills that marked the trail over the ridge. It would be nearly 5 miles, counting the distance across the lake, to reach the ranger's hut.

Charity reached out, tentatively fingering the snow. It had frozen into a hard crust, how hard she could not tell. It did not matter. She would have to try.

Working swiftly she arranged the equipment for his survival in an order he could comprehend and cope with in his weakened state. When all was in place, she went to him and roused him firmly. It was earlier than she had planned, but vital now that he begin to fend for himself. The first step must be to get him on his feet, to try the leg splinted in its makeshift aluminum brace.

She tugged at his arm, forcing him to sit up. He was groggy, and that would make matters worse, but she had no choice.

"Up!" she ordered sternly, pulling his uninjured left leg out of the bedding so that his foot rested on the floor. With great care she uncovered his right leg and gently swung it around, lowering it beside the other.

Pain was in his eyes, but he did not grimace or make any sound. The hurt must have cleared his head somewhat for he seemed to understand that he must comply. It was blind obedience. She doubted that he had grasped the urgency of the situation.

Gripping the armrest of the cabin seat that formed part of his bed, he reached out a shaking hand to her, and together they heaved him erect. He nearly passed out, but held on to the seat back doggedly until the fainting spell passed.

Charity watched him closely, and when the faint pink began to return to his cracked and flaky lips, she pointed to the splinted leg and motioned him to walk. The frame was a narrow U supporting the injured leg from thigh to foot, bending around under his heel to form a rude walking cast.

He took a tentative step, not really putting any weight on the brace, and hopped his left foot a bare inch. Beads of sweat were working from his brow. She began to wonder if she could support him, frail prop that she was under his left arm, should he faint, or stumble, and fall.

It was enough. He had taken the first step. Necessity would force him to try another on his own after she had gone. Carefully she eased him back into the sleeping bag and zipped him up.

He lay back and closed his eyes, face bathed in cold running droplets which she swabbed off. She was nearly ready to go before he opened them again, staring at her boots wrapped to twice their size with extra clothing from her back pack.

For a moment he did not comprehend her reason for the outlandish outfit, but when she selected a long, straight pole from the pile of branches near the door, he began to understand.

She looked at him with a calm smile, pulling on her gloves. "I go to get help."

Jim propped himself on an elbow, trying to remember the chart, trying to remember how far it must be to . . . anything. How deep was the snow? My God, how shriveled she looked.

"Are you sure?" His voice croaked with disuse. "Stay here where it's safe. They'll be looking for us . . . the plane."

"No," she said quietly, "too many days now. Too long. More snow." She turned and indicated the wood and meager food supply. "Now you eat. Small fire. Open door." She popped the hatch an inch to demonstrate. "See?"

His nod was her signal to pick up the staff and open the door fully. Turning back to look at him again, she spoke sternly as to a child, "You wait. Now I go to get them."

An impulse drove Jim to ask the question which seemed foolish when it sprang to his lips, "Please, what is your name?"

The question stopped her cold. She assumed he meant her *name*. She could not mention her true name to him, her tribal name; not to anyone until at death she would whisper it to her firstborn to be held sacred for her in afterlife. It was unthinkable. It never crossed her mind that "Charity Whiteflower" would have been the answer to his question. That was what she had been called, but it was no more a part of her than was the parka she wore or the wood that she burned. These things she would leave to the earth that provided them. But her *name* was part of her soul.

Well! She was not about to die, and he was certainly not her son. She brushed off his request as one that sprang from the innocence of ignorance. With a careless wave she struggled over the waist-high door, tumbling onto the crusted snow. Using her stick to get to her feet, she closed the hatch firmly and began to pick her way across the drifts.

Left alone in the plane, Jim wondered at his situation. With no reference point in time to guide him, he had no idea how long he had been in the wreck. Could the Indian woman be a resident, with friends and family nearby? He wished he had the strength to find his chart to figure out where he was. There were so many things he could not remember. Something about a lake, a trail. He was tantalized with some drifting idea about the mountains, but the more he tried to concentrate the fuzzier the thought became.

After several minutes of the struggle he had trouble fixing his mind on who it was he had been talking with at the door of the plane. Ann's face kept getting in the way of his placing it somehow. It was exhausting work and that damned headache was poking around the edges again. Oh well, sleep would take care of that.

He had a dream of when he was a student with Bud Fallon. They were on his first long cross-country training flight. Bud was in the right seat of the little trainer, pointing down at the beautiful craggy ridges and boulder-filled gorges as they drifted slowly along their course. Jim tried to make out what he was saying again over the drone of the engine. In the dream he was able to push the words back, again and again like rewinding a tape, until he heard Bud's voice whisper clearly into his ear. "Nature is the gal to watch," he warned. "People are only occasionally

harmful—even as enemies. You have to live with Mother
Nature all the time. She'll bide her time, waiting for one
mistake, then slap you down. Don't you forget that."

In his dream Jim felt contented and warm. Slipping
free of all the tension lines, he let himself float into a
peaceful dark oblivion.

It took Charity far less time to cross the lake than she
had imagined it would. For one thing, the snow crust had
held under her padded feet nearly all the way to the far
shoreline. She had broken through several times, but not
deeply, and the staff helped her keep balance. She had not
fallen once. The other assist was from the wind at her back
practically propelling her along.

It would be harder going when she reached the trail
and turned north into the wind. That part of the trail was
uphill, too. She preferred not to think about it. It was hard
enough now just picking her way through the drifted
brush to reach the trail.

At last she reached a level place which she recognized
with difficulty as the point where she had first seen the
stricken plane ten days earlier. The trail was quite different
covered with three feet of snow, but she was sure of her
bearings.

Leaning heavily on the pole, she allowed herself the
luxury of a short rest. Her heart was pounding again,
though not more than could be expected. Two weeks at
this altitude had given her system time to adjust. The wind
at her back soughed a muffled whisper around her parka-
hooded face, cooling the flushed, damp skin. As she stood
getting a second wind, the first flakes of the storm
carromed past her eyes.

Charity dropped her head like a tired dray, and turned
into the whipping gusts to face the uphill grade. She was

measuring the task not by distance, not by time, but by endurance. It would be a parceling-out of strength in exchange for the chunks of upward trail, of buffeting wind. She really felt she could make it to the ranger outpost. She did not speculate on the ultimate cost in terms of her own well-being. Pulling up her last reserves of determination, she took the first step out of the remaining 4 miles.

A considerable distance downwind, his ribs sliding plainly under a coat ruffed against the chill, the cougar tracked his daylong zigzag course for a scent to home on. Desperation marked his every move.

In a small building near the ridgeline, Nate Tomlin was speaking on the telephone. Periodically he would stretch the cord to its limit, straining to peer out of the window of his pinewood paneled office.

"Hell, *yes,* it's started," he said with a tinge of exasperation. "I don't see why you're so surprised. Don't you guys ever watch the TV news down there? You sure must not read the progs." He paused for effect before resuming his needling banter, "I honestly can't see why they put a teletype at headquarters anyway. You clowns don't even go in to tear off the sheets. I'll bet there is enough yellow paper on the floor right now to cover the walls of the state capitol."

Ranger Tomlin slowed his verbal attack long enough to hear out the other party. Then he resumed.

"Well, I guess you *are* going to have to send out for me. I haven't gotten the hang of push-starting a one-ton truck all by myself. At least not in the snow." At this point he let up a bit and laughed aloud.

"OK, Fred, OK. Don't get upset," he continued after another pause. "Maybe you'll draw another good hand after you get me off the hill and I can help you play it." He said goodbye and was just about to hang up when he pulled the phone back for one parting shot, "Oh, and by the way, next time I tell you a battery needs replacing, spare me the crap about saving tax money, OK?"

From the disappointed look on his face as he replaced the handset in its cradle, it was apparent that Fred had signed off before hearing the last indignity. Nate mollified himself in the manner of many solitary vigil-keepers by talking to himself, "You can always count on administrators' gettin' you out of a fix they got you into in the first place."

Tomlin laughed at his own joke as he fired up his pipe. Breaking the wooden match in his palm, he rolled off the head of hot ash and held it in his hand. Force of habit kept him from dropping it into the ashtray for several minutes. Any match *he* discarded would be cold—ashtray or not.

He stood at the window watching the snowfall thicken. It would be an hour before Fred arrived from Lone Pine with the plow and jumper. No problem. Two miles to the notch, and downhill all the way after that following the plow.

A movement 50 or so yards along the widened trail caught his eye, and he squinted through the swirling flakes to make it out. A smile brightened his face upon recognizing the straggled herd of mule deer bounding across the driveway to the station. He counted five does and three bucks, one of the latter a magnificent specimen, particularly for the mountain variety.

"Ho, ho, old man!" he muttered. "Taking the family to the sunny side of the ridge, eh? Well, that's a sign of heavy snow for sure."

The large buck suddenly reappeared, jumping back across the narrow roadway, freezing in a study of statuesque attention on the other side. He remained in that position for a full minute, only his ears giving sign that he was other than a full-color scale sculpture. At last he turned and sprang across to the left again, disappearing after the others with a flash of his white flag.

"Lost one, I guess," Nate mused. "Well, old buck, that's life. Forget your casualty; keep moving the survivors to cut your losses." His mind flashed back to another snowy trail, and he saw himself bending over a bundle in the snow, removing weapon, cartridge belt, and dogtag—then waving his weary patrol back to the trail, back to safety.

A twitching muscle in his face reminded him to relax the grip his teeth had clamped on the pipestem, and he noted that it had gone out. Fingering another match from his breast pocket, he lighted it again, blowing a dense cloud of blue smoke at the window pane. Almost thirty years, he thought; funny how some things never quiet down.

He rubbed the warm brier bowl against the side of his nose, reflecting that it would be nice to spend a week or so with the flatlanders during the storm while the station was closed.

Although she never did actually see the cougar, Charity felt his presence breathing cold terror between her shoulder blades as he tracked her, keeping 50 yards behind. The terror spot crept up her spine and widened with a feeling of dread nakedness. An icy pain pointed through her chest from back to breastbone, nerving her to a more desperate pace.

The hill was long behind her, but the mile of flat trail might have been a 40-percent grade as she willed her feet to move. Her head pulsed with pressure pain, and the cold wind seared her lungs as she heaved it in with rapid, shallow gulps. For a time she felt as though the trail were a white mass that she was pulling toward her by pushing backward with her feet and staff. This perspective dismayed her terribly, and she worried that the ranger station might somehow remain locked in place as she gathered the carpet of landscape, tugging it so tight that it might rip, stranding her forever from her goal.

Eventually she was able to focus on her own relative movement by concentrating on an inner core of strength. She no longer felt her feet and legs at all; sensation in her arms disappeared. Only a great flashing pain between heart and eyes formed the totality of her existence. She kept moving in direct proportion to the intensity of pain, feeding the pain with the fuel of raw determination.

She forgot Puma. Was not even aware when he broke off the stalk, streaking into the deep snow to bring down the weakened doe straggler. She did not hear his shriek of triumph even though it overpowered the howling wind.

The raging pain in her chest and head, a great hourglass of cold white fire consumed all hearing, and so she did not hear the truck until she stumbled into it. Then she saw, through red-splotched eyes, the men stooping to peer in her face.

With one last desperate effort, she willed the pain into her arms and pulled off her left glove. Her fingers clutched something small and metallic. A tiny plastic tag was attached, dangling on a loop of chain. Her mind held it up to them so they would be able to see the tag fluttering in the glare of the headlights, but her arm did not get the signal to rise. A clot of blood was moving through her brain, shutting down the motor circuits, one by one.

She was gone before they got her in the truck, but they raced her 20 miles to the hospital anyway. As he cradled her in his arms, Nate wondered who she was, and why she had pulled off one glove as her final dying act.

Back on the roadway a bright key lay in the packed treadprint of the tire which had pressed it down. The penned handwriting of Jack Laird stood out plainly on the identification tag.

DAUPHIN—N7695R.

It was quickly covered up with snow.

27

"FOR THE SECOND DAY in a row, the record snowfall has closed all mountain passes above four thousand feet. Motorists are advised to avoid mountain roads for all but emergency reasons and cars without chains will be barred from the following locations . . . "

Ann was listening to the midday television news this Saturday as the first groggy act of her morning. It had been two days since the last search flight with Bud Fallon, and each night she had tossed and turned, finally falling asleep with nervous exhaustion.

Turning up the volume on the set, she walked slowly to the kitchen and began to make a pot of coffee, as she strained to hear each word of the newscaster.

"So far four deaths have been attributed to the storm, the most recent being an elderly camper who died enroute to the hospital in Lone Pine yesterday. Authorities know the identity of the victim, but are withholding that information pending notification of kin. The camper, a woman approximately seventy years of age, is thought to have been backpacking alone in the Sierras for over a week. What amazed rangers, into whose station the woman struggled late yesterday, was that she had been able to survive the storm as long as she did. Forest Service personnel in the area say that there are no shelters within miles, and that the woman must have abandoned her pack in a desperate attempt to reach safety before the new storm struck. It is tragic to note that she died literally at the door of the outpost in the arms of one of the rangers. We may never know details of her ordeal because she died without saying a word."

Ann set the pot on the stove, turned up the flame, and returned to the living room. The commentator went on.

"In another storm-related incident, the FAA announced this morning that search attempts for the pilot of a small plane missing on a flight to Reno for over a week have been discontinued. Authorities fear that there is little hope for the pilot, who was alone in the craft and from whom nothing has been heard since his last radio transmission early in the flight."

The announcer continued a string of news items generated by the snowfall, but Ann was no longer listening. She sat on the worn sofa, staring at the screen with glazed eyes. All color had drained from her skin, giving it a yellow-greenish pallor. She did not even appear to breathe as she slouched against the back of the couch.

Angry hissing sounds from the kitchen finally roused her, and she attended to the boiled-over coffeepot. It had put out the flame and the tiny room reeked with gas fumes. The combination was simply too much for her stomach. Gagging on bile, she raced for the toilet and folded to her knees. At first she thought she might pass out, but she waited out the giddiness, savoring the refreshing touch of cool vitreous china under her palms and against her temples.

So it is really true, she thought. Jim really is dead. Everybody has known it all along but me. The thought was like a sharp, physical stab deep inside her, and she rolled to the floor of the bathroom on her side, curled up around the hurt.

It was a long time before the racking sobs subsided and her eyes cleared of the burning tears. Lying there on the linoleum floor, she trembled as the heat of weeping gave way to an aching chill. Slowly she got to her feet and staggered to the shower. She pulled off her nightgown and stepped under the welcome jets of steaming water.

Thought of Jim began to push their way into her mind, but she sidestepped them by concentrating on her schedule for the day. It was Saturday; that meant she would have the graveyard shift again. She would have to check the schedule more closely. Could Dr. Yancey have assigned all that night duty to help her face the dark hours more easily?

It was working. She could feel the cold and tension wash out of her back. Maybe the announcer had been wrong. Those TV people always wrote the news to appeal to the audience. She would have to call up Bud as soon as she got dressed. He was her one reliable source of information.

Poor Bud. He was convinced that Jim was dead, there was no question of that. Several times he had tried to bring her around to accept the idea, always so gently that he barely managed to broach the subject before he switched to another topic.

But Ann simply could not accept Jim's death. Even now, something in her refused to give him up.

Her back was beginning to smart under the hot water barrage so she turned around to face the shower. She winced when the hot jets struck her nipples. How sensitive they were! Covering her breasts, she adjusted the showerhead down to her lower torso.

She dismissed the painful experience and what it signified. It had been over two months since her last period. The night before he left she had nearly mentioned it to Jim but had held off.

She avoided thinking of it now. She would not let herself admit that she was pregnant. Something blocked it—the need to share the discovery with Jim, the terror of facing motherhood alone. She would not speculate.

One fact did manage to nudge itself into place and afford a consolation. Part of him was always with her. It gave her strength.

The following Monday started out badly for Charlie Wise. In addition to its being the blue day, Charlie's start on the week's work was marred by a gigantic hangover. His wife's parents had dropped in unexpectedly Sunday afternoon for a three-week stay through Christmas. That in itself would have been no cause for escape into the bottle, because Charlie liked his father-in-law very much. The problem was that his father-in-law seemed to save his strength for these infrequent visits for the sole purpose of testing his alcoholic capacity with Charlie. Charlie always outlasted the old man by a narrow margin, but the bottom line was that Charlie worked off his liquor while his wife's father was recovering in snoring oblivion.

Charlie's Monday was further complicated by discovering that for the third week in a row the big trash bin had not been emptied by the contract company, and its contents were spilling on the ground. Since his boss would be out of town for the next two days, Charlie took it upon himself to call in a service complaint.

His angry demands were soon quieted by the company bookkeeper, who pointed out to Charlie that since Laird had not made payments for several months, he could keep the trash, with their compliments.

So it transpired that Charlie's first work of the day consisted of making three long trips to the county dump with his pickup, which he had carefully polished just the Friday before. To make matters worse, the bin had to be emptied from within since the sides were so high. He was tempted to remove only enough trash to make room for the day's waste, but after soiling himself and his truck anyway, he decided to clean out the whole thing and be done with it. He would see about getting reimbursed for his mileage when Laird returned.

He had nearly completed the task and was picking up the last of the soggy material from the bottom of the bin when he saw them. At first they did not attract his attention. Discarded vee belts are a common thing around repair facilities. When he picked them up with a handful of wet plastic bags, however, something clicked.

He held them closer. They seemed familiar but out of place. Separating them from the torn and dripping plastic bags, he noted that they were practically brand new, just the barest shine on the bearing surfaces to attest to their ever having been installed. One other curious fact settled in Charlie's still-throbbing brain—they had been cut, each of them, neatly in one place. There was not a trace of damage anywhere else.

He was not sure why, but Charlie decided not to throw them into the truck bed. Instead, he coiled them up and stuck them into one of the plastic bags and climbed out of the bin.

Opening the door of his truck, he climbed in and started the engine. He looked at the wet bag a moment, then shrugged and tossed it under his seat.

"Free Ice, Compliments of Danny's Party Liquor," he said aloud as he shifted through the gears. "I know that place." Then apparently the last word of Danny's logo registered and he belched sourly.

"Yyyuuuk! Never again."

Two days later, the day Jack Laird was due to return, when Charlie was working under the cowling of a Cherokee 140, a thought made him drop what he was doing and saunter over to his pickup. He opened the door, reached under the seat, and pulled out the plastic bag. Slowly he withdrew the severed belts and looked at them closely, checking the still-fresh part numbers painted on the top flat of each.

"Well, I'll be a sonofabitch," he whispered, turning to look toward Laird's office. He knew these belts. They were the ones he had installed on the twin not three weeks ago. Carefully stuffing them back into the bag, he replaced them under the seat of the truck, a bit farther back this time.

When Laird returned that day a little after eleven, Charlie chose not to bring up the matter of the mileage to the dump. In fact, he specifically avoided mentioning the trash bin altogether.

What he did do was watch Jack Laird very closely from that time on.

28

IT WAS ANOTHER rainy afternoon. Ann had to look at the checked-off numbers on the kitchen calendar to verify the date. Two weeks had passed since he had gone. The weather had been unbelievably bad. One storm had passed only to be replaced by another before the skies had cleared of clouds from the first. She spent her free time looking at the skies, the weather forecasts, and drinking coffee.

Snow reports from the mountains were now being given in feet rather than inches. In some places the resorts themselves were beginning to curse the unrelenting daily blizzards, because the frequency of storms closed the roads, and they found themselves cut off from the lowlands—and paying customers.

Ann turned from the window feeling as gray inside as the scene outside. She picked up her coffee and walked gloomily back to the bedroom. There was a call she had to make today, one she had been putting off for several days, hoping against hope that it would not have to be made.

There was a thick envelope lying on the nightstand beside the telephone. It was addressed to Jim, but she had finally steeled herself to open it the day before. One look at the return address was enough for her to realize what it contained. In the frenzied initial search time she had forgotten about the call from U.S. Airways. The letter had brought it all back.

She would have to let them know.

Opening the envelope for the second time, she carefully spread the letter and picked up the receiver. The call went through, and the captain in charge of the training facility heard her out, mercifully sparing her anonymous sympathetic commentary. An alert secretary at his end must have pulled Jim's file immediately, for when he did speak, it was with more than cursory knowledge of Jim's background.

"Mrs. Regan, I have some appreciation of your feelings. Things are as tough as they'll ever be. I don't want you to think I'm raising any hopes, because frankly it looks bad. What I want to say is this: I'm going to hold Jim's spot open for him until his class begins in February. No lousy roll of the dice is going to cheat him, or you, out of that."

Ann tried to thank him, but the words squeaked coming past the tightness in her throat.

He continued, pretending not to hear her cracking voice, "That much *I* can guarantee; the rest is up to Jim and God, I guess."

She managed to thank him this time.

"You call me any time you think I might be able to help. OK? Say, if you run into Bud Fallon, tell him I'm still waiting for a hop in his old airplane, will you?"

"You know Bud . . . ?" The change of pace helped her a bit.

"Oh, yes. Way back . . . You see, Bud sent a letter of recommendation for Jim when he applied." He risked a gentle laugh. "I'd read it to you, Mrs. Regan, but it's supposed to be confidential. I will say this, though; Bud makes him out to be too good to believe. Your husband must be one heck of a guy though. You see, Bud Fallon just never exaggerates."

After hanging up Ann could not quite make her heart decide whether what she had heard was testimonial or eulogy.

"Can't you see that *you're* the one who has to convince her?" Mildred Yancey was talking quietly but intensely to Bud Fallon over a supper that neither was enjoying.

"I just do not go along with what all of you think, Mildred. A person just can't pick a time and say, 'Well, there isn't any hope now; I think I will grieve.' " Fallon gave up on a forkful of chow mein and put it back on his plate.

The movement was not lost on Mildred Yancey. She placed her fork down also and wiped her lips with a napkin. "Oh, I'm sorry, Bud. It wasn't fair to bring up the subject at dinner."

He smiled across the small table and reached over to take her hand.

"Don't you know that dinnertime is when most folks get things off their chests—that and when they're into the schnapps?"

Bud laughed quietly, and they both fell silent for a time, staring thoughtfully first at the table between them and then at each other.

It was a peaceful experience. One that they had shared often in the past two weeks since that evening in the truck sitting outside Ann and Jim's apartment. They never alluded to their moments of silence, simply partaking of each other's company without feeling a need to add to the communication with words or actions.

"At any rate," he said after two or three minutes of quiet, "I really do not think it would matter much to Ann what I said. She is pretty much a gal who follows her own mind . . . and heart."

"She has you bamboozled, too, I see," Mildred retorted. "All that stiff-upper-lip stuff is just a front. I know. I've seen her working her pretty little fanny off like someone on bennies. It just isn't natural. I just can't stand around waiting for her to come apart at the seams."

"She's different," Bud countered. "She's tough—almost as tough as you—" he winked at Mildred; "I don't mean that she is brittle, or uncaring. It is just that if she has to endure bereavement, she is gonna make damned sure that it is necessary." He leaned forward to make his point, "She is convinced in her own mind that the boy is still alive. She wants it to be so, she is almost *willing* it to be so. If you or I could convince her to act otherwise, it would be just that—an act. When the truth, I mean, the *proof,* that Jim is gone finally gets to her, she is going to have to go through it all over again." He leaned back and sucked in his breath. "And the second time will not be softened one bit by the practice session; it might even make it worse."

Mildred sat frowning again, worrying a hangnail on her little finger with her teeth. She gave up on it, looked at the offending triangle of cuticle, and spoke mostly to herself, "I have *got* to take some B12." Then she looked squarely at Bud. "Suppose they *never* find him . . . the plane? What will that do to her?"

"That is something I don't like to think about," he confessed.

"There is something else about Ann that I don't like to think about," Mildred said without thinking.

"What's that?" Bud asked, slightly surprised.

"Oh, it's not important. Just a feeling. Probably my overly dramatic imagination. Forget I mentioned it."

Bud laughed. "Do you think if the shoe were on the other foot, that I could get out of this apartment alive without telling *you* what was on my mind?"

"I don't know what you're talking about." She got up and began clearing away the table. "Do you want coffee here or on the couch?"

He reached out and held her arm, forcing her to look him in the face. "Mildred, you didn't answer my question," he teased.

"It makes no difference anyway, Bud dear."

"How's that?"

"About not letting you get out of here alive tonight."

He waited for the punch line.

"I want you to stay until morning in any case." With that she made off with the dinnerware, leaving him to sort out matters as best he could.

29

EACH TIME ANN HAD the dream, she entered it with the feeling that she might have experienced it before; but although the sequences seemed familiar, she was not quite sure until it faded. Then she would half-waken with the confused dilemma of wondering if this had really been a repeat dream or one of those flashback phenomena by which the brain can fool a person into thinking that all had really transpired before in exactly the same way.

It concerned Jim, of course, and as before she saw him lying in an outlandish bassinet with wicker sides decorated with pink satin ribbon woven into the basket. What made the bassinet so ludicrous was not that it was a strange place for her gangly husband to be sprawled, but that it had wings. They were real wings, formed of ribs and stringers and covered with a taut, gleaming, doped fabric. As she looked from the foolish little wings back into the basket at her husband, she saw that he was smiling at her, a vacant, dreamy smile.

This was the point where the dream usually faded out, and she would wake up, but this time she held on.

She was close enough now to look over the side of the basket and see his hand, lying at his side on the satin cushion. How strange. She had never noticed before that Jim had black hairs curling from the back of his hand. It didn't look like his hand at all . . . yet it was familiar somehow. She let her eyes drift slowly up along his body, button by button up the front of his rumpled pajama top.

Slowly his chin came into view. Ugh! He hadn't shaved. He had a silly smile. What was he doing? Posing for one of those old-fashioned time exposures? His lips were drawn back over . . . his color wasn't really very . . . his nose was so . . . so sharp looking.

Watching patiently for the flaring of his nostrils, she noticed that he was not breathing. For the longest time her eyes were locked on his nose, unwilling to move up to his eyes. Afraid to move up to his eyes.

Finally she did it, half knowing it was a dream-game. She looked full into the faded irises, which stared back at a point somewhere over her shoulder; they were slightly askew, wall-eyed, and they did not blink or move.

When she felt the icy stiffness of his arm with her fingers, she noticed that the rock-hard eyes were crystallized with frost.

Ann's scream ripped her out of the dream. She was still shrieking when fully awake. Lunging for his side of the bed she buried her face in his pillow, smothering out her terrified sobs.

Fifteen minutes later, when she had regained some semblance of composure, she looked at the clock. It was ten A.M. She had been asleep only two hours following her night shift at the hospital. She did not go back to sleep, however, even knowing that she would be working again tonight. Somehow she would manage to struggle through. By working all night she had avoided the emptiness of those dark hours. But now . . .

Desperately she craved a cigaret. Two weeks without one and she felt now as if she were addicted. Well, that would pass. She couldn't smoke—especially now.

But the dream kept coming back throughout the next few hours, reminding her that her retreat into the security of daylight sleeping had been overtaken.

Fear now stalked her nights—and days.

"How about the three of us meeting for lunch?" Bud listened on the telephone for a response. "OK. We'll pick you up at your place in an hour."

"OK. 'Bye, Ann." He handed the telephone to Mildred, who replaced the receiver on its cradle by the bed. Turning back, she settled close to him and rested her head on his chest.

They were silent for a moment then she said, "It's really tough on you, isn't it, Bud? They were really close."

His answer was slow in coming, almost as if he were taking the time to sort it out for himself as he was telling her.

"Yes. Jim has been close—like a kid brother, almost a son, I guess. Ever since he began trading airplane washes for rides, he has been special to me. Ann is different. I've never been able to get that close to her. She seems so capable, so efficient . . ."

"And so beautiful," Mildred added matter-of-factly.

"Well, yes. I'll admit that. You know how it is with people like us, the time goes by, days, months, years. With no kids growing up around your knees to give you reference, you lose perspective. There's no sense of aging. You kinda feel like you just got out of high school a year ago."

"Well," she murmured, patting his thick abdomen, "some things gradually change."

"Yeah," he chuckled. "But I avoid that by never looking in a full-length mirror." He reflected on that a moment. "Anyway, Ann doesn't talk like a twenty-year-old—or act it. Sometimes I wish she would. She doesn't seem like she ever had a childhood."

"Jim is like that, too, though his maturity doesn't intimidate me. I suppose men seem more vulnerable to women, at any age."

Mildred propped herself on her elbows to look Bud in the face. "What time did you say; half an hour?" She wriggled higher along his body, sliding her arm under his neck, and, cradling his head against her, whispered into his ear, "We need to build up an appetite for lunch. There should be time—we can shower together."

They were about fifteen minutes late picking Ann up. She looked so bad, drawn and edgy, that neither Mildred nor Bud had much left of the appetite they had whetted earlier. All three left the major portion of their orders untouched. What Ann needed was a reassurance that neither they, nor the weather, nor statistics could offer.

Though Bud did not state flatly that Jim was dead, Ann noticed that whenever he referred to "search," he avoided "rescue," and assurances of locating anything were limited to "the plane."

"I hate like hell to see you have to go through this for so long, Ann," he said as they were dropping her off at home again, "but it could be spring before we know what really happened out there."

Watching them drive off as she stood on the landing of her outside stair, Ann wished they had been able to come in for a few minutes, but Mildred had to report to relieve

for her shift, and Bud had agreed to meet someone for
parts at the airport store.

Sunday afternoon with nothing to do until eleven that
night. Maybe she would drive out to see George and
Naomi. It would be a change, and the air would do her
good. She simply could not stay in the apartment!

She decided to give them a call first. With all the rainy
weather they might not even be at the airport. Few people
flew on Sunday when it was not pleasant. The ones who
had to would not be stopping at Grant Field, which did not
have an instrument landing system of its own. However,
like hundreds of general aviation fields across the nation, it
did have an approach procedure keyed off a navigational
transmitter some miles away.

Ann was surprised when her call was picked up on the
first ring. She was so keyed up that when she heard
Naomi's cheerful voice, the impulse to visit assumed
greater importance than she was quite ready for. She
began a confused stammering of the reason for her call,
and before she realized it she was crying over the telephone.

After she had gained enough control to speak coher-
ently, she assured Naomi that she would be able to drive
and that it would not be necessary for George to come in
to pick her up. Within minutes she fled the apartment
and got the old sedan moving toward the freeway. The
drive took only a few minutes, and soon she was pulling
into the parking lot at the rear of the hangars behind the
Feisters' office. Angling the little Dodge into the closest
stall she was surprised to see three people huddled under
as many umbrellas directly in front of her car. Naomi,
George, and Bud wore matched looks of apprehension as
they waited for her to get out. Naomi was fumbling with a
fourth umbrella, which she had obviously brought to protect Ann from the hissing rain. In contrast to the other

three, which were standard black, the uncooperative umbrella, when it finally popped open, nearly stabbing George in the ear, proved to be a bright red floral.

Ann smiled and cut the engine. "Thank God for the geraniums. For a minute there I thought this might be Act Three of *Our Town*." She was laughing, a bit louder than she intended, as she stepped out and allowed them to convoy her to the line shack.

30

A VICE PRESIDENT of his insurance company called Thad Monte a week before Christmas with instructions to contact his client and give him the news that a bank draft for over half a million dollars was on deposit in his name at the local bank. The amount represented the face value of the policy plus interest from the date of loss.

Ordinarily Thad was happy to bring news of claim settlement to his clients, for the cash usually represented salvation from complete or partial financial ruin. In the case of a private aircraft owner, the settlement check frequently meant that necessary repairs could be made on a rumpled airframe so that the pilot could get flying again. Thus he was a kind of angel in times of distress.

He did not feel this way about Jack Laird's claim. True, the investigation had yielded results that pointed to an entirely legitimate claim, but he had an uneasy feeling about the thing. His wife, Shirley, would have felt the reason lay in the fact that there had been no proviso for the pilot of the plane. They had not mentioned the insurance once since his awful admission to her three weeks before.

Privately Thad had counseled Ann to press for civil damages against his client's company. That this was professionally unethical did not deter him in the slightest. Thad was a pragmatist in the ways of right and wrong. He knew that Laird carried liability coverage to protect his company, therefore himself, from lawsuits, and Thad believed strongly in the protection of the innocent. He even gave her the names of a few lawyers.

Ann had thanked him but said she would rather wait to let Jim handle any suit if he thought it justified. She made it clear that she had no liking for Laird or his method of doing business; it was just that her information had come secondhand by way of her husband. It would be better to let him decide on that after the rescue was effected and the facts established.

All this had been in the first week after the disappearance of the plane, when she was firmly convinced of Jim's survival. Thad had not broached the subject with her since. There would be time enough after they located the wreck.

The real reason for his reluctance to announce to Laird the happy outcome of his claim lay in the disproportionate values of policy and property. Thad did not believe in windfall profits, particularly when they dropped only from the tree under which the insured had spread a net. None of these dollars would be bruised by contact with a mortgagor before falling into Laird's lap. He had owned the plane outright—the only one in his entire inventory for which some bank did not hold paper. Thad did not know how much Laird had paid for salvage rights when he bought the plane in Mexico, but he was reasonably sure the price had been less than a hundred thousand.

The whole thing left a bad taste in his mouth.

He elected to phone Laird the news instead of going in person with him to the bank.

When Laird realized who was on the line, Thad could feel the eagerness in the man's suppressed manner.

"Yes, Thad. How's the family? You and Shirley take those kids skiing yet?"

"No, haven't had the time." The idea of snow providing anything but tragedy was somehow grotesque in the circumstances, and he hurried on to his point. "Listen, Jack, I have good news on your claim—the draft is in the bank. All you have to do is go down and sign the release papers to effect the transfer to your account."

There was silence at the other end of the wire, and by the time he answered, Laird had mastered a nearly solemn tone.

"Well, that is welcome news, Thad. Now maybe I can satisfy all the banks who have been after my hide these past few weeks. That money will go a long way toward getting me out of deep water, believe me. I had a lot tied up in that plane."

That's a lie, Thad thought, wishing he did not dislike the man so, wishing he could believe the words, wishing it was merely compensation for a pile of scrap aluminum they were talking about, and not the incidental flesh and bone wreckage of his friend mixed somewhere in the heap.

"Thad?"

"Yes?"

"Thought I lost you there." Laird cleared his throat and spoke tonelessly, "The check is for the full amount, isn't it?"

"Yes, well . . . no. What I mean is, there is an additional amount for daily interest from the date of loss— about twenty-five hundred more, I believe." Thad was speaking mechanically. "I have the exact figure here if you want me to look . . ."

"No . . . That's fine . . . no need, no need. I can check it when I get to the bank."

Both men fell silent for an uncomfortably long time. It was Jack Laird who ended the conversation. "Listen, Thad, I want to thank you for pushing this through for me. We little guys really understand what 'agent' means in times like these. Well, I'll be getting back to you."

Laird was not even aware that his agent failed to say goodbye but simply hung up without a comment. He was too busy thinking about the money.

Thad was thinking what "agent" meant to his wife, to Jim Regan, and . . . to Jim's surviving widow. Jack Laird had not even *mentioned* Jim . . . Ann. . . . God, how callous the man was!

In one more hour it would be December 23. Ann had nearly staggered into the hospital to report for the night shift. Her eyes burned with sleepless irritation, her nerves were raw with exhaustion. She had not had more than two hours' continuous sleep for more than a week. The nightmare was by now a reflex triggered by merely lying down and closing her eyes. She managed to escape it only by catnaps in the chair in front of the television. On the backs of her hands and between the fingers, small hives had begun erupting.

The smell of holiday evergreens assaulted with their mockery of her mood, and Ann at last began to allow logic to invade the optimism of her intuitive defenses. It had been four weeks today at noon. What possibility could there be of his survival?

Even if he had survived the crash uninjured there could be little hope. That thin jacket he had worn. The lack of food—immediately she became nauseated thinking of the small block of cheddar she had used to make his sandwich lunch. Even the store of food Bud had carefully itemized for her as part of the survival pack in the plane would long ago have been used up.

"Mrs. Regan?"

Ann realized that she had not been paying attention to the report being given by the nurse she was relieving.

"I'm sorry. What did you say?"

"Are you feeling . . . all right?"

"Oh yes," she responded. "I'll be fine. Just not enough sleep, I guess."

When the report was completed and she had assumed care of the floor, Ann stepped into the doctors' lounge, deserted at this hour, and switched on the television. At quarter-past eleven she should be able to catch the weather forecast.

It was in progress. The animated weatherman was dancing through his routine.

"So to recap, my friends, the outlook for the holidays is good. We should have clearing late tomorrow, with a definite prospect for sunny skies on Christmas Eve. That little system east of the Hawaiian Islands probably will not affect us until Christmas afternoon or evening. Soooo . . . holiday driving should be good. Just tell your out-of-town relatives to plan to stay with you for a few days after the holidays. By then the next storm should have passed on through."

Ann snapped off the set and began making the rounds of her floor, checking on each patient, administering the prescribed medications and generally bedding down the floor. She did her work almost by rote, thankful that there were no complications to upset what promised to be a quiet night.

So the weather would clear sometime tomorrow afternoon. She was not surprised that she felt no elation. The chances were remote indeed that a search would be reopened with the prospect of a forty-eight-hour hole in the pattern of record-breaking storms. Her one possibility was Bud, of course. It was not fair to ask him to go on another wild goose chase, with the odds a million to one that a single search plane would happen to cross the site of the downed plane or that the wreckage could be spotted anyway under a four-to-six-foot-thick blanket of snow.

Her intuition murmured weakly that Jim would find a way to let them know where he was if only they could get close enough. But if he were alive, why hadn't he signaled somebody when there were dozens of planes crisscrossing the Sierras searching for a sign weeks ago?

Ann sagged into the nurse's station chair to begin making entries recording her floor check in each of the twenty-three patient charts. The fatigue even showed in her handwriting as it jerked erratically across the page.

Briefly a memory of her sitting in Jim's lap with his arms holding her gently but securely sprang into her mind and then faded. The thought was so comforting she tried to will it back. It would not return, though, and it sharpened her sense of longing so that she closed her eyes and turned back her head, yearning for the feel of his shoulder on her cheek, the pulsing of his throat against her nose and lips.

It was no good. The ache in her chest and throat tightened all the more for her desire.

Trembling, Ann got up and went to the water cooler. The first cup slipped from her shaking fingers before it was half filled. Leaving it rolling in the puddle at her feet, she took another, drinking greedily as though parched.

As she stooped to clean up the watery mess, she wondered if she might be losing her mind.

31

LEO KEMP'S EXECUTIVE twin flashed over Owens Valley southbound at 200 knots. The plane's altitude was shoulder high to the craggy white wall of the Sierra Nevada off its right wing. As the craft gained the lower reaches of the widening valley floor, it gently turned the corner of the great wall and leveled out over the flats of the Mojave Desert.

"Would you look at that, Bruce!"

Leo Kemp indicated the sugary coating of the desert floor ahead of the airplane.

"That *is* a rare sight." The young pilot on his left whistled as he too marveled at the sparkling beauty of the snow-dusted wasteland below them.

"It looks like southern California has spread the VIP Christmas carpet for us. I just hope they didn't go *too* far. God knows, I've had enough cold weather this past month. I'll be glad to soak up some sun again."

His pilot nodded agreement as he turned to look at
Kemp. "It's been a long four weeks. I don't see how you
keep up the pace. I'll bet you haven't averaged more than
five hours' sleep a night for the past month."

"Well, I'll admit it, Bruce. I *am* tired. But . . . it had to
be done, and I'm glad we could pull it off."

"I guess the merger is pretty much in the bag, huh?"

His boss winked. "Can't say. You might upset the market with that kind of information. Let's just say that things
worked out pretty much as I had hoped they would."

Bruce Logan adjusted aileron trim and leaned back,
watching the wingtip scribe a perfect line across the distant
mountains.

Neither man spoke for some time. Finally Kemp broke
the silence, "Say, Bruce, you don't have a heavy date in
San Diego tonight, do you?"

Bruce shook his head. "No. No plans at all."

"Then I'd like to land at Grant Field on our way home.
There is a dealer in used airplanes I need to talk to." Kemp
said nothing beyond that, but he was thinking. His own
sources had advised him of fund-shifting to close an
airplane deal which mysteriously never materialized. Although no money was lost, the person responsible could
not be found. A quiet investigation had turned up the
name of Jack Laird. Kemp, for reasons he would not admit
even to himself, wanted to speak to the dealer privately.

It was nearly noon on the twenty-third of December
when the gleaming little transport whistled in to a feathery
landing, chirping three distinct tireprints on the short
runway at Grant into a blustery 15-knot crosswind. Bud
Fallon approved of the arriving pilot's technique with only
a fraction of his attention. He followed the plane's progress, wondering idly if it would be able to make the cen-
terfield turnoff without using brakes.

Ann Regan stood beside him, also watching the twin. She had never looked worse. There was a desperate nervous exhaustion which added ten years to her face and an irrational bent to her normally well ordered mind. She had just asked—pleaded—that he try once more to find Jim.

Bud knew that the way he handled her request could have a profound effect on her recovery from what was by now the assumed death of her husband. He also knew she was acting out of desperation. What had him upset the most was that she still had not accepted the fact of her husband's death, after four weeks, and that it was tearing her up inside.

Mildred was right, he thought. I should have been brutal with Ann at the first. The longer it took to get confirmation, it seemed, the stronger became her conviction that he was still alive.

He decided that he would refuse to recommend any further searching, and he would tell Ann as plainly as he could why she must face up to the facts for her own sanity and the safety of everyone involved. Already there had been one close call with a pilot nearly getting trapped in a tricky high-altitude canyon because of inexperience and overzealous attempts to do his job.

They watched as the unfamiliar twin pivoted to a stop near the gas island and cut its engines. At last, as the two occupants of the plane debarked not fifty feet away, Bud turned to Ann. Gripping her arm almost fiercely, he faced her, cutting away her last hopes.

"He's gone, Ann," he said, beginning to grieve himself. "You and I knew that before the others did. Whatever chance he might have had, weeks ago, is over. There is no reason to force others to take chances with their lives on a fool's errand. God knows, and so do you, that I'd trade my life for that kid and you. But that won't work, and I have to do what I should have done weeks ago—prevent you from hoping even one more minute."

"Oh, Bud" was all she said, but she repeated it with such reproach that it did him in completely. He could not go on.

Ann slipped out of his grasp, and slowly wandered toward Naomi's office. He watched her numbly, as the door burst open and the portly woman rushed out to gather in what was left of Ann. He was completely oblivious of the withering look Naomi sent in his direction.

Someone was speaking to him. He heard the question twice and still did not comprehend. The speaker was young, like Jim, and that did not help. An older man was standing close by, giving him a strange look.

"I asked if you knew where Jack Laird . . ." the young man stopped abruptly. The older man, about his own age, Bud guessed, came forward and stood beside them.

"Sorry . . . we seem to have come in at a bad time." The voice went on smoothly. "Can I help in any way? My name is Leo Kemp," he went on, extending his hand, which Bud shook dumbly, "and this is Bruce Logan."

Bud was confused and embarrassed. He was like an automaton, explaining the situation about Ann, bubbling out the story of Jim's disappearance, dimly thankful that he sounded like he was maintaining emotional control, at least not crying like an old woman. His face above his lips felt frozen, eyes drying in their sockets because he had forgotten to blink, but the words came pouring out. He became aware that his monolog was being interrupted by sharply worded questions from the listening men, and that at one point the younger of the two suddenly sprinted for the parked airplane. He was back in a moment, asking questions again, dates, times, headings, estimated airspeeds; he was busily turning pages in some kind of journal.

Suddenly there were no more questions. Both men were bending over the open pages of the log. He heard one say, "That must be it. The time certainly jibes. Let's get a chart."

The older man turned to Bud. "Mr. Fallon, we picked up an ELT signal south of Bishop on the day you mentioned. Do you think it could have been from the plane you are missing?"

Bud stared at the man dumbly, as the meaning of his words sank in.

"It was of short duration," added the young pilot, "like an accidental transmission. At the time we thought it might have come from a radio shop, because it started a minute or so after the hour."

Could it be? Bud hoped that at last he could find the plane and put Ann's delusions to rest. He heard himself urging the men into George and Naomi's office to consult the wall chart. He made the introductions, wishing Ann were not there until he was certain.

The figures worked out. They were able to triangulate, from the bearings Bruce had recorded with times, on a point where the plane could have gone down.

Bud ran back to his parts store across the ramp and returned with copies of hourly satellite photographs taken on the day of the flight. All his work with the weather people was about to begin paying off, grimly and belatedly.

"Here. You see?" Bud said, pointing a finger at the cloud cover. "This is where he would have first noticed it. He probably turned east to get over the ridge before running into the weather. Without radios, he would have to do that to stay VFR."

For some reason Bud kept looking at his wristwatch, consulting it as if to back up his analysis. He looked at the others and went on, "He would want to stay on the Inyo

County side so if it got bad he could land at Lone Pine, or maybe Bishop."

"Bud, his proposed en-route altitude wasn't high enough to cross there," Ann said quietly. "Remember what the Flight Service people said about his plan?"

Bud thought a moment. "That's right, Ann. But he had planned to go up along the route faced with lower mountains. I'm sure he would have increased altitude if he turned east." But looked at his watch again, and this time it spoke to him. He remembered the conversation between Jim and Jack Laird. The suggestion, almost insistence, that he switch tanks after one hour on the mains. All at once the puzzle cleared away like fog under a hot sun.

"It was fuel starvation," he said to the still room.

"How do you know, Bud?" asked George Feister.

Before he thought of the consequences Bud answered, "That was when he switched to the tip tanks, George. Either there was a stoppage in the lines, or he got some bad gas."

It was not until he heard the low cry from Naomi Feister that he remembered where the gasoline had come from. The cause of contamination usually came from the airplane tank itself, he knew, but he was unable to reassure Naomi on that point.

He looked to George for help but saw that he, too, had been struck painfully with the possibility that fuel from his pumps had caused the accident. Both George and Naomi tried to make the best of it for Bud's sake, for they realized he had not even thought before he spoke, but the damage was done, and Bud added to his increasing mountain of misery the fact that he had hurt his friends.

The group broke up after an hour's planning for a search the following day. It would take more time to reopen the official search, because the reported signal had been heard by only one plane, for such a short period of time that it might prove unreliable. There were the additional factors which added up to a delay, and these included the facts that the search was no longer considered a life or death situation, the morrow would be Christmas Eve, and the weather was forecast to get bad again on the twenty-fifth.

32

AN AIRPORT IS a neighborhood community unto itself. As such, it fosters a rapid spread of gossip. Barely an hour had gone by before the news of the ELT signal had spread to the only cafe on the field, and with it the speculation that Regan's flight might have gone in because of bad fuel. One of the first listeners to this tale as he sat nursing a late-afternoon beer in one of the corner booths was Jack Laird. When asked, he made no comment beyond saying expansively that George and Naomi were careful in their operations and that he would find it hard to believe that their pumps had been the cause of such a calamity, although he did allow, adding a factor no one had mentioned before, that "Their equipment *is* quite old."

Laird did not quite realize why he had taken steps thusly to add suspicion while seeming to exonerate until much later in the afternoon. The idea struck him with its brilliance, its extra margin of guarantee.

That night he would sabotage the Feister underground tanks and pumper truck by charging them with water.

It would be so simple! The wash rack, a concrete pad with a spigot and hose, was adjoining the gas pumps. This facility was provided by George as a convenience to customers to enable them to hose down their airplanes.

Laird thought through the plan several times to be sure it would go smoothly. He would need an extra length of hose to reach the fuel-truck and ground-tank fill pipes. When it was quite late he would drive to the wash rack, soap up his car to provide a reasonable cover for his being there, and when "not a creature was stirring," so to speak, fill Feister Fuelers' stockings a day earlier than usual.

He waited until Charlie Wise had gone home for the day before going out to the shop to pick up a 100-foot length of hose. When it had been carefully stowed in his car, he drove to a restaurant in town to treat himself to a quality meal. He even celebrated with a few drinks in honor of the approaching holiday. Just before the dining room closed at eleven, he left and headed back to Grant Field. As he suspected, no one was around but the single patrol car that checked incoming vehicles and aircraft. Laird waved to it, shouting something that passed for "Burning the midnight oil again." The lone security officer recognized him and waved back.

An hour later, his job nearly completed, Jack Laird saw a plane entering downwind for landing. He knew the security patrol would drive to the taxiway to check on the incoming flight and see him at the pumps. Quickly coiling up the hose, he hung it on the holder, raced for his car, and managed to make it to his own office and park just before the security vehicle cruised by. To the officer in the cruiser it appeared that Jack was finished for the night and just leaving.

But Laird was not quite through his preparations. Returning to the work shed he hunted around for a 5-gallon gas can. When he located one, he filled it with water from his own tap and lugged the heavy container to his own twin Beech.

Using care not to spill any on the ground, he split the 5 gallons of water between the two main tanks of the old airplane. Before returning the fuel can to the shop he shook out the last stubborn drops and left the cap off so that it would be completely dry by morning. Then he got into his car and drove home.

The fact that in his haste to avoid the patrol he had forgotten to remove his own extra length of hose from the one hooked up to the wash rack never occurred to him. Too many drinks after dinner probably. It should not matter much. The two hoses were identical in color and manufacture. In fact both of them had been bought from Bud Fallon several months earlier. Nearly everybody at Grant Field had one.

The first thing George Feister did each morning, after opening the line shack and turning up the heat, was drain the fuel sumps of his ancient surplus gas truck. Today he waited a little longer than usual, deciding to have a cup of Naomi's coffee before starting his routine.

By the time he got out to the truck, he discovered a man sitting on the cab step waiting for him. The stranger introduced himself.

"Mr. Feister? I'm Bill Short from the FAA office. Mind if I watch?"

George Feister reserved a special treatment for anyone on "official business," be he businessman or bureaucrat. A visit from the government people piqued him especially, however, and his response was civil but chilly. He went about taking his first fuel sample from the sump with the air that Short was not even there. His lack of concern was well-grounded on the conviction that high personal standards of quality control gave him no cause for concern.

He would expect to find traces of water condensate, for, after all, that was the function of the sump. He was shocked, however, when the quart jar he used for sampling turned out to be three-quarters filled with water. Dumbfounded, he turned to the inspector to show him with the air of one who had made a rare archeological find.

Tossing the first liquid aside, he quickly drew another, then another, and still another, until he looked for all the world like someone bailing out a sinking dinghy. He was aghast.

The inspector was noncommittal, quietly taking notes. They moved to the pumps, checking each carefully, but found no contamination at any of them. Without being asked, George, who had been joined by Naomi, hurried to the underground tank caps. A preliminary dip of his measuring rod brought up the tell-tale globules of water along the bottom foot of its length.

"What does it mean, George?" Naomi asked, wringing her hands.

"It means we stop selling gas until I find out what the hell is goin' on here; that's what it means."

"I'm sorry about this Mr. . . . . Mrs. Feister," the official said quietly. "It *would* be best to shut down until your equipment is checked."

George did not hear the comment. He was deep in thought, angry at something he could not identify. Suddenly he spoke to Short, "Say . . . how come you happen to be here the one day I have water contamination?"

Short answered carefully. "Apparently you may have had problems before, sir. You see, I'm here at the request of an insurance company reopening the investigation of a casualty loss. One of their clients—insureds—complained that a second plane had purchased contaminated fuel here a few days ago."

"Jack Laird."

"I'm afraid I'm not at liberty to say. In fairness to the complainant, however, I must add that I've just checked the aircraft in question. I drew nearly a gallon of water from its sumps."

After the inspector had left, George locked the pumps and hung a large NO GAS sign on the island.

"Oh, George! How could this happen?" Naomi whispered to her husband in the privacy of the office. "We really *did* cause that boy to crash." She was close to tears.

"Bullshit, Nome. For one thing, it didn't just *happen*. For another, I could pump gas outta that truck and those pumps right now and all day without gettin' a drop of water in a plane. The filters and baffles would keep it out."

She was not following his line of explanation, so he faced her, gripping both her arms, and spoke quietly but harshly, "Listen, babe, some bastard is out to make us look bad. Why, I don't know. Now count on me in this. Our gas didn't put Jim down. Something—or somebody—else did that. How that water got in the tanks I don't know, but this is for sure—the water in the truck had to be *put* there. I always fill the truck from the pumps, and they are runnin' clean—we just checked them."

Feeling her ease perceptibly, he softened his grip. "Just give me time, Nome. I'll find out what and why and who, and I got a pretty good idea right now. Why don't you drive to the bakery for some donuts," he said, suddenly changing the subject. "Bud and the others will be here soon. They'll want somethin' to eat before heading for Lone Pine."

She nodded, swallowing a hard lump; following his direction with a docility brought on by helplessness, turned to get her purse.

At the door she stopped and spoke in a hoarse whisper, "Now George, don't you go and do anything foolish. I don't want you to get hurt. Just . . . act your age . . . please."

The telephone rang as she closed the door. George nearly jumped when he recognized the voice at the other end. His face deepened into a scowl as he spoke.

"Yeah, Charlie. Funny; I was just thinkin' of you."

"I figgered you might be, George, that's why I called."

"Charlie, I was wonderin' if you had any idea how come an FAA guy knew I got water in all my gas." His voice was hard, more than insinuating.

"Lay off me, George! I ain't got time to give you sweet talk. I guess you think you got good reason to put the finger on me, but you're dead wrong."

"Somehow I don't feel convinced, Charlie," George retorted drily.

"OK. Let's leave it at that. Do yourself a favor though. Keep yer big mouth shut, and stay away from this end of the field until I show you somethin'."

Charlie pressed on. "I'm bringing that insurance guy—Monte. I'll see the two of you in an hour. Now for God's sake, keep your lip buttoned."

George's curiosity was gnawing at him now, but his temper was slow to cool. "You better have something worth all the trouble."

Charlie's voice was quiet and serious. "It ain't perfect, at least not yet—but it will be worth the trouble."

In the pay phone booth next to the cafe, Charlie hung up and glanced at a number scribbled on a torn piece of paper. Depositing a coin, he waited for the tone and punched out the new number. While he waited for Thad Monte to answer, he felt in his windbreaker pocket to make sure they were still there.

They were. His fingers closed around the belts in their plastic bag, holding them tightly, as he spoke to the insurance agent.

33

SOMETIME SHORTLY AFTER five A.M.
Mildred Yancey's clock began a low, annoying buzz. She
swatted it silent before it had time to build into a full-
throated alarm. Long years of practice popped her out of
bed, turning the light on before she was fully awake. On
her way to the bath she pinched one of Bud Fallon's toes to
rouse him also.

He was nearly dressed by the time she came dripping
back, wrapped in a mammoth towel. A rumbling, nonde-
script greeting escaped his lips as he struggled with an uncooperative zipper. Mildred stood appraising him for some
time before starting her own clothing selection. It was
more than nice being with him these past few weeks, she
decided. In fact, their affair was beginning to flower rather
than fade. She was discovering a mutual dependence and
reciprocal fulfillment with Bud, and for her that was a
novel, if not unique experience.

"Where have you been all my life?" was what she had asked sometime last night, after a particularly fulfilling sexual interlude. They had both laughed quietly at that, because by no stretching of their imaginations could either conceive of the other's matching needs of earlier times. But they were different people now, "right" for each other because of the years' slow molding of their diverse lives.

When he looked up from buckling his belt, she felt awkward in an almost forgotten, girlish way, thinking of her nakedness under the towel. A blush heated the back of her neck and spread up under her ears.

"Finish in the bathroom, Bud Fallon. I would like some privacy to dress, if you don't mind."

Raising his hands in a signal of surrender, Bud backed out of the door.

"Whatever you say, lady. I'm going." He slowed the exit long enough to add, "Say, could you call Ann to make sure she's up?"

Alone in the bathroom, he did his best to freshen up for what would certainly be a long day. He wished he had a razor; he could not face again the one he had borrowed from Mildred the night before. There were dried nicks still smarting near his Adam's apple which attested to the validity of the commercials claiming the razor had been "designed especially for a woman."

He was not used to the role of drop-in lover, nor did he consider their relationship to be that casual. Although he had spent five or six nights sleeping with her, there was enough of the old-fashioned about Bud to exclude deliberate preparations for those overnight eventualities.

The nature of their affair, in that it had been precipitated by Ann's loss of Jim, was something that had caused him concern. On more than one occasion he had alluded to this unfortunate circumstance to Mildred, who had wisely pointed out that had they not been so emotionally stirred by that situation, they might not even have noticed each other.

Bud had been surprised not so much by the apparent lack of "romance" in her analysis as he had been by his own acceptance of that probability—and his own undiminished joy in spite of it. He decided that it was something like finding out that there was no Santa Claus, but being old enough to appreciate the fact that human love was the greater miracle after all.

Mildred was just hanging up the telephone when he stepped back into the bedroom. She was already dressed.

"Line busy, or no answer?" he asked.

"Neither. Ann is up and ready to go, and I'm cleared at the hospital."

He whistled. "Boy, you sure move fast in the morning!" Then he looked at her with a trace of confusion. "What do you mean about the hospital?"

"I'm going along with you."

"I don't understand . . ."

"Look, Bud dear, both you and Ann are so emotionally involved in this thing today, I'm worried about your taking chances you might not under ordinary circumstances. Let me go along to supply a cool head if nothing else."

He was pleased that she wanted to fly with them, but one look at her determined face was enough to convince him that he would have had to let her come regardless of his wishes. He gave her a long look, then kissed her lightly.

"Let's go, Amelia," he said, taking her arm and steering her out the door.

At the airport they met Ann, who had picked up Leo Kemp and Bruce Logan at their hotel. Naomi and George were also there, an hour earlier than usual, to see them off, but the pair were not themselves this morning as they passed out hot coffee and donuts to the group.

Mildred noticed the absence of their normal gregarious behavior, George's frowning, monosyllabic gruffness and Naomi's puffy red eyes. She remembered Bud's agitation of the night before, and wished she could say something to reassure the couple, but realized nothing anyone could say would help.

Bud, Leo Kemp, and Bruce Logan were talking quietly at the wall chart, plotting courses, taking notes, planning flight strategy. Ann stood directly behind them, listening to every word. In back of her was Mildred flanked by George and Naomi.

When everything had been talked out, the three at the wall turned around to face the others. How much like a funeral it is, Mildred thought, watching the tableau. Ann's back was straight and brave, her head erect. This will be rougher on her as the day goes by, Mildred continued to muse, unable to shake the requiem mood.

She was totally unprepared for the shock of seeing Ann's face when the young woman turned to face her. She was beaming! Eyes sparkling with suppressed anticipation, eagerness to be on with the flight radiating from her smile.

Dear God, Mildred Yancey thought, her mouth dropping, aghast. She still thinks we'll find her man alive!

The trip to Lone Pine was uneventful but turbulent. On the way up, both Ann and Mildred confessed to airsickness, due partly to the fact that they had not had a proper morning meal. Bruce Logan and Leo Kemp had delayed their departure for thirty minutes to compensate for the lower cruise speed of Bud's airplane. An aerial rendezvous over the small town had been arranged, and a discreet communications frequency agreed on.

By the time both planes converged into loose formation, Bud had to suggest landing before beginning the search. His crew was quite sick, and it would be pointless to attempt anything under those circumstances.

"Yeah," he said by radio to the twin circling with him high above the airport, "I think we'd better get some ground under their feet and some grub in their stomachs."

"OK, two-four Papa, you go first," Bruce replied, "We'll follow you in."

On the way down Bud regretted having to descend over 10,000 feet to the valley airport without having used the advantage of altitude for an hour's search. Climbing back up to get high enough to clear the precipitous eastern wall of the Sierras would be time-consuming and a needless waste of fuel. He would have to refill the tanks, adding extra weight, to compensate for the time loss, and ridge flying in a heavy, sluggish airplane was something to avoid.

When the high-winged Cessna had rolled to a stop in a transient parking space, Bud talked himself through the shutdown procedure, trying to make up his mind. The big Jacobs finally rumbled into silence, and he spoke, "Come on, gals. Let me spring for breakfast; that'll fix you up."

Outside the plane they waited on the ramp for the others to taxi up and shut down. As he looked first at Mildred then at Ann, Bud decided to make the first search pattern of the day alone. They wouldn't like it much, but neither woman would be of much help until they got over their airsickness. If they spent two hours on the ground after eating something, perhaps he could take them up later. The more eyes the better.

He managed to convince them of the practicality of his plan as they ate. Ann pleaded at first, but finally gave in when she realized that she *would* be a liability rather than an asset to the search effort. The promise that she would be included in the second flight lessened her disappointment considerably.

Mildred questioned Bud closely about his solo flight,

and did not appear to be completely satisfied even when he assured her that he would maintain plenty of terrain clearance during the search.

Outside the small restaurant they all watched as he took off and began a steep circling climb to reach a safe altitude for ridge crossing. As before, Bruce delayed takeoff for several minutes, since the supercharged twin could reach the same height in a quarter of the time.

"I wonder if it wouldn't be better to use a faster plane," Mildred ventured, peering up at the slowly rising 195 from under the shade of an upraised hand.

Bruce laughed softly. "Well, Doctor, that old bird might look slow climbing up there, but it will fly circles around us when it comes to poking in and out of those mountains. That's where speed is a real drawback." He joined her in following the progress of the glinting aluminum toy roaring ever higher into the nearly purple mountain sky. "We'll have to stay higher and make wider turns; he can get closer to the deck."

Mildred Yancey dropped her eyes to look intently at the young pilot. "I'm not sure that I am happy to know *that!*"

Bruce flushed, concerned that he might have opened up a can of emotional worms. He added a bit hastily, "Oh, what I mean is that the one ninety-five's wing loading makes it a safer plane at low airspeeds. I'm sure Mr. Fallon will not take any risks."

Mildred was silent, staring at the laboring speck in the sky. She answered with an air of finality which precluded any further reassurance from Bruce, "Knowing the way he feels about things, I'd not be sure about that at all."

High above them, Bud monitored the slow windup of his altimeter and put on an oxygen mask. After he turned on the valve, he patted the glareshield and spoke in a rumble that nearly matched the growl of the struggling engine, "Wish I could give you some too, Jake. Maybe after this is over I'll see about gettin' you a turbo."

Some time after he had observed the twin take off below him he called on the plane-to-plane frequency.

"This is two-four Pop at thirteen five. How are you doing?"

Bruce's voice crackled back in his headset immediately, "We're out of six thousand for one four point five—about five miles north with two-four Papa in sight."

"OK. I'm heading across the hill now. Let me know when you're overhead, or if you lose me."

The two planes headed for their prearranged search area and began a methodical pattern, covering the patch of mountains southwest of Mount Whitney which coincided with the triangulation plot Bruce had roughed out from his notes. On the chart the area seemed small enough, 4 or 5 square inches, but when translated to the actual terrain of ravines and craggy ridgelines, the problem took on staggering complications. Searching an area of flat country is difficult enough. Mountain work is almost overwhelming by comparison. Added to the terrain considerations, of course, was the deep cover of snow changing the shapes of even the mountain peaks themselves.

Two and a half hours went by as they laced back and forth over the granite and snow, rarely seeing anything to attract their attention. On those occasions when something did, Bud would methodically examine the questioned spot, dropping down to near treetop levels, planning his entry and exit from the inspection pass with close precision, and then executing the maneuver as though on tracks. Each time, although he always gave it a second look from a slightly different angle, the results were negative.

Finally he gave up the pattern in deference to sagging fuel gauges, and pointed the blunt nose of the plane toward the pass above Lone Pine. As he tracked over the ranger station, he remembered what George had told him about Ann the last time the three of them had flown through this notch. Dipping his right wing, he gazed out over the frozen lake. Too bad Jim couldn't have landed there—all that open space. The ice was covered with a heavy blanket of snow, but even if it were 6 feet deep it would not hide the outline of a large airplane.

Something about the lake troubled him. It was definitely within the corner of their search area, and after he had refueled, he would include it in the afternoon search. He looked at his watch and whistled to see that it was already twenty after one.

"Well, *maybe* we'll get as far as the lake," he said to the airplane, "but it will be awful late if we do."

Bruce called him at that point, asking if they might precede him in the landing. Since their plane was pressurized, they could get down comfortably more quickly. Bud agreed, grateful that someone else would have to give Ann the bad news for a change.

Several minutes later, as he was turning downwind for landing, the lake intruded once again. A picture of Jim's plane formed slowly in his mind, and with a shock he realized what the suddenly interrupted ELT signal could have meant. How long had they heard the signal? About ten minutes.

An image of the gleaming airplane sinking slowly under the icy water of the lake held him in a trance. He saw the tail of the plane slip under the surface with a great froth of bubbles. He could almost visualize the short whip antenna of the crash locater sticking briefly above the water. With a great effort he wrenched his mind away from a vision of Jim clawing at the escape handle as the water numbed him to slow-motion.

Heads turned all over the airport as Two-four Papa slammed to the asphalt, screeching her tires and bouncing awkwardly into the air again. The engine roared at such mistreatment, and by the time Bud had the plane safely on the ground, he had had a very close encounter with the fence at the far end of the runway.

It was the worst landing he had made in thirty years, but the embarrassment was lost to him. As soon as he had jumped out of the parked plane, he began asking locals if anyone could tell him when the big lake on the other side of the ridge had first frozen this winter.

34

BUD HAD CONSIDERABLE difficulty finding anyone with hard information about the lake. Several pilots at the airport had overflown the pass dozens of times during the early winter season, but none could pinpoint exactly when the first skin of ice covered the lake. Estimates ranged from October to December. Someone told him that the ranger who manned the small station several miles from the spot would probably know, but the outpost had been closed for nearly a month.

After a few telephone calls with frustrating results—caused by the fact that it was, after all, the afternoon of Christmas Eve—he finally reached the man at his holiday address on a ranch near Bishop.

"Sorry to trouble you at home, Mr. Tomlin," Bud began when his party answered, "especially on Christmas Eve."

"No problem. Everybody calls me Nate. What can I do for you, Mr. . . . ?"

"Bud . . . Bud Fallon. Look, Nate, we're doing an air search for that plane lost a month ago on a flight from Grant to Sparks."

"A twin? Only the pilot aboard? Yeah, I remember the bulletin."

"Well, we have new information that could put the plane down somewhere near the big lake a few miles southwest of your station. I need to know whether the lake was frozen over on the day of the flight."

"That's easy."

"Then you know?"

"Oh, yeah. The plane was lost on the day of the first big snow, right?"

"Yes . . . yes," Bud repeated.

"Well, the day after, I was making a game check along the trail above the lake. It was covered with snow then."

Bud began to feel a rising hope. "Then it had to have been frozen before the snowfall?"

"Oh sure. It gets a tad warmer when it snows. There would have to have been ice there first."

Bud nearly gasped, "I was afraid the plane might have gone in and sank. We might never have found the . . . body."

Nate's voice turned a shade more solicitous. "I get the idea that you knew the pilot; right?"

"Right. There isn't much chance, I know, but I thought we might get lucky and spot the plane. The widow is going through particular hell right now, you see."

"Sorry to hear that . . . for her and you." He paused. "But one thing, Bud."

"Yes?"

"Don't count too much on that ice thing."

"What do you mean?"

"The ice *was* sound when I saw the lake during the

snow; I mean there were no dark spots that would suggest
mushy ice underneath. But that doesn't prove it was strong
enough to support a big plane, especially if it came in
hard."

"I see," Bud murmured.

"I have to be honest with you, friend," the voice said
quietly.

Bud sighed and spoke tiredly, "And I appreciate that,
Nate."

Both men were awkwardly silent for a time, then Nate
Tomlin spoke.

"That old mountain has been hard on us this year, first
your friend's plane and then the old Indian woman."

Bud struggled with the shift in conversation at first, but
then he remembered the news stories about the lone
camper who had died in the snow some weeks earlier.
"The backpacker? Was she found near here?"

"Yeah. Stumbled into my truck as we were pulling out
from closing the station. She died before we could get her
down."

"I didn't know the truck hit her . . ."

"Oh, it wasn't like that. We were standing still when
she staggered into our headlights and kinda bumped into
the truck. Actually she was dead before I scooped the old
gal up. Just a bag of bones. I'll bet she didn't weigh eighty
pounds."

"Did she die of exposure?"

"No, the doc down here said it was probably massive
stroke from all that walking. She was over seventy, they
tell me."

"Did she live up there . . . have a cabin or something?"

"No. She wasn't one of the local people. Actually she
was from an old folks' home down your way. Nobody
seems to know what she was doin' up around Mount

Whitney; all alone at that. No family either. Real mystery.
She must have been camped out somewhere for a couple
of weeks, though. The people at the home say she had
been missing since the middle of November.

"Funny thing. When I bent over her she had pulled off
one glove and she kept trying to tell me something with
her eyes. Whatever it was it was mighty important to her,
'cause she was in real pain. Pity we'll never know what it
was."

Nate Tomlin pulled himself away from the story.
"'Look, Bud, I hope you find the plane, but don't take any
more chances today. There is more weather comin' in. I'd
hate to hear that you ended up with your plane decoratin'
one of our local Christmas trees."

Bud thanked him for his help and reassured the ranger
that he had no intentions of letting that happen.

By the time he returned to the others in the pilots'
lounge near the restaurant, it was nearly 3:30. A glance at
the late afternoon sky confirmed that a high overcast was
adding its shadow to that of the mountains towering above
the town.

Ann's face was drawn with apprehension as she rose
from her chair and started toward him.

"Did you find out anything?"

"He's not sure about the lake, Ann. It was frozen over
before the snow, but whether it was solid enough to support an airplane he couldn't say."

"Oh, Bud. Please let's go and look. I feel so strongly
that he might be up there. Even today I knew where it was
on the way up, sick as I felt. We were miles south when we
crossed into the valley, weren't we? But I could feel it
pulling me out the window; it was on your side, blocked by
another mountain peak, wasn't it? I didn't even have the
chart, but I know the lake was there!"

Bud shrugged. "Yes. It was there. But, Ann, that . . ."

Ann fixed him with eyes blazing with conviction. "The plane is there, too. And . . . and so is Jim."

He looked at the threatening sky again and thought, *Ann, Ann, you're asking us to take too many chances.* With lead in his chest, he realized that he would have to refuse her. Suddenly he caught the sound of a pickup sliding to a stop on the gravel ramp. He walked out to meet it, thankful for the reprieve. Ann followed closely behind him.

"Hey there. Are you Bud Fallon?" The words curled easily around a battered pipe cocked in the speaker's mouth. Bud recognized the voice of Nate Tomlin, and introduced him to Ann. The ranger tactfully refrained from mentioning anything about the crash, and went directly to his point.

"After you hung up I got to thinking that it wouldn't do any harm to have you look over these things." He indicated a parcel lying on the seat beside him. "These are the effects of the Indian lady. They are keeping the . . . her here hoping to locate next of kin."

Bud accepted the paper-wrapped bundle and carefully untied it on the tailgate as Ann and Tomlin looked on. The garments were mostly small-sized men's wear, something out of an army surplus store. Even the underwear might have been a man's—thermal top and bottoms. As Ann watched she felt a vague closeness to the wearer beginning to absorb her. A weak suggestion of wildflower scented the collection, probably from the soap she had used; this and the overall cleanliness of everything testified, even in death, to the fastidiousness of the woman.

Something bothered Ann. For a moment she could not quite put her finger on it. Then it hit her. There were no personal articles in either the pockets or the paper sack.

She turned to Nate Tomlin, who was looking at her with a respect mixed with sympathy. "Is this all?"

"Yes, that's it. Why, is something missing?"

"Well . . ." She seemed at a loss to explain. "It's just that there is nothing personal here . . . not even a comb."

Tomlin nodded, smiling at her perception. "We wondered about that, too. Probably she was making a run to beat the snow. Decided to leave everything at her camp to travel light. She probably knew all her camping gear wouldn't help if she got caught anyway."

Fallon shook his head and muttered, "Damned shame. To think she made it all the way just to end up dying when she got there." He was folding the clothing to put it back in the bag. He started to zip up Charity's jacket, but when his fingers closed over the zipper tab, he opened them again bending to examine the metal pull. A short length of wire had been threaded through the eye of the tab, probably to make it easier to operate the fastener with mittens or gloves. What caught his attention was a disc of lead, smaller than a dime, into which the wire was imbedded.

Bud felt the skin of his neck begin to crawl, and he let out a low whistle. The other two followed his eyes to the dull gray metal, watching as he turned it over. On the reverse side were impressed the letters B.F. Bud was trembling. "This is the tamper seal from the survival kit I gave Jim when he left! She must have been with him until the last storm, Ann."

Ann took the soft lead disc from Bud after he had untwisted it from the jacket. She was having difficulty controlling her voice. "These are your initials!"

Bud looked at Nate in despair. Now they had positive proof that the plane was nearby, and the pressure to find it would force him into a deadly corner of recklessness, despite the certainty that Jim could not have survived.

Nate Tomlin saved him from confronting Ann with this. "Mrs. Regan, you must know that your husband is certainly dead after all this time. I know the terrain up there. There is barely a chance that he survived the crash. Even if he did there is not much to hope for. The fact that this poor soul"—he indicated the sad bundle of clothes— "found the plane doesn't change much. Remember, she walked out a month ago."

It was as though Ann had not even heard him when she spoke. "Could she have walked to your station from the lake?"

"The trail goes past the lake. Yes, but . . ."

"Let me keep this . . . please?" She held the amulet-like seal out to him in her open palm.

"Of course, and when the weather clears I'll personally . . ."

But she had turned him off and was tugging at Bud. "Hurry, Bud. We haven't much time."

Fallon shrugged, trying to feign nonchalance. He shook Tomlin's hand briefly. "Well, thanks, Nate. We really appreciate your help."

Ann and Bud returned to the cafe to report their discovery to the others. Despite the weather, they agreed to make one more try. Leo Kemp suggested that Mildred accompany them in the twin as insurance against air sickness. Bud agreed, secretly relieved that she would be in the other aircraft, safely above all that cloud cover moving in over the peaks.

Mildred must have read his mind. "Just remember when you're poking around those mountains," she said softly. "Killing yourself to find a dead friend would be a terrible waste. You can afford to be generous; you've had one love to fill your life. Just remember not to throw away mine."

Twenty minutes later, as the old highwing single banked again toward the snow-choked notch in the ridgeline, Bud noted that a broken layer of cloud was moving in under the high overcast. He called to the twin circling higher behind him.

"Can you tell how high the tops are?"

"Roger. Looks like we will be IFR if we try to stay above you this time. I think we better not risk it."

"OK. If you can, why don't you get on top of the overcast layer. It probably isn't more than fifteen thousand. I'll just keep talkin' on this frequency to let you know if we see anything. We'll beat it out of the lake area if this bottom stuff starts lowering on us."

"Roger, Two-four Pop, just don't get caught. The stuff west of here looks pretty bad. You might be in snow before long."

As planned, the two aircraft crossed the ridge. Once above the top layer of cloud, Bruce used navigational radio fixes to establish the twin over the lake and began a standard holding pattern.

Several thousand feet below, Bud eased the 195 into a shallow glide toward the lake. When he had reached a reasonable altitude that offered the best compromise between safety and effective sighting, he set the airplane up for powered slow flight. They would not have much time, from the looks of the scud moving in. One or two circuits of the lake would be all they could manage before making a dash for the notch and clear air on the eastern side.

"Keep your eyes peeled, honey," he spoke to Ann when they began the first run. "Tell me the second you see anything odd."

Ann nodded, her eyes glued to the landscape below. Her teeth were clamped so tight that the muscles of her jaw balled into peanut-sized knots, and her clenched fists pushed down against the soft flesh of her inner thighs.

Bud studied the rippled snow patterns of the lake surface. He was looking for a depression, a darker shading, anything that might reveal the outline of a refrozen hole in the ice.

"There's a broken tree, Bud," Ann said.

Bud thought grimly, how many millions of broken trees there must be in the great Sierras! But he took action on her report as a matter of habit. In a search you checked out *everything,* no matter how trivial it might seem.

"Point it out when we swing around." As he spoke, the plane circled like a roping horse turning smoothly back upon the point. This time he kept the area on his side of the plane, banking slightly so that they both could see.

"Right there," Ann said, reaching her arm in front of him to point. "Here, let me put the wingtip on it."

Bud let go of the yoke and watched as Ann moved the big cantilevered wing down in a series of circular bobs until she got it steady, holding it on a point around which they slowly turned.

"OK, I've got it," he said squinting into the deepening murk and resuming control of the plane. Bud studied the tree carefully as they circled. It was an old pine. Near the top, at the bottom of its symmetrical crown, the otherwise perfect circle of branches was slashed with a deep vee, marking the place from which a major limb had been ripped. Down along the trunk, a livid scar pointed a long tapering finger at the ground, marking the place where the falling member had ripped away bark and underlying fiber until the heavy branch at last had torn free.

It was a fresh wound, all right. "Good eye, Ann. That's the kind of clue we're looking for. Now, look around the area to see if you can see any other damaged trees, or anything that looks disturbed or out of place."

He swung the plane back over the lake to make another pass, noting with some apprehension that it was becoming darker by the minute. They would barely have time to get back before the dim light failed completely. The thought of being forced on instruments was something he pushed into the back of his mind, where it rested uncomfortably with the memory of Mildred Yancey. It would be a very iffy situation to be forced to climb on instruments at such a high altitude, surrounded by the highest mountain peaks in the country, into clouds he knew had the probability of heavy icing.

"One more look, Ann. Then we gotta get outta here."

On the way back to the tree Bud noticed that part of the branch was sticking up out of the snow. It was propped at a strange angle—as though resting on a large boulder hidden under the snow. He strained to make out the outlines of the rocks, cursing the failing light.

Reaching for the panel, his fingers found a switch and flipped it on. Out on the underside of the wing a landing light blossomed, sending a stabbing beam straight down. Bud left the old-style lamp in its retracted position and walked the beam up to the branch. Something flashed back the lamp's reflection on the ground.

Bud's pulse quickened, and he jammed the throttle forward, sawing the big plane into a tight, but careful turn. Ann looked at him with mixed expectancy and alarm. He spoke carefully, afraid to raise premature hope. "I saw something reflected in the landing light. We're goin' back over the tree again. Look at the lumpy spot on the ground just under the scar."

On the third pass they both saw it, a jagged shard of aluminum jutting up through the branches of the fallen limb. Suddenly, like a design blended into the mosaic dots of an eye-examiner's color chart, the muted outline of the plane stood out.

They did not speak to each other. Ann had unfastened

her seat belt and was standing slightly behind Bud in the roomy cabin, her head next to his, hand on his shoulder, bracing herself against the G-forces of the wide turn. Her eyes burned out the window with his, into the virgin snow.

"No signs of life, but we're gonna make sure." Bud's voice drifted in on her consciousness like a grating saw blade, cruelly shredding her concentration. She looked at him, formulating a protest, when she realized that he was giving a report to the twin circling high above them.

"Now look closely, honey, I'm gonna drop a flare. Don't look at it, though, look at the plane. Look for tracks in the snow, any sign of activity."

Suddenly the area under the plane bloomed into brilliant detail as the belly-mounted tubes of the old plane fired a parachute flare into the gloom. The ground appeared to sway, tilting to the swinging oscillations of the descending magnesium torch.

They saw nothing, no footprints, no signals, no signs that anything had moved near the plane for weeks.

Bruce Logan's voice was in his ear. "Two-four Pop. The three of us think you had better get out of there. The stuff on top is really building."

Bud acknowledged quietly, "Roger, we're heading out now. It's the plane all right, southwest corner of the lake, about thirty yards on shore, up against a tree. You copy?"

"Gotcha, Bud." Bruce knew why Bud had given the detailed location, but he refrained from commenting on the possibility that he and Ann might not be making the report themselves. He depressed the mike button again. "No signs of life." It was a statement of corroboration, not a question.

"Correct. Negative life signs." Bud added as an afterthought, "I'll give you our progress every minute 'til we make the pass. We're over the lake now, halfway, about four hundred feet actual."

"OK, we're on the line."

Ann was still standing in a half crouch behind Bud's seat, turned toward the window, hands and face pressed against the plexiglass, straining to watch as the parachute flare dropped slowly into the snow and winked out. She was relatively blind for a few seconds, blinking swiftly as though that would speed the return of sight. Slowly the dim outline of the tree returned, shrinking as the plane lunged for the far side of the lake. She kept her eyes locked on it, unable to accept the marker for what her logic demanded it must be. An agonizing need to leap from this departing plane, to run back to the tree, to claw him out of the snow nearly possessed her, and she pressed so hard against the window that the vibrating plastic touched one eye, searing it with pain.

Three red balls of fire looped up to match the burning sting, and she had to close her eyes and let them wash with tears. Reopening her eyes, she was startled to see the same three red comet lights claw down from their height, racing for the lake.

She screamed, pounding Bud's shoulder, afraid to take her eyes from the dropping red blobs. She knew he had seen them too, because the plane suddenly wrenched itself into a violent left turn, and she went crashing to the floor and slid against the opposite side.

Bud did not apologize. He reached a hand back to help her without ever taking his eyes off the place from which the lights, now gone, had apparently come. She heard him talking excitedly on the radio as she regained her seat and buckled in. The plane was level now, descending in a shallow glide back toward the corner of the lake. She could no longer make out the tree, but knew where it was with every vibrating sense of her thrilled body.

At that moment a faint trail of sparks, like a flipped cigaret butt, arched directly in front of the plane. The lead spark exploded into three blinding red suns, each looping its separate course up and over the wing behind them.

Bud was shouting, "Red star cluster! Red star cluster! He's using the old Very pistol!"

As they approached the shoreline, Bud pushed the prop into high pitch and firewalled the throttle. The tachometer bounded to redline and flickered there, registering the protesting snarl from the deafening engine. This time Ann was ready for the climbing turn, and the left wing pivoted on the old tree as if it were tethered there.

She was not listening to the radio conversation; all Ann knew was that at last the others knew what she alone had cherished through the nightmare weeks.

"Listen, Ann . . . *Ann!*"

She found her voice and answered with a squeak.

"Ann, I'm gonna put it down on the lake. It is gonna be a rough landing . . . probably tear up the plane. I want you to find the emergency radio and survival pack behind the back seat. Leave it tied down until after we stop moving. Then get the stuff and crawl out of the plane. If I can't manage, call Bruce on one twenty-one point five using the portable transmitter. He's listening now. One more thing. Turn off your oxygen and strap yourself in the back seat— I'll need the center of gravity as far aft as I can get."

"Bud . . ."

"Save it for later, Ann. We have to land anyway. The pass is closed by now, and we couldn't climb out of here through that stuff if we had to."

Bud began total concentration on positioning the plane for landing, and he was not aware that Ann had moved out of her seat until he felt her kiss on his cheek as she moved to the bench seat in back.

When he was abreast of his approximate touchdown point on downwind, he triggered the second electrically fired flare and turned on the landing light. After waiting a moment to get enough distance, he dropped the left wing, lowered flaps, and circled to the final approach, keeping the blinding light of the flare blocked with his left wing and talking himself through the landing ritual.

"Now this might be your last landing, old girl. Don't let me down. Keep that heavy chin up so I can drag you in real ladylike."

He nudged the tail lower, trimming all the pressure off, coaxing the heavy craft to the edge of a stall, settling to within a few feet of the snow whipping below the spring-steel fixed landing gear, milking every ounce of lift from the ground effect as the plane slowed. He knew that the instant of touchdown she would go over on her back; the high altitude meant his over-the-ground speed was more than what the indicator read. He was not looking at it anyway. This was all by touch, the near-instinctive adjustments made in deference to the mechanical individuality of a machine he had flown for years.

"It will be very soon now, old girl," he said, watching the shoreline weave closer in the flickering light of the flare behind them. The nibbling trout-strike of imminent stall vibrated through the yoke and up his arms. In a blur of right-hand movements, he shut off fuel, closed the mixture and, at the first cough of the fuel-starved engine, killed the mags and cut the master.

His timing was perfect, and he felt the tail hit the snow the instant he hauled back on the wheel with both hands. The wings stopped flying and the plane dropped her long front legs into the racing snowdrifts. The deceleration was sudden and violent, smashing the nose down and wrenching the fuselage slowly over onto its back. Bud was glad he'd had the foresight to install shoulder harnesses.

"OK back there?"

"I . . . I think so."

"Look, Ann, be careful about unbuckling; you're upside down. Hold on to something so you don't break your neck getting out of the belt. If you can wait, I'll get undone and help you."

It was not more than two minutes before they had extricated themselves and were standing outside on the inverted wing of the plane.

Bud immediately raised Bruce on the portable radio and made his report. Despite himself, he could not keep the shake out of his voice. After a terse but jubilant exchange, he said they would call again after locating the other plane. Then he added, "Tell Mildred I'll try not to catch cold." It was not what he wanted to say, and the joke was corny, but she would understand, he thought; she would understand.

He lifted the bag of survival gear over his shoulder and stepped off into the deep snow, forging a path for Ann to follow close behind him. The position of the plane was easy to spot because of the tree, but they could not see the wreckage at all even though they were not more than a few hundred yards from it.

In their eagerness to cover the distance they wore themselves out plunging through the deep drifts. It took ten minutes for them to gain the edge of the lake and a few minutes more to find the buried plane.

As they approached it there was no sign of activity. The hatchway door was completely covered with a smooth drift of fresh powder. Then, just as they began to claw away at the snow, a branch rose up above them with a tattered flag of orange cloth and began to wave weakly to and fro.

They scrambled up on the tail, using branches from the fallen limb for support. Walking cautiously, they inched their way on top of the fuselage toward the front of the plane. The flag was protruding from a hole in the snow.

Bud aimed his flashlight at the waving branch to where

it disappeared through a raggedly cut hole in the roof of
the cabin.

"Jim?" Bud shouted hoarsely, "Jim, can you hear me?"
Bud thought he heard a sound, but it was beginning to
blow with flurries from the first of the new storm, and the
sound might have been the scraping of the rude flagstaff
against the jagged metal hole.

Frenzied, they tumbled into the snow beside the plane
and clawed to find the buried door. At last they located it,
cleared an opening and tried the handle.

It was frozen shut.

Bud tugged open the pack he had been carrying and,
giving Ann the flashlight, reached in and pulled out a small
hatchet. After hacking away at the sealed edge, he managed to sink the blade between the door and jamb. Puffing
with exertion, he pried at it by pushing with both hands
against the handle. On the third try the door popped open
with a rending groan, and he pushed it up against the stops.

Ann aimed the flashlight into the dark hole of the
cabin, flicking it toward the pilot's seat with her shaking
hand. In the eerie light she saw that it was empty. A
movement to her right pulled her hand and the light
around to the back of the cabin.

She stared at the blinking, bearded face for several
seconds before she realized it was her husband. Dropping
the light with a clatter inside the cabin, she slid after it and
rushed over to him. The slanting beam from the fallen
flashlight accented his sunken cheeks and hollowed eyes.
She knelt on the floor beside him, cradled his head in her
arms and kissed him again and again, great sobs convulsing
her out of a month-long grief.

Bud joined them quietly and waited for Ann to get
control. A soft, rasping whisper brought her weeping to a
temporary halt and she bent her ear to Jim's lips to catch
the words. They were loud enough for Bud to hear.

"Gee, honey, I was afraid you were still mad." Jim struggled with the words, but in the light she could make out his grin under that awful beard. "I always knew you'd come back, but what the heck took you so long?"

Bud found his voice at last and answered for her.

"Merry Christmas, Jim," he said, but then he lost it again.

35

ANN AND JIM WERE at last delivered to their apartment by Bud and Mildred late Christmas evening. Those two friends stayed only long enough for Bud to set up the miniature tree Naomi Feister had decorated and sent along, and for Mildred to lecture them not to be so violent in their reunion so as to damage Jim's leg cast—or themselves with it. With that they had left.

For a moment, as the young couple watched the lights of Mildred's sedan pull away, they stood awkwardly at the window. Ann stared at their half-reflection in the dark pane almost as if she were watching strangers. Her husband looked so different—bearded, twenty pounds underweight, hunched over the still-unmastered crutches. She turned to him and looked up into his face, a bewildered expression of joy mixed with disbelief in her eyes. For the hundredth time in the past twenty-four hours, she reached out for him, touching his arm, caressing his back, encircling his waist, leaning into the thin body for tactile reassurance of his presence.

Jim slipped the left crutch out from under his arm and propped it against the wall. He held her close, pressing his face into her hair, inhaling the wondrous fragrance of her, pressing his fingers gently into the softness of her back, feeling the tenseness leave them both in this, their first private moment in a month.

By the time they had negotiated the short distance to the bedroom, they had managed to leave a trail of most of their clothing behind. Jim was dimly aware of how smoothly this was accomplished, but later he wondered how he had manipulated the zippers and hooks with only one free hand—the left one at that.

After she had stripped off her stockings and lay back on the bed, a momentary shyness overcame Ann, and she covered herself with the pillow. Jim smiled down at her, mildly embarrassed at his own urgent tumescence, and slid awkwardly on the mattress, gratefully shucking off the right crutch with its draped and tangled inside-out shirt.

Looking only at her face, he bent to kiss her long on the lips and gently slipped the pillow out of her grasp. His hands ached for the roundness of her breasts and he yielded to the longing.

Ann reached up for him and pulled him down, and they were caught in the wonder of rediscovering what they had missed in the long emptiness of their separation.

Several times throughout that night they awoke in the half-light of the bedroom and embraced tenderly, wordlessly, testing the dream for its reality, never fully trusting deep sleep, and never mentioning to each other why they were glad to have forgotten to turn off the lights in the living room, visible down the hall.

It was not quite daylight when Jim opened his eyes to her kiss, finding her robed by the bed with a tray of steaming cups in her hands.

"Get up, you lazy loafer," she smiled brightly. "It's time to go to work."

He blinked at her sleepily. Clearing his throat, he reached for the cup she held for him and grumbled, "Sorry about work. My office is closed for repairs." A flicker of concern crossed his face as he thought of the fact that he was indeed out of a job. A freelance pilot does not accrue sick leave. He sipped thoughtfully at the cup.

"Hey!" he exploded, after swallowing the first taste. "How come the tea?"

Ann laughed lightly. "Isn't it good? So much better than that sour old coffee."

Jim looked at her closely. "Boy, you *have* changed. What happened to my old wife, the coffee-and-cigaret freak?"

She did not answer immediately, but reached back to the tray and picked up a fat business envelope decorated with a skimpy red stick-on bow. Handing it to him she whispered, "Merry day-after-Christmas."

He took the package from her, turning the sealed plain envelope over in his hands, then looked at her in confusion.

"Well?" she asked impatiently, "aren't you going to open it?"

Carefully he slid his finger under the lightly sealed flap and opened it. When he saw the U.S. Airways logo on the letterhead, Jim's hands began to tremble. Shaking out the folds of the letter, he clutched it in both hands and began to read it greedily. His eyes alternated between the neatly typed message and Ann's delighted face as the marvelous news slowly registered.

She anticipated his next move and checked him just as he was about to leap from the bed. "Hold it, buster, you have a bum leg; remember? Let's not get carried away and break your cast."

They talked excitedly about the job for some time, with Ann filling in the details about the captain's promise to hold Jim's spot until he could make it. The memory of that call sobered Ann briefly, and Jim caught the change, took her into his arms, and held her quietly for several minutes.

"That's why I got you up so early," she said finally. "You really do have to go to work—or call in at least. Their office is two hours ahead of us. I have the number."

Jim continued to sit beside her on the bed, lost in thought. He pulled her close again, tucking her head into the hollow of his neck. "It was pretty tough on you . . . all those weeks without knowing anything."

It was not a question, but she nodded anyway and pushed tightly against him. He went on, "I had this desperate need to let you know that I was still alive."

He had begun stroking her arm absently. "At first I was absorbed with the pain of my head and leg, and then with the sheer effort of survival . . . and then," he swallowed hard, remembering, "the loneliness after the old woman left."

Ann squeezed his hand and waited for him. "You see, the one thing that kept me going was the thought that you were here . . . that you would *be* here no matter how long it took for me to get back. Then one day the realization of the awful strain you must have been under just knocked the wind out of me. I knew that trying to keep up hope under those circumstances for all those weeks would have cracked me up." He shuddered to think of himself in her position.

Raising her head from his shoulder, Ann grasped Jim's arms and turned him so that they were looking into each other's eyes.

"Yes, it was bad," she replied soberly, "worse than I could ever describe. And you are right; it probably would have broken you to have gone through the same thing. But you see, love, I had a very definite advantage."

She smiled brightly, and he marveled at the sudden lift in her mood.

"What kind of advantage?"

"I knew you could never leave me . . . not completely."

"Well, sure. The memories . . . "

"More than memories," she laughed. "More than love even. Something tangible."

He caught it then, more from her shining eyes than from the words, and cheated her out of her announcement.

"You're going to have a baby." His tone was soft with awe, and Ann was glad to have heard him say it rather than the other way around.

They sat together on the bed for quite a long time after that, not saying anything, just holding hands and looking at each other.

Some time later, when Ann came back from getting breakfast things at the corner store, she found him looking quietly out of the window. He appeared strangely sad.

"Did you make the call?" she asked, somewhat apprehensively.

"Yes . . . Well, not to the airline—not yet." He looked at her, standing with the groceries clutched in her arms. "I made a call to that place the ranger said claimed the body of the old Indian woman."

Ann set the bag on the counter and turned back to stand beside him. "What did you find out?" she said gently.

Jim looked at the floor. She could see a struggle working in his eyes.

"There isn't much. Somebody from an Indian agency claimed the remains . . . had her cremated. They couldn't tell me about where she is now. 'Final disposition' is the way they put it."

Ann waited. This was his own private hurt. She felt outside, unable to help.

He went on, "I know she was very old and could not have had much more time, but I can't get over the fact that she died trying to get help for me. I didn't even know her name until just now. 'Charity Whiteflower.' It certainly fits, doesn't it?"

Ann nodded silently, taking his hand.

"For a time . . . there in the plane . . . I think she thought I was someone else, someone she knew from before . . . someone she might have loved. I don't know—I was pretty confused myself most of the time."

They sat together on the couch. Jim held both of Ann's hands as he struggled for the right words. "I have this terrible feeling that the poor woman led an empty life, no one to love . . . do you know what I mean? And she spent it all on me. I would have died, you know. I must have been out for nearly a week."

"But, Jim dear, you shouldn't feel so low," Ann said, hoping to find some point of reassurance. "The poor woman was able to accomplish something heroic in her life. Not too many people can claim that."

"Well, it isn't easy to be the one saved, especially when it was at the cost of somebody's life."

"Yes, she should have stayed in the plane. You did tell her not to go. Remember? Maybe she was confused, unbalanced."

Jim looked at his wife with pain in his eyes, "That is what bothers me the most. You see, she never touched any of the rations in Bud's pack. She fed us both on what she had brought. When that was gone, she must have known there would not have been enough for two. No, she knew what she was doing."

Ann caressed his hand lovingly. "Please don't feel bad for what she did, Jim. I am deeply grateful to her for having brought you back to me. Maybe she knows that now . . . wherever she is."

Ann saw tears form in his eyes for the first time since she had known him. Somehow that made her husband dearer to her than before.

"The thing that really hurts," he said, "is that I never even got a chance to thank her."

Ann took her anguished husband into her arms and shared his grief. Somehow she knew the test of the last month would bring them a deeper union. Above all she had the father of her child back from death. She accepted the gift without constraint.

"Thank you, Charity Whiteflower," she murmured.

36

BY THE TIME Thad Monte and Charlie Wise arrived at the Owens Valley airport, the severed wing of the wreck was already thawing out in a heated hangar.

"Boy, that was quick work!" Charlie commented, puffing as he lugged his set of inspection tools.

"A half-million still stirs the souls of claims adjusters, Charlie, even in these days of inflation," Thad said drily.

They met the FAA inspector on the ramp and proceeded directly into the hangar.

"The rest of the junk will be hauled out with a Skycrane, I guess." The inspector paused to knock ashes from his pipe. "We got the port wing and engine out with a light rig a couple of hours ago."

The three men quickly located the alternator, which was missing a belt, as expected. That in itself could not be considered a cause for the crash.

They moved to the intact wingtip fuel tank and removed the cap. Inside, under the full load of gasoline, they saw a large chunk of ice blocking the fuel line.

The inspector whistled. "Now *that* is what I call fuel contamination."

The implications were not lost on Charlie and Thad. They could see the official report wording. "Crash caused by fuel contamination. Causes: improper preflight procedure; faulty equipment maintenance by fuel dealer a contributing cause."

The inspector was still peering into the tank with a flashlight and what looked like an oversized dentist's mirror. "The only thing I can see under that slush is a piece of metal." He straightened, rubbing his back. "Probably a stray rivet dropped in when the plane was built."

Charlie was at the open tank like a ferret. "Where is it?" he demanded.

The two men crouched over the small opening. Charlie moved his flashlight over the inside of the tank.

"Down lower, toward the after end . . . see it there by the seam?"

"Yeah." Charlie squinted along the beam of light. "It don't look like no rivet to me, though. Let's see if we can fish it out."

After several tries with a length of wire, he finally lifted the small object clear of the tank and placed it in the investigator's open palm.

The three of them looked at it silently. Thad Monte shrugged and turned away. "Just looks like an aluminum shaving to me."

"No," said the FAA agent. "It's too regular for that. It's a clip of some kind. See how it has been crimped?"

Charlie suddenly grabbed the agent's wrist and picked up the curved aluminum strip, turning it at different angles close to his eye. He turned pale with excitement and nearly danced.

"Godamighty!" he croaked, "that's it!" He looked at the piece once more to reassure himself, then looked at the others. "That no-good murderin' sonofabitch." Thrusting the metal back into the investigator's hand, he ran for the door. "Fer Christ sake, don't lose that. Wait here. I'll be back."

The two men looked dumbly at each other and at the clip, and were still in the same positions when Charlie came rushing back. He was holding the bag of cut vee belts in his hand.

Thad began, "Charlie, you've already shown us the belts. They didn't cause the . . ."

"Not the belts," he shouted, pulling them out and letting them fall carelessly to the floor. "The goddam *bag!* It was the plastic bags! They were underneath the belts when I found them in the trash!" He held the crumpled plastic up for them to see. It was ripped at the shoulder as though the person getting at the contents had not tried to unfasten the neck of the sack. The wrinkled blue words "Free Ice" blazed up at them.

They looked on incredulously as he pointed out the tiny aluminum ring crimped around the gathered plastic. The inspector held out the one resting in his hand.

It was a perfect match.

The two men looked at Charlie for an explanation. "Don't you see? Laird put a bag of ice into the tip tanks before he gassed the plane. It was cold, in the twenties, the little gas in the tanks wasn't warm enough to melt the ice-cubes. That way Jim wouldn't see any water when he did the preflight, because the stuff was still frozen. Then Laird made sure he topped off the tanks with warm fuel from the underground tanks at the Feister pumps."

Thad Monte's jaw muscles bunched as he spoke through gritted teeth. "All that ice was water by the time Jim took off. Laird knew it wouldn't get to the engines until Jim switched tanks—when he was over the mountains."

"Yeah," muttered Charlie, and suddenly he was thinking of a small wad of masking tape stuck on the wall chart in Jack Laird's office. "He had it all figured out, all right." He reached into his pocket and pulled out a handful of change. Turning toward a pay phone in the corner of the hangar, he said, "I'm gonna tell Bud Fallon to keep an eye on Laird 'til we get back."

The FAA investigator looked at Thad with meaning. "I think you and I have some important calls to make, too."

Late that afternoon Jack Laird was sorting through his desk to put things in order before leaving on a long vacation. He was quite pleased with the way things had turned out. The nagging guilt he had experienced whenever he thought of Jim was now erased because of his rescue.

His other crimes did not cause him the least concern. He put them all into the category of clever business dealings. Oh, they were illegal, but he did not consider them any worse than the manipulations of the insurance conglomerate he had just bilked of a half-million. Perversely, his greatest regret was that he was not able to crow about it to anyone.

A shadow fell across the window, and he looked up to see Bud Fallon approaching the door with a large grocery sack in his arms. The door swung open and crashed against the wall. Fallon strode toward the desk, ignoring the rebounding door, which thudded to his shoulder and bounced to the wall again.

"Well, hi, Bud. Good to see ya. Howza kid comin' along? Jeez, but that was a lucky break. I can tell ya now that I was pretty busted up when I thought . . ."

Fallon did not say anything, but the look in his eyes was murderous. He set the grocery sack on Laird's desk with a sodden crash, and propped his bunched shoulders on stiff arms, fists pressing hard on the marred wood as he glared at the seated salesman.

Laird's patter had dribbled off into silence and he began to experience real fear.

When Fallon spoke finally, the softness of his tone was in such contrast to his fierce look that the effect was more frightening than if he had shouted.

"A friend of yours—and mine, now, I hope, because it seems we have all misjudged him—this friend tells me you have a very interesting wall chart." He turned away and walked up to the large map on the opposite side of the room. "He tells me that you have amazing powers of precognition. He says you had the crash site marked on your chart on the very day the plane went down."

Fallon's finger shot up to the dot of white marking the tear where Laird had removed the tape weeks before. Laird's eyes bulged to see the tiny mark, for he had not noticed until now that the tape had removed the spot of ink when he pulled it off so hastily.

"You were a bit off at that. About eleven miles southwest, I'd say," Fallon went on, his voice now taking on an edge.

Laird decided he had better fight back, for appearances. The spot on the chart meant nothing.

"Now look, Bud, I think you're makin' a fool of . . ."

"Oh, and another thing. Charlie said your green hose was missing. I looked all over for it. Guess where it turned up? George Feister must have stolen it. I found it at his wash rack a few minutes ago. Thought he could rip you off, I suppose. But he didn't know that Charlie engraved your name on the brass couplings—did you know that? Thorough fellow, that Charlie."

Laird was tensing; this was getting blacker by the minute. He gambled a wild shot.

"So Charlie was the one to try to blame the Feisters
. . ."

Fallon ignored him, pressing mercilessly. "Charlie and
Thad are on their way back from Lone Pine, right now.
They should be in any minute. Some guy from the FAA is
coming along, Laird; he wants to ask you some questions."
He paused long enough to pick up the paper shopping bag.
"They want you to have this to think about until they get
here!"

With that Fallon upended the sack on Laird's desk.
Two sodden bags of party ice tumbled out, one of them
falling wetly into Laird's lap. Fallon gave the paper sack a
shake and two hooplike vee belts bounced crazily off the
desk, sagging into a staggering roll before flopping to rest
on the floor.

"Now . . . about my promise," Bud Fallon growled and
started to reach across the desk for the rising Jack Laird.

A voice at the door stopped Bud before he could get
his hands on the shrinking salesman. "I'm afraid that will
have to wait, Mr. Fallon." Bud turned to see a police officer walk into the office followed by Thad Monte, Charlie
Wise, and another man who must have been the FAA
investigator.

The young deputy sheriff took Bud firmly by the arm,
but he was smiling as he spoke in a gentle voice, "We really
have to read the suspect his rights. You wouldn't want to
incapacitate the man and invalidate an airtight conviction,
now would you?"

By the time Jack Laird had been taken away in hand-
cuffs, Bud had regained most of his composure. Charlie
Wise grinned at him with regret. "I suppose it was stupid
of me to call you about the evidence, Bud. I shouldda
figured you might pull a barroom act." He looked wistfully
after the departing patrol car. "I know how y'feel. I'd like
to get a piece of him myself."

In the end they settled for a drink to celebrate at the local cafe. Charlie Wise felt better than he had in years. He was just itching to tell Bud how he had arranged to have his old Cessna hoisted up by helicopter off the lake and trucked back home. It was hardly damaged. He and Bud would have it fixed in no time.

Maybe with a little luck he could get it back in time for Bud and Mildred's wedding. Charlie's eyes sparkled; what a surprise *that* would be!

37

SEVERAL MONTHS LATER, after Jim's leg had mended and he had completed training with the airline, Jim and Ann dropped in on the Fallons. They were barely seated when Bud sensed an urgency in the younger couple unlike their mood on previous visits. He looked at Jim and asked pointedly, "What's on your mind?"

Ann smiled and thought, How much like Mildred he's become.

Jim shifted awkwardly and answered, "Well, unfinished business is what you could call it, I guess."

"It's Charity Whiteflower," Ann added quietly.

"It probably seems silly," Jim said, "but I can't seem to get her out of my mind. She . . . something, anyway, keeps poking around in the corners of my mind. I keep wondering what she was looking for up there in all that wilderness." He waved his hand idly as if to shrug off his words, but his face betrayed deep turmoil.

Ann reached over and took his hand. "Jim is upset that the old woman had no family to claim her, especially after the heroic thing she did for him."

Mildred cut in gently, "You mustn't feel guilt for her death, Jim. That would certainly spoil her memory. It is a pity she could not have survived to realize she saved you, after all she must have gone through, but you can't change that," she added with finality; "nobody can."

"Oh, I know all that, but it's no comfort." Jim's eyes clouded with some private memories. Then abruptly he spoke to Bud. "Could we borrow the one ninety-five?"

Bud was surprised at the apparent turn of subject. "Well, sure, you know that. The old bird flies better than ever since Charlie and I put her back together. When do you want her?"

Ann chirped excitedly, "We were thinking of flying up there to see what we could find out about Charity. Jim has made phone calls, but it's not the same."

Mildred jerked erect. "Now look here, young woman, you could deliver any day now. I don't think it's a good idea to complicate things."

Ann laughed. "That won't be for another two weeks, according to your own estimate. Besides, it's only a two-hour flight each way—with a hospital at both ends."

Mildred finally gave grudging acceptance if not approval, and Bud cautioned Jim privately to make sure Ann used oxygen in the higher altitudes.

They left early the next morning into a warm sky blue with the last days of spring. It was a beautiful flight all the way up to Owens Valley, and not a single cloud obscured the majestic Sierra wall when they landed.

Renting a car at the airport, they drove to the address of the reservation, which Jim had been given over the phone by the Indian Affairs official. After several false starts, they finally located a man who seemed to know as much about Charity Whiteflower as could be expected of anyone under the circumstances.

He was quite old, but he rose to greet them from the porch of his small home as they parked the car on his packed-earth driveway. Even without the ceremonial costume he was wearing, his leathery skin and dark eyes marked his ancestry.

"I hope you won't mind the tribal garb," he said easily, extending his hand to each of them. "I thought that, considering the nature of your call, this might lend some respect to the deceased." Then he waved them to a cluster of rocking chairs under a nearby tree. "My name is Bill Pitana—that is a short version of Pitanakwat, which, from what I've heard about your narrow escape, you will identify with." He chuckled and looked at Jim. "The word in Shoshonean means 'pine-nut eater.' "

With a rush Jim was swept back to the long days of solitude and the vision of the old woman painfully shelling pine cones and teaching him what parts were edible. He savored again the pungent taste of the pine needles she had also forced on him.

Their old Indian host appraised him with a smiling look of understanding. Taking Jim and Ann by the hand, he stood between them and nodded. "Yes, our old friend, the Tubatulabal, did well. It was a good end, and" —he indicated Ann's swelling figure—"a symbolic exchange!" Then he laughed at his own seriousness. "You must pardon me, friends. I'm afraid that I am incurably romantic. Even the university could not cure me of that."

They liked the old man immediately, and as Ann watched Jim, she could see the weight lifting from him as their long visit stretched into early afternoon.

Most of the conversation centered about Charity's tribal background—very little about her life apart from what Jim had been able to piece out in his many telephone calls.

The old man had been educated in anthropology and had lived a portion of it himself. He explained that Charity had apparently been seeking out her ancestral home, but having been raised far to the south, she had inadvertently started her trek on the wrong side of the Sierras.

"The Kern River Indians lived in the valleys on the other side," he said, sweeping his arm toward the granite wall rising several miles to the west. "It would have been easy for her to take the bus to Kernville and hike along good roads to the south fork of the Kern River. Of course," he chuckled, looking at Ann, "that would not have helped your husband."

He fell silent for a time, eyes downcast, and they wondered if he had not dozed off. But when he looked up they knew that he had been deep in thought because his tone had changed; become serious—more than that—mystic.

"I sent for her personal things, from her home—we Indians can manage that, cut red tape. Also, I have her ashes here in the house—she should not have been cremated. They buried their dead as we do." He waved that thought aside, "No matter." He paused again. "There is one thing among her belongings which troubles me. I'll get it now." With that the old man rose and walked with difficulty across the yard to his house.

When he returned he was carrying a metal box and a white leather pouch. With an almost ritualistic deliberation he placed the metal container in Jim's lap. "Those are her ashes," he said simply.

Turning to Ann he extended the leather pouch, gripping the gathered top with one hand and cradling the underside with his other palm. She took it, a thrill of expectancy heightening her confusion.

He sat between them as before. Jim stared down at the macabre burden in his lap. Ann examined the deerskin pouch closely. It was quite old, but soft and supple. A white flower design had been worked into the leather with beads and quills. The top was secured with a pale ribbon intricately worked through the leather.

The old man startled them by beginning to chant a soft melodic air. It lasted only a few minutes. When he had finished he got up again and stood facing them, motioning them to rise with him.

"Now, my young friends, I am not sure whose ashes these are in the flowered deerskin, but Charity guarded them through her life. We must complete her trust."

With those words he carefully untied the ribbon and spread open the mouth of the pouch. Turning to Jim he reached out and carefully pried off the lid of Charity's tiny casque. Then he took Jim's elbow and gently guided his arm and the metal urn, tilting it so that the ashes spilled neatly into the leather pouch.

After he had retied the ribbon, the old man took the empty urn from Jim and patted the deerskin bundle. Ann and Jim stepped closer, moved by the strange ceremony.

"You must leave now; the wind will soon be on the ridges." He pointed to the pouch. "Can you find the headwaters of the Kern?"

Jim nodded, still not quite able to speak.

"Pick a place on your way back, you will know where," he said with conviction. "And you, soon-to-be-mother, keep this," he tapped the deerskin, "as a token of love."

With that he turned and made his way to the porch, mounted the steps, entered the house, and closed the door silently behind him.

Shortly after noon a pair of gracefully cantilevered wings soared over the lake high in the Sierras. When over the southern shoreline, they banked in a graceful turn and pivoted around a shattered pine.

"I think I see where you mean. I can make out the broken tree limb."

"That's the place. Now do you see what I mean about being hard to find?"

"It's a miracle you ever found me."

They continued circling low over the breathtaking wilderness. Then Jim turned the plane slightly to follow a rugged canyon south of the great white mountains. A raging stream, charged with spring meltoff, twisted its way between the feet of the crags. At some point, which neither Ann or Jim could be sure of later on, the river abruptly turned, creating in the hook a grassy curving meadow of wildflowers.

Suddenly Ann gasped and tugged at Jim's arm, "Look, down by those rocks! Is that a lion?"

Jim peered down following her pointing finger but could not make it out. "Could be a cougar—mountain lion. I can't see it." Something prickled at his memory, giving him a strange thrill, but it passed before he could make anything of it.

"It's gone now. Disappeared into the rocks." Regret tinged her voice. "He was beautiful."

They were silent for a minute as the plane continued to circle easily. Then Jim looked at his wife and spoke in a voice that surprised even himself with its gravity.

"We will do it here."

Without a word Ann lifted the pouch which had nestled in her lap and gently untied the faded ribbon. Jim cranked open the small window on his side and heard a tugging whistle as the slipstream rushed past the opening.

Taking the flowered vessel from her, he held it open near the sucking draught of air. In a few seconds the pouch was empty, the ash drawn out and mixed in a nearly invisible stream. He looked inside but there was not a trace of gray anywhere on the glove-soft deerskin.

Ann took the pouch and smoothed it on her knee, tracing the delicate flower design with her fingertips. "How beautiful," she said. Almost immediately she felt a strange new stirring within her. There was no hurry, she decided, but she checked her watch to time the contractions just the same.

Later that evening as he and Ann shared a mutual wonder in their child, Jim admitted to the release of the melancholy that had oppressed him since Christmas. Somehow the counsel of the old Indian man, the ashes, and the birth had combined to put his mind and, he hoped, the spirit of Charity Whiteflower to rest.

They fell silent for several minutes, watching the newborn weakly groping with her mouth. Ann guided the tiny lips to her breast and winced, then laughed with Jim as the infant sucked lustily.

"We all need help from others, at one time or another," she said, and kissed her husband on the cheek.

"Ann," Jim asked quietly, "What gave you the idea to name her Terry?"

"Theresa," she corrected; "after St. Theresa. But we'll call her Terry."

He laughed gently. "OK. But you've had it picked out for some time?"

"Yes, a long time. You might call it repayment of a debt . . . a token."

She was quiet then, absorbed in the infant. When she looked up again, she said, "Do you know what they called St. Theresa?"

He shook his head.

"They called her 'The Little Flower.'"

They felt a deep peace envelop them. It was so intense that Jim's skin prickled on the back of his neck. Ann took his hand and placed it over hers on the nursing child.

EPILOGUE

At the lake the cougar lazed in a puddle of waning sunlight, his mind satisfied with the preoccupation of digest-
ing a full stomach. A late afternoon breeze, harbinger of
sunset, rippled patches of the alpine water, but nothing
else stirred.

A few hundred feet away in a small meadow, a dark
young man stood hipshot with the irked air of someone
who had been waiting too long for an overdue companion.
Occasionally he would cast impatient looks at the sun,
measuring its interminable passage.

At last he caught a movement at the edge of the clearing. His demeanor quickened and he straightened,
smoothed hands over his hair, adjusted the ceremonial
headband across his brow, and folded his arms—assuming
an attitude of indifferent control.

As the girl glided into the meadow, she appeared not
to notice him at all—although her steps led in his direction
only. When she was but yards away, she stopped and bent
over to pick a small white flower from the profusion of
blooms dotting the mountain grasses. She stook and dal-
lied, fixing the blossom into the top of a jet braid reaching
nearly to her waist.

It was altogether too much for the young man. With a
soundless whoop he leaped forward and swept her into his

arms. Carrying her cradled lightly across his chest he drank deeply of her long kisses. Finally he raised his head to look exultingly toward the snowy peaks.

Under the sharp angle of his jaw, Flower of the Great White Mountain saw the large vein pulsing in his throat. A small weldline marked the old wound. Tenderly she kissed the scar and spoke soft things in his ear.

He put her down then, and she led him into a wooded glade fragrant with pine and aster. They passed over the sunsplashed earth as though floating.

For a moment they stopped directly in front of the cougar, amused by his contented yawn and curling tail. But he could not see or smell or hear them.

Nor did they ever again cast shadows.

ABOUT THE AUTHOR

Jack Rowe has been a pilot for many years. A native of Wilmington, Delaware, he served with the 7th Marine infantry in Korea. He lives with his wife Laura and their nine children in Orange County, California, where he teaches writing and literature. This is his first novel.

DATE DUE

APR 0 4 2007